THE FINAL MELODY

Cecilia Randell

Book Three of The Forgotten Trilogy

Print ISBN: 978-1-7339745-2-3

eBook Published 2019

Editing by Heather Long

Front cover image by Covers by Combs

Published by Blue Wren Publishing

author@ceciliarandell.com

🌸 Created with Vellum

This one is for the Cat.
I may or may not have already dedicated something to the Cat.
I do not care. The Cat deserves many dedications.

Contents

Previously...   ix

Chapter 1   1
Chapter 2   13
Chapter 3   23
Chapter 4   25
Chapter 5   35
Chapter 6   43
Chapter 7   49
Chapter 8   61
Chapter 9   69
Chapter 10   77
Chapter 11   85
Chapter 12   87
Chapter 13   93
Chapter 14   105
Chapter 15   123
Chapter 16   141
Chapter 17   151
Chapter 18   161
Chapter 19   173
Chapter 20   175
Chapter 21   191
Chapter 22   199
Chapter 23   205
Chapter 24   215
Chapter 25   225
Chapter 26   233
Chapter 27   237
Chapter 28   245
Chapter 29   265
Epilogue   287

A Note From The Author   295
About the Author   299

Previously...

Shar stepped back, his gaze still on the trees. He paused, head cocked as though listening to something. Then he twisted his head, meeting Bat's eyes. He gave her a sweet smile that nearly broke her heart as words from two months ago came back to her. Even if you were our doom, we would embrace you.

Her throat closed. "Wait." Her words came out as a bare whisper. "Wait, Finn. Not yet."

A scream slashed through the morning air. It was deep, yet shrill, a million voices crying in pain—or crazed rage.

Mell's eyes slid closed. "Well fuck me."

Dub spun to face her, but he didn't look to her. He locked his gaze to Finn's, then nodded. Finn's lips thinned and he took a breath.

"What are you doing?" she asked, her heart pounding.

Finn ignored her. He raised his hands, palms down and fingers spread, then with a twist of his fingers, brought his palms together.

Her last sight before appearing in a green field bathed in the soft glow of dawn: a horde of grotesque and squat men in ragged *red coats and hats spilling from the brush and leaping from the limbs of trees, all heading with dripping teeth and rusted blades toward her defenders...*

Chapter One

Bastie,

Well, I suppose I will continue writing you notes. Do not worry, I will not send them. I know you must be busy with something.

But writing these helps to settle my thoughts, and I do need settling right now.

So, here is my question.

How far should one go for the ones they love?

- Bat, a goddess who found her heart only to have it ripped away by little men with red coats and sharp teeth

P.S. Yes, I am aware this note is a bit dramatic.

BAT

a rolling field stretched out before her, filled with brown grasses and scrubby purple shrubs. There were patches of green, but it wasn't the rich color she was used to. Instead of stone walls, the land was divided by uneven rows of small trees and bushes. She took a breath and the cool air of the morning filled her lungs with the sharp and musty scent of livestock and heather. In the distance, low hills rose in gentle waves. The sun crested over those hills, the contrast turning them black under the blanket of pale golden light...

What had just happened? What had she just seen?

Where...?

She spun to face Finn, her harp case swinging in a wide arc behind her. She had her mouth open in readiness to harangue him into going back for the others, for her men.

The guardi captain already had his phone to his ear. "Get your asses there now! Cu Chulainn and three others are dealing with a nest of Fear Deargs." Pulling the phone from his ear he looked down at Bat as Mell laid a comforting hand on her shoulder.

"They'll be fine," Mell said, his voice steady. He radiated assurance and confidence, but Bat wasn't sure she trusted it. As she knew, Mell could project emotions he did not truly feel.

Her stomach churned and she swallowed even as her eyes narrowed. She glared first at Mell, then Finn. "Take us back right this moment." Her voice didn't tremble, and she bit back the pride she felt at that accomplishment. She

2

had just found Shar and Dub. She refused to contemplate the idea that she could lose them so quickly.

Meera appeared before her, the two other banshees hovering at her shoulders. Their packs were in a small pile near the huddled group of few a few yards away. "We'll go," she said.

There was a familiar darkness in the banshees' eyes. It was the same expression Anubis would assume when a human's heart was shown to be heavier than the feather of Ma'at—when that heart was to receive pain and condemnation.

"No." Finn's voice was flat. "No one is going back there. Dub, Shar and Cu Chulainn are some of the best warriors, not to mention you've seen a bit of what Ari is capable of. My guardi team is also on the way. They will be able to handle the Fear Dearg." He paused. "And it was only one nest."

How could he say that? *Only one nest?* "That was one nest? There were hundreds of them." Bat turned to face him fully, wracking her mind for a suitable threat to force his compliance. "If you don—"

"There were not hundreds, there were a few dozen," Finn said, cutting her off.

Her heart continued to pound as fear receded and anger grew. Power—the power that Dub and Shar had helped her to grow—surged through her limbs and settled in her palms. *No one* was allowed to talk to her like that anymore, not even a man she had grown to love.

Especially a man she loved. The edges of her vision faded as she focused on the hazel-gold of Finn's eyes without really seeing them. No, her mind was filled with sharp teeth and ragged red coats.

"*Realta...*" Mell's cautious tones did nothing to ease the tension and power that rode her.

Finn didn't flinch from her stare even as she raised her hands and laid them along his chest, her power pressing into him. She did not send it deep, instead she created a film of heat just below the skin. Her chest hurt with the fear of losing her not-men... she would make Finn hurt in return...

What am I doing? She blinked and focused on Finn's face. His eyes were wide and his mouth pinched, but he had not drawn away or attempted to evade her. She pulled her power into herself and made to step back, but he brought his own hands up to capture hers against his chest.

"They really will be all right, *acushla*. Do you think I would have left them as I did if there was a chance we would not see them again?" His hands were warm around hers. Her fingers curled in and dug against his chest.

"No," she said. "No, I do not believe you would leave them to die. But..."

"Goddess, this is a small group of fae who have come together *just* this morning—and most of them do not work well with others. To throw them into a battle at this point is the height of foolishness." A lock of red-gold hair fell over his forehead as he bowed his head toward her. "Plus, there are those who the enemy has been very diligent in searching for, for the last couple of days—and the harp. I could not allow us to stay there, if there was even a chance that something could happen to you, the

4

harp, or the human. There is a much larger battle ahead of us, and we cannot afford to lose the war due to a mishap during such a small battle."

Bat understood what he was saying—his words echoed her own earlier thoughts. At the same time, he was also telling her to leave Dub and Shar behind to fight those… *things*.

"Give them twenty minutes. If we don't hear from them in that time, I will take the banshees and go. But, please trust me, goddess. I would not insist upon this if it was not necessary."

Twenty minutes. It was not a long time, but it was also forever.

"And think upon this," he continued. "These are warriors who have survived countless battles and wars against opponents much larger and more numerous than a nest of Fear Deargs. They have fought against those wielding soul-blades and worse. Nothing so meager as what amounts to a pack of hopped up rodents will bring them down. Trust *them* as well."

He was correct. She was surely panicking over nothing. Her not-men were fine warriors. She had seen this in her visions. Pulling her hands from Finn's, she stepped back and faced the entire group: Finn, Mell, Meera, the other banshees and fae and sluagh. Killer stuck by her side, his head and ears up in alert readiness. "I will allow this." The words were among the most difficult she'd ever had to say, despite her assurances to herself. "And while these twenty minutes are passing, we will meet each other officially, so that we might be able to 'work well together' as Finn has said." She would not be able to stand still and simply *wait* to find out if Finn was correct in his estimation of the situation back at the cottage.

Ailis snorted. "So, what, ya want us to go 'round the circle and share with everyone our names and powers? Kind of like the first day of Primary?"

Bat nodded, not quite sure what Primary was, but the suggestion was sound. Ailis was very clever at most times. "Yes. This. It is a good idea. Unless you all know each other already? I know many of your names and faces from the pub, but I must admit I am not familiar with your skills and powers."

The green-haired fae snorted then grinned as quiet chuckles spread through the group. These escalated until laughter roared through the morning air, Mell and even Finn joining in.

Bat stared at the assembled group, brows drawn. This was not a laughing matter. Killer barked, the sharp sound cutting through her allies' inappropriate mirth and drawing their attention back to her. Finn quirked up an eyebrow. "Well then, let's begin," he said as the last of the laughter faded away.

Meera stepped forward. The banshee's brown eyes were narrowed and her lips pursed. "I'm after thinking ya didn't know we came over with the Fomoiri."

It wasn't a question, but Bat answered nonetheless. "The banshees were mentioned at the same time I found out *any* of you came from Egypt."

Meera's eyes widened as her fellow banshees moved to flank her, one with hair dark enough to match Bat's and the other sporting bright red waves. "The O'Loinsighs didn't tell ya?" This was the redhead.

Bat's gaze flicked to Mell, whose head hung in exasperated resignation. "No, they did not. But this has been resolved." Her chest tightened at the mere mention of her not-men. How many minutes had passed?

Meera glanced at the other two banshees, who nodded. Then she turned back to Bat. "Well, banshee is not our original name. I will not tell it to ya, as we left that existence long ago, but we can do more than wail for the dead." She waved a hand toward the banshee who had yet to speak.

The dark-haired woman stepped away from the others, opened her mouth, and wailed. But this was no sound Bat had ever heard. This was not the crying of mourners or the weeping of those who had lost the ones they loved. This was rage and destruction wrapped into a scream that both terrified and fascinated—and it was directed at a small tree about thirty feet away. The trunk and limbs trembled, then exploded in a burst of splinters and leaves.

Bat tilted her head, considering. "This is a useful skill," she said. She turned to Meera. "All three of you can do this?"

Meera nodded, a slight grin on her face. "Our aim is a little rusty. I wouldn't trust it in close quarters, or for precision targeting, but for general mayhem and destruction, we're yer girls."

Bat looked to the redhead who had seemed so frustrated with not being able to join in the action back at the cottage. "This is what you had wanted to do earlier, in the battle."

"Yup. Neasa, by the way. The grumpy one is Teagan." She gestured to the dark-haired banshee.

7

Bat nodded. "It is nice to officially meet you. I have seen you in the pub." *And seen the way you flirt with my Mell.* But she held those last words to herself. She next turned her attention to Faolan, the sluagh who had saved her harp.

"I've got my shadows, and they're very good, my shadows," he said. The sluagh had taken on his more human-like aspect, but the gray tint to his skin was even more obvious in the morning light, and red eyes glowed from his wrinkled face.

Another sluagh stepped up. Like Faolan his form was human, but the shadows were even stronger under his skin. "Ya don't know what the shadows do, do ya?" He didn't wait for an answer. "I'll tell ya. They hide, and they trap. They can burn with cold, and they can stretch like a whip. I'm Carrig." A shadow uncurled from him and stretched toward her.

Mell stepped forward, probably to intercept the thin tendril, and Finn caught his shoulder, shaking his head in a subtle gesture. Finn met her gaze and the message was clear—this was an official greeting of some kind, or a ritual, and she needed to complete it.

Bat held out her hand as the rope of shadow hovered just in front of her. It flicked, much like the tail of a cat that is contemplating whether to bite or purr. Then it wrapped around her hand, and cold seeped into her. The cold of lonely nights and an extinguished fire, of empty hearts and stern condemnation. It was not pleasant, but it was also not malicious. It simply *was*.

Flash. A shadow on a pale horse with glowing eyes, chasing after a

8

fleeing human. A criminal. Behind the shadow rode dozens of others, atop steeds in a range of colors. Still more figures ran beside those horses, while others flew. Dark hounds coursed over the ground beside the hooves of the ghost-steeds. It was an army of shadows, all out to capture and punish the evil human.

She blinked, coming back to the mist-covered field. She had just been shown the Wild Hunt Shar had once mentioned. They hunted the wicked and the lost, he had said. Though their justice that she had just seen was cold, it was still a similar purpose to her own. She could understand these sluagh.

"It is nice to meet you, Carrig," she said, keeping her hand steady in the grasp of the dark tendril twined around it. If the sluagh thought to disconcert her with his shadows... well, she had lived with much worse. *I should make sure he meets Anubis some day, then he would know shadows.* She sent a pulse of her power into the shadow, warming it slightly.

The sluagh's red eyes narrowed then widened and he whipped the shadow from her palm. Faolan chuckled as though he knew just what she had done. "And this is Dalaigh," he said, gesturing to the third sluagh, who hung back in the crowd, a large pack strung across his back. Bat nodded toward him, and the gesture was returned.

How much time has passed now? Surely twenty minutes is not this long?

"I'll go next, then, shall I?" A golden-haired man stepped forward, his frame slender.

There was a sharpness to his features that reminded Bat of some of the drawings she'd seen of fairies in her

9

Idiot's Guide to Ireland. Had the book at least gotten *this* correct?

He bowed, the move graceful, and Ailis and Mell snorted in unison. The slender man ignored them. "Eoghan, at yer service, goddess. Ailis said there was a bit of fun to be had, so we're along for the ride." He gestured vaguely toward two others, a man and a woman, who stood near Ailis and shared the same sharp features. "These are Cliona and Ogma, and no, not *that* Ogma—this one's parents simply had no imagination."

Bat's brows rose. She had no idea who *that* Ogma was, and she was not sure it truly mattered. "And what can you do, Eoghan?" Was this her chance to find out more about the trooping faes' powers? And Ailis's?

He shrugged. "Oh, a little of this, a little of that."

She frowned as disappointment and frustration filled her. Allies being evasive was not something she should have to deal with. Ailis stepped up behind Eoghan and slapped the back of his head. "Just tell her, ya dunce. Now's no the time ta be a gowl. Tell her what ya can do." Ailis gave Bat a decisive nod and poked Eoghan's shoulder until he shook her off and sighed.

"Right then. Well, glamour's my main, as it is for most fae. I can do a bit of enchanting with smaller objects, and have a bit of nature-speak. Ogma's good with the animals, and Cliona's been known to... befuddle a male or two. Could come in handy."

Bat studied the female fae, Cliona. There was something about her... and many of the males gathered had taken to casting sneaking glances her way. Bat's gaze cut to Mell and Finn, only to find their eyes locked on her own. A bit of the tension riding her eased, and she realized there was, *perhaps*, a bit more healing her emotions needed to do.

"Good," she said, pulling her attention from things that did not matter at the moment. If she began thinking of her relationships with her not-men, she would think of Dub and Shar and begin to worry again… "These will be useful skills to have."

Finn's phone went off. He snatched it from the pocket of his jeans and held it to his ear. As he listened, his expression darkened. Bat's stomach clenched.

Chapter Two

SHAR

*S*har swung his axe, slicing through yet another Fear Dearg—those little vicious cousins to the leprechaun—and sending the body flying through the air to land against the trunk of an oak. The tree shuddered, both abhorring Shar's use of his axe and accepting the blood sacrifice. The trees were truly neutral, unlike the solitary fae, but they were willing to help those who spoke to them.

Another of the small creatures jumped on his back, its nails jabbing into his muscles as it sank its teeth in his shoulder. He grunted, ignoring the pain as he reached behind, tore the pest away, and then flung it at a half dozen other Fear Deargs heading his way.

Dub let out a roar as he spun, his sword a steel blur, gems winking at the pommel. It had been made for him by Giobnu—the original Smith—and Dub never failed to keep it close, tucked away in his personal pocket of space —well, except for that one time.

"Behind you!" Cuchi shouted, sprinting in Shar's direction.

Shar spun and ducked, just in time to avoid another face full of fangs. There was a squelch as Cu Chulainn's sword cut through the small body. *At least he's on our side this time*. Shar hated to admit it, but the sidhe was an accomplished warrior. Hell, he'd defeated the brothers once. Granted, their hearts weren't fully in the fight, not after what Derbforgaill had pulled, but Dub and Mell could be quite capable when they put their minds to it.

Another of the small, red-clad Fear Deargs came into reach of his axe and he swung, catching it just under the chin. He also knew he himself was no slouch. Not when he had something to fight for.

Bat's visage, the last glimpse he'd had of her just before Finn transported the main group away, flashed before him. Her eyes had been wide, her face pale, as she spoke quickly to the guardi captain. Shar had tried to tell her with a look everything would be fine. The trees had warned him what was coming, and it wasn't anything they couldn't handle. He wasn't sure he'd succeeded.

A low coughing sound came from a pile of red coats, and Ari's arm shot out from underneath them, his many-jointed fingers and razor claws coated in blood. He hooked those claws into the back of a Fear Dearg and tore it away, then the next, until he stood amidst a circle of bloody and torn bodies.

The remaining small fae, less than a dozen, retreated to the edge of the trees. Hovering there, they whispered to each other, the sounds no more than spare chittering. What were they doing...?

More come. You must leave, protector. The ancient oak shared a pulse of urgency with him.

What was coming...? He shook his head. It didn't matter. "Dub," he called out. "We need to go, now."

His brother turned to him just as four guardi appeared on the path from the trees to the cottage, fully equipped with dull black armor and short swords. One man had an axe similar to Shar's, though not quite as large.

"Took you long enough!" Cuchi said, not taking his eyes from the tree line.

"We still need to get out of here," Shar said, again. "There's more coming, and no use continuing this fight now." He stepped back, putting himself farther from the trees. "Everyone, get over here." He and Dub were going to have a serious talk after this about putting *someone* in charge. They wouldn't be able to continue on as they had, with Bat more of a consultant than anything, and the brothers and Finn acting with "cooperation." Once the fighting started—and who was he kidding, it *had* started— there needed to be *one* person in charge.

Dub's eyes narrowed on Shar, but he nodded and eased backwards, refusing to turn his back to the coming threat. Ari copied him, stepping lightly over the twitching pieces of the Fear Deargs he'd torn open. They would heal, eventually, if those pieces were lucky enough to find their way back to each other. Just like the sluagh they'd fought off would recover.

But what was coming through the trees was neither sluagh nor another pack of Fear Deargs.

Tree roots shook in soft vibrations and leaves rustled in the still air.

Fir Bolg, the ash whispered.

Like the sluagh, the Fir Bolg stuck to the bogs and the dark, they could call upon the shadows, and they tended to hunt those who'd been lost to wickedness. Unlike the sluagh, they possessed an inner savageness that no amount of living among the "civilized" would ever erase.

The newly arrived guardi shifted into a defensive circle, facing out. "It looks like you got this covered," a female guardi said, though she was careful to keep her attention on the Fear Deargs.

"It's Fir Bolg. Get over here. *Now*." Shar didn't need to argue with allies who were late to the battle. He gripped his axe handle as the trees' vibrations became strong enough to feel through the soles of his feet. *It's the Hunt. The Wild Hunt. Run.*

Shar froze, his heart pounding. *The Wild Hunt*. The trees were warning him, trying to keep him and the others safe. But fighting against the Wild Hunt was not something the oaks or ash or even the rowans could do— not when the Hunt had someone's scent.

Cuchi's head lifted, his nostrils flaring, and his eyes widened. "It's the Hunt!" he shouted, calling out the warning before Shar was able to wrap his mind around the fact that *the Hunt* was after *them*. Their enemy was not simply Fir Bolg or more sluagh, but the Wild-fucking-Hunt.

This shouldn't have been possible. A few sluagh or Fir Bolg swayed to Balor's side he could understand—but the Hunt as a whole? They could be vicious and merciless, yes, but they tracked those who were *lost*—lost to wickedness or apathy or who could not find their own way anymore. They did not hunt on behalf of anyone but themselves. They remained... neutral.

No longer. *Balor is persuading those who have been neglected and lost. It is not a far stretch to imagine him seducing the Hunt.* If Bat had not come to Ireland when she did, how many more would have already gone to Balor's side? How many of the solitary fae would have decided they'd had enough of not being seen by their own gods, would have hungered for the acknowledgment and recognition Balor had promised in Bat's dream?

Shar suspected it was thanks to their little goddess that so many of the solitary fae remained watchful in their territories.

Dub had reached Shar by then. Ari loped over to stand beside the brothers, his needle teeth bared in a fierce grin. The guardi also made their way toward Shar, though they weren't moving fast enough for his taste, trying too hard to maintain their formation.

The woman twisted and met his gaze. "Go. We'll delay them, try to lead them away." Then she grinned, echoes of The Morrigan in that smile. "It's been a while since I've had the opportunity to take on the Hunt. If nothing else, yer goddess has brought back interesting times."

Shar gave her a sharp nod, uncertain if the woman cursed or praised Bat. He wanted to protest that *none* of this was Bat's doing. Instead, he looked to Dub.

The oldest brother's face was grim, but at least he hadn't fallen into a battle frenzy. It would have been

17

impossible to get him away if that had been the case. Was he, too, thinking of getting back to Bat?

It was a redundant question—of course Dub would be focused on their goddess. Hells, his brother had been focused on her long before she ever stepped over the pub's threshold on that fateful St. Paddy's day.

Shadowed shapes twisted through the trees' trunks without revealing themselves. Some carried the bulk of giants, and others were slender as a Starved Man. The Hunt was closing in.

It was time to go. Dub and Ari stood just a bit in front of Shar and facing out. Cuchi stood on Shar's blind side. Turning his head to face the guardi captain, Shar frowned. "Now is a good time." Why was the guardi hesitating in transporting them out of here?

Cuchi gave an answering frown. "Not yet."

Dub twisted around, his scowl fierce enough to frighten pixies into silence. "The Hunt's not after us, or them. They'll go for the human, and the harp, once they realize their true prey is no longer here. We're no' stupid." He turned fully and squared up with Cuchi. "Get us out of here and back with the others. The guardi can by-damned be useful in this for *once*, and at least delay them."

Cuchi cast a disparaging look upon Dub then turned his attention back to the trees, eyes narrowed. Shar didn't care either way about past blood and old grudges, not now. "What are you waiting for?"

The shadows grew thicker until all Shar could make out were slivers and snips of tree trunks and leaves. A low growl reached them.

"That. I was waiting for that." Cuchi flicked a finger at

the circle of guardi and they fanned out to advance on the tree line.

Where were the howls, the stamping hooves and neighs and other sounds of restless beasts? Why did the Hunt not attack, or rush the defenders where they stood in the open clearing?

A Fear Dearg grinned. "Ye're ta late. We've go' th' scent no'." Then it and its fellows disappeared into the shadows as suddenly as they had appeared.

"Gobsmacking balls of shite." Cuchi cursed and pulled out his phone. "After them!" he shouted to the guardi.

The four men and women rushed the tree line, no longer worried about stealth, and their war cries rang stark in the still morning air.

Then Cuchi twisted his hands, and the four of them were gone. *Finally.*

BAT

She studied Finn's face, looking for a clue as to what put that look of apprehension on his face. "Understood," he said, and tucked his phone away. Lowering his head, he stared at his boots for a good five seconds before sighing. "That was Cu Chulainn, he—"

Mell's phone went off, and then Ailis's a moment after.

Bat's gaze darted between the three, searching for any telltale signs of what the news could be. Mell's expression closed down and his emotions pulled back into a blank and impenetrable wall. Ailis's brows pulled together and her lips turned down in a subtle frown then lifted into a wicked grin. Finn continued to frown as his eyes slid closed in what looked like weary resignation.

Ailis finished first. "That was Ciara and Con. They missed us, what with the whole Fear Dearg attacking and the leaving early. They're going to meet us just outside of Londonderry."

Cliona's head jerked back. "Con's joining the fun?" A smile, nearly as wicked as Ailis's, crossed her face.

Con, a kind old man who'd helped to give her directions on her first day in Ireland. She'd run into him a few times since, either at the pub or at Ailis's store. What was so special about him?

"Dub and the others are away, safe for now," Mell said, interrupting her musings.

She jerked her head around to stare. Where were they?

"Dub says they're about half-way to Londonderry, they'll meet us at Finnegan's just outside of town. And—"

"The Wild Hunt is after the human," Finn finished. "Criedne and the rest of my team are attempting to keep the Hunt distracted, but they won't be able to manage it for long. We need to get moving, now."

The Wild Hunt. They were supposed to go after those who had morally lost their way, those who had committed crimes, who were wicked. They were the ultimate neutral force in judgment. They did not show mercy, but they also did not pursue unsuitable targets.

Why were they helping Balor? Had he come to them in dreams and made promises, twisted their perceptions of right and wrong just as he had attempted to do with her?

Then another thought came to her. The Morrigan said

only a few fae and sluagh knew what was happening with Balor. But how could that be if he had swayed The Wild Hunt to his side?

It seemed there were many more players in this than the Irish gods knew.

Bat peered through the assembled fae to where Daniel stood, the set of his limbs and slumped shoulders screaming weariness. His eyes were less wild, but confusion still pinched his brows.

Had she made a mistake in insisting they wait here for the others? Should they have continued on to Londonderry and gotten farther away from the Hunt? Doubts clung to her like the dark mud of a flooded Nile, but held none of the mud's life-giving properties.

And where did this new wave of uncertainty come from? It reminded her of her hesitation in beginning anything with the brothers, and Finn. It seemed there were more wounds in her soul than she had yet spotted.

Shaking off the useless musings, she stepped up next to Finn. Bat gave him a nod, indicating that it was time to go.

"We'll finish this up at Finnegan's, then, and regroup." Finn gestured the rest of the fae closer. They gathered their packs and then, with another twist of his hands, Finn took them away once more.

Chapter Three

SCATH

Finnegan's. The voice whispered to him. *Go to Finnegan's. You will find them there.*

Scath eyed Alatrom, who sat in his plain wooden chair, at a bare wood table, in an office that overlooked the shipping yard of northern Londonderry. It was only a facade for the humans, of course. Most of the Clan's business was conducted aboard *The Golden Crane*, the clan leader's yacht.

The wooden chair creaked as Alatrom leaned back. A bulk once massive with muscle was now running to fat, though the head of the Crane clan remained a formidable Fomoiri.

Lies. Scath wasn't sure if it was his own thought or the voice's—Balor's. The connection had formed decades ago, beginning with subtle whispers in his dreams. He'd recognized his former leader almost immediately. And he'd found out soon after that the Crane brooch Alatrom wore on his chest was a fake, a lie—just like the man.

Alatrom slammed the report he was reading down onto the desk. "Damn tithes are going to be the death of me. Whose brilliant idea was it to set up an excise tax on peacocks?"

And whose brilliant idea was it to put peacocks on our ships? But Scath knew better than to ask the question aloud. He didn't have enough support *yet* to depose the oaf as clan leader. Once Balor was back, though, the Fomoiri King would need to know his clan leaders were loyal to him and him alone. And Scath was that, utterly and completely Balor's man.

Until it was time to act, Scath needed to play his role of loyal lieutenant well.

Chapter Four

Bastie,

Have you ever been so happy you had trouble moving?

Well, I now know what that feeling is like.

Things are moving extremely fast now, and they are
beginning to get away from me.

I have to wonder about my adequacy as a goddess. A deity
should be better at managing her existence.

- Bat, an overwhelmed goddess

BAT

She peered around the narrow alley. It was very like the one behind her pub, only there was no garden here. Finn, Mell, Daniel and the rest crowded together around her, blocking most of her view.

It was only a couple of minutes after they arrived that a rust-red door swung open. A short blond man stood there. He was stocky, with a full beard, and something about his demeanor reminded her of Cu Chulainn—arrogant and all too full of himself. Their gazes met and the edge of his lips curled up in a smirk before he shifted his gaze to Finn.

"That all of ya?" the man asked.

"For now." Finn's voice was hard.

"Well, get in here then. I'm after strengthening the wards. Won't hold for long, not with The Hunt, but they'll do for now." The man pushed the door wide and stepped back.

Finn leapt up the short steps that led to the back stoop and caught the edge of the door before it could close. "In, now," he ordered.

The pixies wasted no time, zipping into the building in bright streaks. Mell nudged the banshees to get them moving, and Bat grabbed Daniel's left arm while Old Mike supported the human's right side. She moved him through the door and the rest followed close behind.

They trooped though the kitchen and out to the common room of the empty pub. "Now what?" she asked Finn as their small band of mismatched immortals found seats for themselves around the scattered tables.

"Now we wait. We'll give them thirty minutes."

She nodded. "And then?"

"Then we get away from the Hunt."

She nearly rolled her eyes, but restrained herself. It was a bad habit that she didn't want to pick up.

Ailis did it for her, though, the whites of her eyes showing. "*That* is obvious."

"We get a boat," Mell cut in. His tone was harsh.

"We'll wait until Dub and Shar are here to discuss it," Finn said.

It took a moment for Bat to catch on. The only place she knew of to get a boat would be...

Their father.

As much as she hated it, it was a good move. "It would be smart," she said, avoiding Mell's gaze. "We need to assess where his loyalties lie. Sometimes the best way to sort enemy from... well, not-enemy, is a direct confrontation."

There was silence.

"You're right," Mell said. He moved to one of the tables, pulling Bat along with him and into a seat. "But we need to wait for Dub and Shar so we can discuss the best way to approach him."

"I think..." she trailed off. She didn't want to say it.

Ailis sent her an understanding glance before joining the other trooping fae at a corner table, leaving Bat to her discussion with Mell and Finn. The pub's owner, Finnegan, had gone behind the bar. He leaned against it, a deliberate expression of boredom masking his thoughts.

Then he straightened and strode to the back door. Bat sat up in her seat, her gaze following after him and her heart pounding.

They're here. Cuchi and Ari came through the doorway first. Then Dub entered, his clothes torn and bloody. She scanned his body, taking note of each injury, every scrape and cut and bruise. Her gaze moved past his as the last figure filled the doorway. His long hair had come loose and blood had splattered across his face and eyepatch, but he was *here*. Killer ran to them and sniffed each man in turn, his tail working in swift sweeps of welcome.

They were *all* here.

She slumped back in her seat, the anxiety and nervous energy that had been keeping her going leaving in a rush.

They were safe, and they were here.

"*Storeen*, is that any way to greet a returning warrior?" Dub's usual frown was absent and his eyes crinkled at the corners.

Was he teasing her? Now? *Perverse wanker*. "If I could walk right now, I would have leapt on you in joy, but my legs don't seem to be working," she said, her relief turning to giddiness. Her lips stretched into a wide smile.

Dub scowled. "What's wrong with your legs?"

Ah, that was the grumpy not-man she knew.

"Nothing," she said. "I just…"

"She's been in a bit of a tizz since we transported away," Finn said.

"Since we left them behind, you mean." Bat crossed her arms over her chest.

"*A stor.*" Shar waited until she looked at him. He held his arms open. "Come here."

Then her legs found their strength. She leapt to her feet and ran to him. He scooped her up against his chest, one arm under her butt, the other snaking around her waist. Wrapping her legs around him, she snuggled into his chest, ignoring the scents of blood and sweat that invaded her nose.

They remained together for only a few seconds before Dub cut in. "Hand her over. My turn." Hard hands wrapped around each of her arms and she was lifted away from her giant pirate. She hung in Dub's grip for a half second before she was placed back on her feet. He spun her around to face him and their gazes locked, bright lapis-blue meeting dark brown.

Dub's hand cupped her cheek and he lowered his head, resting his forehead against hers.

"I was afraid I'd lost you," she whispered.

He frowned. It was his concerned frown, though. She pressed her cheek into his palm.

"I'm not that easy to get rid of," Dub finally said. "None of us are."

Bat nodded, the sensitive skin of her cheek rubbing against his callused fingers. "I know."

They left it at that. There were possibly more things she could or should say, but in that moment she didn't feel that any more words were necessary.

Cuchi cleared his throat. "No special greeting for me, goddess?"

Bat glared at him. He chuckled and raised his hands.

She still did not like this man who had once hurt her not-men in a ridiculous battle over a woman who was long gone—she assumed. But she had managed to find a wary peace with him over the last few days.

Stepping away from Dub, she gathered her scattered emotions and fought to put her mind back on the task at hand, something that was surprisingly difficult for her to do.

"How long do we have?" she asked.

"The Hunt?" Dub asked.

She nodded.

Finn and Dub exchanged a glance as the rest of the

gathered immortals looked on. Tension and anticipation rode heavy in the air despite their silence.

"No more than a half day at most," Finn finally said.

"Then we need to ma—"

"Incoming," Finnegan shouted.

Instantly, those who had sat sprang to their feet.

"Shit, we should have had more time." After a short glance at Bat, Finn spun around and grabbed Daniel. The guardi threw the human over his shoulder. "No time for arguing or arranging now, goddess." He turned to Dub. "We need a boat."

Dub's face darkened, but he nodded. "Not the way I wanted to do this," he muttered.

Bat's hands crept up. One clutched at her necklace while the other gripped the strap on her harp case.

Flash. Cu Chulainn beside the stone vessel. Blood poured from a wound on his head. He reached up and wiped his fingers through it, then smeared the red substance over the lip of the stone. It glowed, light turning the blood to rubies. There were four other similar stains, ranging around the circumference of the vessel. Ailis, Finn, Dub, and she herself stood beside them.

Bat pulled her harp from its case and strummed a light tune. The cauldron hummed in answer, resonating with the notes Bat pulled from the instrument. As she continued to play, the cauldron began to emit an aura of… longing. It longed to return to its original purpose, to birth something new, something sacred.

Bat continued to pluck the strings. The harp was working its magic, not just on the cauldron, but on all those gathered around it. As the song carried away from where she stood, she became aware of a battle in the distance. Gradually, the sounds of fighting faded away.

Daniel appeared before her, but he was no longer the human tourist she had so briefly met before all this began. His eyes glinted a deep green. Blood was smeared across his face and clothes.

"Thank you, little goddess," the man who was no longer Daniel said with a wicked grin.

Bat blinked.

"Finnegan, can you get a feel for how many of them there are?" Shar called out.

The bar owner closed his eyes, a look of concentration on his face. "No more than half a dozen." His eyelids twitched. "Don't think it's the Hunt, doesn't have the right feel." His eyes shot open. "You've probably got about ten minutes before they break through my wards." His tongue shot out and flicked, almost as if he was scenting the air. "Tastes like... clan."

Finnegan strode out from behind the bar. Dub fully turned away from Bat as they squared off. "Just what did you O'Loinsigh brothers get me into?"

Bat's mind swirled with the meaning of this new vision. *No time to sort it right now.* Then Finnegan's words registered. Had the brothers not told him what was going on? Was he not to be trusted?

This was too important a question to be left unanswered. She reached out with her mind and searched his heart. She didn't really have the power to spare, but this was necessary.

There was darkness there, but it was not... malicious.

He had the potential for wicked actions and deeds, but he had not yet tipped over the edge into evil.

She made a decision, not giving herself time to doubt. "Balor," she said, stepping a little to the side so she could face Finnegan directly. "We have gotten you into a situation against Balor, who is trying to escape from death." *And become a god,* she added silently. But that was something she couldn't let anyone know of.

Finnegan's eyes rolled much like Ailis's had and his lips pressed together. He looked torn between horror and laughter.

The laughter finally won. "Ya expect me ta believe that The Evil Eye is coming back, *now?*"

Bat didn't back down. "Yes. And you will need to come with us from this point." They couldn't leave him here, not now that they had already been tracked. Either he would be in danger, or he could reveal their numbers and what he had heard so far of their plans—not that they had said much to him.

Flash. A boy, no more than three, cowered at the feet of a swarthy giant who had a red eye painted on his forehead. The boy was covered in bruises, and one of his arms hung at an unnatural angle.

"I will not let him hurt you again," was all she said. The words were general enough, but Finnegan flinched.

"Who *are* you?"

Bat turned her head to Dub, her expression questioning. Had they not told this not-man anything?

Dub shrugged. "He owes me a favor. I was cashing it in for the use of his place for a few hours. Finnegan's a good man, but he's like me. Doesn't like to poke his nose in politics and power plays." The last was said with a resigned sneer.

It finally occurred to her how hard this must have been for her not-men. In a matter of days, they'd gone from a relatively peaceful and quiet life in their pub, to being embroiled in the very things they had avoided for centuries—*politics and power plays*. Although, it was less about those and more about a grand quest to save the world.

And my mind is wandering again. I need to pull together. I will make this right to them—and Finnegan—somehow.

"No time," Finn said, his voice commanding. "Even if that's not the Hunt, we need to get out of here. This is no longer a secure location." He planted himself beside Bat, Daniel still over his shoulder. "N—"

A bone-shaking roar thundered through the night.

And under it, Bat could have sworn she heard Finn curse. "Well fuck me, the dragon's here."

Chapter Five

Bastie! I met a dragon!
Or, sort of. I didn't get to see him as a dragon.
But I definitely met one.

- Bat

BAT

"*D*ragon?" she asked no one in particular. A thrill of excitement shot through her veins, pushing aside everything else.

The entire room stood frozen. Not, she noted, that they had moved all that much since arriving at the pub. *I wonder if we're all in some sort of shock.*

But, no, there was Ailis with a smug grin on her face. The men of ba looked just as excited as Bat, their needle teeth showing in wide smiles. The banshees were intrigued while the trooping fae stood with hips cocked and arms crossed, bored.

These were not the reactions she'd been expecting. But, maybe they were used to dragons? Maybe they didn't really care about the Hunt being on their trail? Maybe she'd misread the earlier situation and the Hunt wasn't all that bad?

"Ooh, now there'll be blood," Neasa, the red haired banshee, said.

Or, maybe there were simply all insane. This was a valid possibility. She recalled how exhilarated Dub and Finn had been when they returned after retrieving her harp from the Dubros, and the light that entered Shar and Mell's expressions with talk of the coming battles. They were not happy about Balor seeking to return to life and the threat of war, no. But they *were* excited about the promise of battle.

So, yes, they were all crazy. Who got excited about war?

Unbalanced warriors, that was who. Unbalanced warriors and insane immortals.

Finn sighed, went to an empty seat, and dumped Daniel into it.

"Wha..." The human looked around, dazed. He was getting worse.

"We'll give it five minutes, but I doubt Con'll need that long," Finn said.

Why do we keep having to wait *so much?*

"Ummm..." Bat raised her hand and everyone's gaze shot to her. "Does this mean our original plan is... how do you say it... shot to hell?" That was actually a phrase she'd been waiting for the perfect opportunity to use, and now seemed to be the right time. "I mean the fact that someone has found us so soon, not a dragon showing up," she hurried to add.

Mell laughed and a tendril of amusement wrapped around her mind. "Not shot to hell, *realta*, more shoved off the road. Just means things will be a little more rough."

"We'll let the dragon finish things, then talk." This was Dub. "He'll buy us the time we need."

Silence fell over the room and Bat shifted on her feet. She was growing restless, though she wasn't sure why. Well, she knew part of the reason. It was the waiting thing. Why were they all just standing here, not doing anything? Not talking, not planning, not fighting, not continuing to meet each other. Not even drinking.

Since when had she become too impatient?

Caw. Einin settled on a table in the middle of the pub.

Where had she come from? Was the raven actually a raven, or was she some spirit The Morrigan conjured? Annoyance pulled Bat's face into a frown.

You're restless because you're running out of time, Egyptian goddess.

Why do you just pop up like this? I thought Einin was supposed to assist us. So far all she's done is disappear and reappear without warning.

A dark chuckle sounded in Bat's mind. *Getting feisty are you? I don't mind it, but if you encounter any of the members of the Tribunal, I suggest you don't let any of that attitude show, or give away that you've been... gathering power.* The Celtic goddess paused. *I can't stay connected long, but I promise to leave Einin behind as my eyes for as long as I can.*

Bat didn't believe her.

And you have Cu Chulainn. Use. Him. You'll be going to the sea soon, and my influence there dwindles to almost nothing. The raven cocked its head toward Saoirse, the brown-haired woman who had claimed to be a guide, but who had yet to fully introduce herself. *At least you've made one ally from the oceans.* Einin locked her beady eyes on Bat once more. *Don't doubt yourself, goddess. There is a reason you are the one here, sorting out this mess. So, trust your instincts. You are restless because you need to move. You are worried about your companions and their ability to act together because you should be. You doubt them because you should. Do not doubt in yourself.* This last was repeated with a slow and emphatic cadence.

Einin ruffled her feathers and settled back down. The Morrigan was gone. Bat returned her attention to her companions. The O'Loinsigh brothers stood in readiness, their attention on the doorways and shuttered windows. Cuchi stared at Einin. Ailis stood closer to the banshees now. Finnegan had stepped back, putting more distance between him and the raven. The sluagh were huddled together and Neall the Far Gorta had joined them. The men of ba formed their own group. Pixies glittered in the air over where Killer guarded Daniel and Old Mike. The two leprechauns she only knew by sight were with the older, gray-haired woman and Saoirse.

Muffled grunts and growls filtered in from the street in front of the pub.

You doubt them because you should…

That's what The Morrigan said. No, she hadn't personally scanned everyone, and she wasn't sure if Ari or the other men of ba had had a chance to do so before the attack.

They needed a boat, yes, but before any of that, she needed to finish checking over the allies that had joined them. It was not something that could be put off simply because the urgency to find a safe base of operations had increased.

Five minutes. That was what Finn said. Now that she had something she could do in that time, her restlessness slid away.

Who to start with? Her gaze found Meera and the other banshees. These were immortals who once lived in Egypt. They had travelled the oceans along with the other Fomoiri and the men of ba.

And they were strong. She shivered at the memory of a demolished tree.

Bat would begin with the banshees.

Still looking in their direction, she shut everyone else from her mind and allowed her gaze to unfocus. Bat concentrated on Meera first.

As with Finnegan, there were shadowed places on her soul, wounds and bruises in her spirit caused by things that Bat could not even begin to imagine. There was a potential for wickedness, but there was no actual evil. The stain a corrupted heart and mind left on the soul was unmistakable, and Meera did not possess it.

Bat sighed in relief. She had not wanted to lose Meera as an ally, or as a friend.

She had just turned her attention to Teagan when a

soft knock came from the front door. "Bat, are you guys there? It's Ciara… and Con."

Bat recognized the voice as the pixie who once loved a leprechaun. A leprechaun murdered simply because he was in the wrong place at the wrong time and had stepped into the middle of a centuries-old feud.

Finnegan's eyes closed and his brows drew together. A few second later he nodded, crossed the room, and opened the door to reveal a petite woman, an old man, and a giant hound flanked by two more around Killer's size. The latter sniffed, then bolted across the room towards Killer, and began examining the pup with licks and playful growls.

Bat smiled at the small reunion as Ciara and Con stepped into the pub.

"Well and now, that was fun." Con stopped a few paces into the room and looked around. "This it then?" he asked.

Finn snorted and Dub grumbled. Mell's amusement increased. Shar sighed.

"Yes, Con, this is it," Finn answered.

"Not much to look at," the pudgy man said. Except he wasn't a man, he was a *dragon*.

Bat had figured it out.

Finn shot him a glare that didn't last long. "Did you at least capture one of them so we could interrogate them?"

Con grinned. "Now why would I be going and doing that?"

"Con."

"Two of them bolted as soon as I showed. And the others… well, I was hungry, and it's been a while since I let my true form out." The last was uttered in a sheepish tone. Then the dragon turned to Bat. "I hear we're having a bit of a scrap with that old fucktard Balor."

Bat's eyes widened. While she was now used to the harsh language, it was shocking to hear it come from such a kind looking face. Con, even from their earliest meeting on her first night in Ireland, had been nothing but polite. "Umm, yes. He is refusing to stay dead."

Con chuckled. "Can't have that, now can we?" He crossed his arms over the slight paunch around his middle. "So, what's the plan?"

Finn, Shar, and Dub all sighed. Bat returned the old dragon's grin. "That's what I want to know as well."

"Now we get a boat," Dub said. "And figure out how they knew we were here." His lapis eyes focused on Finnegan. "Sorry, friend, but you'll need to come with us." Dub must have come to the same conclusion Bat had as soon as she knew they had been found—they couldn't risk the barkeep remaining behind, for their sake and his.

Finnegan's lips tightened then relaxed, and he nodded. "Yeah, the goddess there said as much."

Con clapped his hands together and rubbed them. "Let's get to planning, then."

Chapter Six

MELL

*M*ell had his emotions on lockdown. He'd pushed them deep, so deep *he* didn't even know what they were.

He knew himself well enough to know it was necessary.

Why do we even have to do this?

He knew why. It was just...

Returning home was never easy. Especially when that home consisted of an indifferent mother and an abusive ass of a father. At least they were only meeting Da. Ma had been living at the property near Dublin for the last couple of centuries, so he didn't need to worry about running into her. Sometimes, he thought he despised her more than his father. At least his father had *been* there, and, in his own sick way, at least he had *cared*.

Anger stirred and he pushed it down into the recesses

of his mind, imagining it as a black hole from which nothing could escape....

He, Shar, Dub, Bat and Cuchi stood on a shallow balcony overlooking the harbor below. Weak morning sun shone through the fine haze that hung in the air. It would be burned off by the time noon rolled around.

Only a few ships were docked. Most were smaller freighters. One, however, stood out. A large yacht, the design sleek and powerful, floated at the end of the quay. *The Royal Crane*.

"You ready for this?" Dub asked. He, more than anyone, knew just what Mell had gone through over the years. By the time Shar was born, Mell had been spending as much time as he could outside of the hellhole called home.

Bat slipped her hand into his and gave a gentle squeeze. He knew she'd seen something about that time in at least one of her visions. She hadn't said what it was and he hadn't asked. He didn't need to know what she saw—he'd lived it.

He also didn't need to talk about it. No, what he truly needed to do was put it all behind him, once and for all.

"I'm ready," he answered.

"Everyone remember their roles?"

Affirmatives came from all around.

Mell smirked, though there wasn't much mirth involved. Their roles weren't really *roles* at all. They weren't going to act in any way, or try to be cute and trick Da. No, they were going to go in there and lay it all out. They were going to assess Da's reactions to what they had to say. They were going to do their best to monitor every single person on that ship, every single clan member gathered around their father, and they were going to determine the level of the Crane Clan's involvement in Balor's return.

If there had been more time, subtlety would have been the best course. But, as Bat had pointed out after Con dealt with whoever had come for them at the pub, there *was* no time.

So, they were here to confront Da and gain a boat. It sounded much more simple that it really was.

Mell snuck a look at Dub, who'd pulled out his phone. He knew his brother was thinking of trading the brooch for cooperation and a boat if Da turned out to simply be oblivious of Scath's manipulations instead of in on them. Mell wasn't about to allow that. He'd thought it over, and he had a plan.

Dub hit a few buttons and the speaker on the phone rang out in the mid-morning air.

"*Hello.*"

Mell's fingers twitched in Bat's grip. That voice was as harsh and grating as ever.

"Da," Dub said. They'd agreed he would be the one to handle their father, and Mell would let him, right up until it was time for him to take over.

"*My boy.*" A dark chuckle came over the line. "*We weren't expecting you for another week or so.*"

"Some things have changed."

"*Have they now?*"

"I will not play with you, Alatrom. We will meet at the main boat in ten minutes."

Silence. Then, "*I am already there, no need to wait. You and*

45

your companions may enter now. I'll expect you in a few moments." Then he hung up.

So, Da had eyes on the harbor and knew they were there already. Not a surprise. Those last words also meant Alatrom knew that Cu Chulainn was with them, and that he could transport them directly aboard the yacht.

Also not really a surprise.

Alatrom was never stupid. Oblivious to some things that he didn't want to see or acknowledge, yes, but never stupid. It was the reason they had decided on the direct approach.

"I'm ready," Cuchi said.

Mell's fingers twitched again. He didn't mind the giant idiot as much as his brothers did. All his animosity for the guardi stemmed from the fact that his *brothers* had been hurt by the sidhe in one way or another. And the fact that Cuchi kept trying to flirt with *his* goddess…

Though, his behavior *had* grown a bit more respectful since Bat had cast the curse on the guardi.

Which was exactly why Cuchi was here instead of Finn. One, they trusted Finn to manage and protect the other fae while the O'Loinsighs handled the boat. Two, due to that curse, Cuchi *had* to protect the brothers.

"Go," Dub said.

Cuchi twisted his hands and a moment later they were on the deck of the yacht. A startled bird scrambled out of the way, its colorful feathers trailing behind.

"Is that a peacock?" Bat asked. "Why are there peacocks?"

The pure bewilderment in her tone startled a laugh out of Mell. Some of the tension in his shoulders melted away.

Gods and goddesses, he loved her. He loved her straightforward attitude. He loved the look on her face when she encountered something new. He loved the way her lips quirked and her head tilted. He'd become fascinated with guessing which new words would come out of her mouth next. He loved her truthfulness, and the way she held his hand in silent comfort.

He just... loved her. One day he'd work up the courage to say the words out loud.

The deck was empty except for the lone bird, but Mell knew better. Da had eyes on them. Mell loosened his hold on his powers enough to scan the ship for emotional signatures. One, two, three... twelve. There were twelve Fomoiri aboard, including his father.

It took a few seconds, but a man appeared at the top of a companionway. He was bulky, like most Fomoiri, and his shoulders filled the narrow passageway. "This way," he grunted out. He turned his back and headed back down.

Mell narrowed his eyes. Even though it had been a while since he'd come around, he thought he knew each of his father's men. The clans of the Fomoiri did not change quickly, or often. He tugged on Bat's hand to keep her beside him and took his place behind Dub. Shar followed, and Cuchi brought up the rear.

He couldn't help but compare this yacht to the last *Golden Crane* he'd been aboard. That one had been a beautiful galleon, which Alatrom had somehow taken off of a Spanish captain. The sleekly modern lines of this newest version of the *Crane* were lacking compared to the warmth of the rough wood of the older one.

The man halted outside a pair of doors at the end of

the gangway, knocked twice, and pushed the door open. "Ya can go in." Again the words were curt, almost disrespectful.

It has *been a while since we've come around.*

They entered the office.

And Mell once more confronted the man who had turned his early years into pure torture.

Chapter Seven

Dearest Bastet,
How does one deal with someone they do not like, but
cannot bring themselves to hate?
I think the answer to this question will be very important.
The more I think on it, throughout my existence I have had
many people like this my life...

- Bat, the goddess who apparently still has much to learn
about life

BAT

She tightened her grip on Mell's hand as he pulled her into the office. He wasn't giving off any sort of emotional tendrils, but she could imagine some of what he must be feeling based on the one vision she'd seen.

Her life had been nothing like his, but she did

understand how it felt to have those who were supposed to care for you turn their backs. It was not a pain easily recovered from. Mell had been one of the ones to show her that she could belong again, that she could be whole.

She would do what she could to help him heal from his own pain. She would do whatever he needed her to do. And for now, that was to continue to hold his hand and make sure he knew she was there.

Their father—Alatrom, he was called—sat behind a wide desk, the top of which was a mellow and warm wood. The office itself was mostly white, the decorations minimal and delicate; a slender vase in one corner, a painting of a sunset on the wall behind him, a pastel rug under their feet.

It all provided a stark contrast to the man who called this room his domain. His dark hair grayed at the temples, and his hands and face were gnarled from centuries in the sun and the salt-wind of the ocean. While his frame had begun to run to fat, he was still heavy with muscle.

He was an older and rougher version of Dub, frown included.

Bat smiled. She couldn't help it. Was this her not-man in a millennia or two?

"Well now, and that's a pretty sight," Alatrom said.

Mell's fingers tightened over hers and Bat returned the squeeze. She kept her smile in place; after all, there was no harm in exerting a little charm. There was no way she would fall for anything this monster said, not after she'd seen this darker side in her visions. "I am Bat," she said.

"Bat." Alatrom's eyes narrowed.

"Yes."

"Not heard much about you. Why don't we visit for a bit?" He flicked a finger at the brothers. "You lot can wait outside." He didn't acknowledge Cuchi in any way.

"No," Bat said.

"No?" He gave her a displeased frown—the same one Dub used. She suppressed the urge to laugh. If she told the oldest brother just how much his father reminded her of him, no doubt he would give her that same frown.

"There is no time. When everything is done, I may consider your request." She had no intention of spending time alone with this not-man, but arguing over something so trivial was a waste of time.

"*Realta...*"

"Hush. Now is not the time to be distracted. All of you will need to take chill pills."

Alatrom choked on nothing. It was satisfying to see. "I see..." he finally said. He tapped his desktop a few times. "Then just tell me why you're here."

"We—" Dub started.

"Not you," his father cut in. "Her."

Interesting. "Why?" she asked. She had a feeling his answer would be important to evaluating his true intentions. She opened her mind and senses, delving into his soul. She would need to recharge somehow after this, but she could push out enough power for this scan. This one was important.

"Because," Alatrom was saying, "I know these boys, and they will twist their words to suit their own needs, even unconsciously. I want to hear it from you."

Mell sucked in a breath, Dub let out a low rumble, and

Shar grunted. Cuchi remained silent. No one was attacking them, and he was not part of this drama.

"Why do you think I will not twist my words as well?" she asked. She needed a little more time to dig into this Alatrom. "I am with them, after all."

"Because you, Bat The Unifier, are a goddess who has set her own fate and made her own choices, and the last I heard, you were very passionate about a little subject called justice." A smug look overtook his face. "You will tell it to me exactly as you see it. I can make my own decisions from there."

She tilted her head. He knew much more about her than he'd earlier implied. However, she detected no corruption in him.

It was unexpected. In fact, his soul was cleaner than Meera's, which was even more surprising. *How could* this *man…?* Had he tricked her senses somehow?

Do not doubt yourself. Those had been The Morrigan's words. This not-man had a fairly clean soul, and he asked for the blunt truth. Should she give it?

Bat took a leap of faith—in herself.

"Balor seeks to come back." She didn't take her gaze from him for a moment.

Only the slightest widening of his eyes told her that this was not what he'd been expecting. It meant Balor had managed to keep the knowledge of his activities away from an otherwise well informed man. Balor's resources were extensive and those he'd swayed to his side were extremely loyal. But at the same time, not all fae and immortals were aware of what was to come, and this cut down on the potential for additional chaos.

"Explain," was all he said. He sat in his chair, his back straight and his palms now flat on the desk.

Such arrogance. Bat decided to let it go for now. "When Balor was slain in the battle of Mag Tuired, a portion of his soul escaped into an effigy." She thinned her lips, thinking how to explain things. "You are aware that the pieces of a soul will always seek to be reunited?"

Alatrom nodded, the movement sharp on his stiff neck.

She hesitated on the next part. The actual operation of the soul blades was a secret of the Celtic deities, and was not one for her to reveal on her own. Well, not any more than she had already let slip to her companions. Bat settled for the simplest explanation. "Well, that small piece of soul is allowing Balor to reach into the world and communicate with potential allies. He's spent centuries wiggling onto people's thoughts and souls. We know for a fact he has influenced a good portion of the Wild Hunt if not the whole of it, at least a few sluagh and Fir Bolg, a portion of the Fomoiri…" She took a breath and said the last. "And at least one of your own men, who is working behind your back."

He scowled, but that was his only reaction. There was no surprise this time, only anger.

"Who?"

This time she did look to Dub, who nodded. "Scath," she said. "You had put a scrying spell on the invitation sent to the pub for the clan gathering. There was a secondary spell laid in, allowing the caster to piggyback on the first spell. That caster was Scath."

She gave him a moment to digest that information.

His gaze softened and focused over her shoulder. After a moment he rolled his shoulders and sat forward. "That proves nothing."

"Except Balor acted upon information he could have only gained by spying through the invitation."

"And how do you know I was not the one who acted upon that information?"

"I know," she said simply, still following her instincts.

Flash. Alatrom stared down at a bloody and beaten Mell. He had named the boy himself. Mell, for he was the joy of the clan, had been from the hour of his birth. But Alatrom had found out the boy was not his son, and that joy turned to rage. He stared down at the all too fragile figure crumpled at his feet. Protectiveness warred with anger, and turned into something new. Determination. Mell was not his, no, but he would turn the boy into a proper Fomoiri. It was the only way to clean up the mess his wife had made...

Alatrom stared at her with wide eyes, his lips parted. "Why are there stars in her eyes?"

"Every damn time," she heard Cuchi mutter. Bat could almost feel the guardi's eye-roll.

Alatrom shook himself. "Let's say I believe everything you've just said. Why are you here?"

Bat gave him a smile. She could not like this not-man, but now she could not bring herself to hate him. She had wanted to, but she kept finding pieces of her not-men in him. Dub's grumpiness, Mell's flirting and charm, and Shar's protectiveness, even as warped as the last had become.

"We need a boat," she finally said.

He let out a booming laugh. "Ah, now this, I understand. This is business." He crossed his arms over his chest. "And what will you give me in exchange?" He shook his head, his expression admonishing. "I don't just give things away, girl. That's not how it works around here."

Mell stiffened and Shar moved to stand directly behind her, his heat pressing against her back.

Dub strode to his father's desk and leaned forward, placing his palms flat on the surface. "I have let you have you fun, old man. But this stops here. You do not disrespect our goddess."

Alatrom's brows rose, the rest of his expression unfazed. "*Your* goddess? Does The Morrigan know about this? Last I heard, no one was allowed to worship—"

"She does." Cuchi's deep voice out through the room and halted the budding argument.

Everyone twisted their heads to look at him.

He shrugged. "The Morrigan *is* aware and she is making an exception for this case." He rolled his eyes. "Can we get back to the negotiations now?"

It was Alatrom's turn to shrug. "Of course. So, as I was saying, *goddess*, what will you give me?"

Dub's eyes closed for a brief moment before popping open, determination written cleanly on his features. "I have something you've been looking for." He reached for a small pouch on his belt.

Mell dropped her hand. "Dub, stop," he said. His anger cut through the air like a blade, glanced over Bat, then was quickly subdued. The men jerked. Mell approached his father, his shoulders stiff and his hands loose at his sides. He was angry, yes, but he was controlling it. "You dare to ask a price for this? Fine." He held his hand out and cream-colored card stock appeared in his fingers. He slammed it onto the desk. "Here is your price."

Alatrom looked down. Gold lettering winked back at him. "It's the invitation to the gathering."

"It is. It's what you get in exchange."

"I don't understand." There was a flash of something in the clan leader's blue eyes, something that Bat might have called sorrow, but it was gone too quickly for her to be sure.

"I'm giving you a way to keep this clan from falling apart, if it hasn't already." Mell's tone matched his posture, stiff and cold. "Use it to track Scath. Unless he's here?"

"He's not. He went out last night and hasn't returned."

Oh. Was he one of the people Con ate?

Mell smirked, as if he already knew what Alatrom's answer would be. "Then use this as a way to find him. We reversed the scrying spell and linked it to the scryer. *To Scath.*" Mell nudged it with a finger. "See for yourself."

Alatrom didn't hesitate. It was another thing Bat could respect about him. He placed his hand flat over the luxurious paper.

Then his lips thinned to white lines and his face went red. "That bastard," he growled out. He locked gazes with Mell, lapis blue and warm brown clashing together. "You'll have the ship. I can't give you my best, but it'll be fast enough." He stood, his color returning to normal as he scanned the five people in front of him before settling on

Dub. "Did you keep up with your mariner's classifications?"

"Well enough," was the answer.

Alatrom grunted. "How many does it need to carry?"

The men hesitated. Bat did not, she had already made her decisions about this not-man. "About thirty-five."

"Any of them know how to operate a boat or engine?"

That was not something she knew the answer to, and she looked to Dub.

"Probably. Either way, we'll make do without the crew."

"Huh. All right then. I'll keep it small so it's easy to manage. Quarters will be cramped, but since this isn't a pleasure cruise..." He opened a drawer and picked up a phone. "Get the Blue Heron fueled and ready. You have one hour." Hanging up, Alatrom turned to Dub. "You'll get your boat."

"Thank you." The words sounded as though they would strangle the eldest brother on the way out.

Again, that flash of emotion appeared in Alatrom's eyes, the ones that matched his eldest's so well. He locked those eyes on Bat as though he wanted to say something, then turned back to Dub. "You keeping her?"

"Dammit Da," Mell ground out. His hands curled into fists and trembled, though no stray cuts of anger leaked out. "Watch yer mouth."

"Yes," Shar said from behind her, speaking for the first time since they entered the room. One of his arms went around her middle and pulled her back into him. "She will be staying with us."

Alatrom's gaze went unfocused and then he nodded, as

though coming to some kind of decision. "After this, do not bother to come back. I can't have my clan known to have ties with an Egyptian deity, and I cannot have it known my sons are shacking up with her." He glared at Dub. "Ye'r out."

Shock replaced Dub's frown and Shar's arm dropped from around her. Mell's shoulders sagged before tensing once again. The office seemed to darken even though nothing changed in the light atmosphere.

"You bastard," Mell growled out as he lunged across the desk, catching his father with a powerful blow to the jaw. Papers, pens, and folders went flying as they crashed into the wall behind the desk.

Alatrom didn't fight back. He took each punch until Dub and Shar finally recovered from their shock and pulled their brother off of their father.

"It's enough, Mell," Shar rumbled, his thick arm around his older brother's neck. He tightened his hold just enough to keep Mell in place.

"Not enough," Mell spit out. Anger slashed out from him once more, uncaring this time about what it hit. The blows weren't physical but mental, and Bat flinched.

She started toward Mell as Dub spoke. "It is enough," he said. He stood in front of Mell and grabbed his face, forcing his brother's gaze to meet his. "It is *enough*. We have what we came for. And now it's time to go." Dub's voice was low and even, as though he spoke to a wild animal that needed both coaxing and taming.

Bat laid her hand on Mell's arm and stroked. She didn't try to say anything, but she hoped that her touch would help him regain his control. It took a few minutes, and in all that time none of the room's occupants moved.

"Fine," Mell finally said and rolled his shoulders against Shar's hold. The giant hesitated only a moment then dropped his arm. Mell gathered Bat to him and held her close, burying his face in her hair. She slipped her arms around his middle and stroked his back. Twisting her head, she was able to catch sight of Alatrom from the corner of her eye. A look of... tenderness appeared through his forming bruises and split lip, before it was quickly wiped away.

Dub spoke from beside them. "We accept your terms, old man."

"We are no longer part of the Crane Clan," Shar added.

Bat's hands stilled on Mell's back as she realized what had just happened, what Alatrom had done.

He'd set them free. He had given them what they wanted. *Everything* they wanted.

Do the brothers realize what their father has just done? Do they realize it was for their sake, and not only for his own? Bat had no doubts that this was done for them. Oh, Alatrom had meant very word, he really didn't want to be associated with an Egyptian goddess, even if it was a tenuous connection; but that was just his excuse.

He had done this because, despite everything, part of him still loved his sons.

Bat had no proof, nothing except the flickers of expression she had seen, her brief flash of vision, and her instincts.

She also knew she wasn't wrong.

She twisted in Mell's hold just enough to be able to

catch Alatrom's gaze once more. Then she nodded. It was an acknowledgement that at least one person knew the truth of what had just happened in this room.

Alatrom picked himself off the floor. "Well, and now that's settled, I have business to attend to. Namely, the eradication of a traitor." He strode for the door. "Ya can all see yerselves out. The boat's up at the Keeley Docks. They're expecting ya." He hesitated with his hand on the doorknob. "I'll contact ya when Scath is taken care of."

Then he was gone.

For some reason, there was a pressure behind Bat's eyes and they burned.

Chapter Eight

FINN

*F*inn sighed in the late morning sun. He was north of Londonderry now, somewhere along the coast on an uninhabited stretch of rocky shore. It was just his luck he'd been relegated to baby sitter for this next interlude in their quest for the cauldron, Tir Hudi, and stopping Balor.

Babysitting. That's exactly what he was doing— babysitting a group of fae who didn't get along on the best of days. Without Bat around to focus their attention or pints of Guinness to mellow them, they'd reverted to throwing childish insults and sulking in their shadows.

The only ones not causing any trouble were the human, Old Mike, and Con—the latter was having too much fun watching the chaos.

"Look, death breath, I am not interested in your woe is me tale. I'm only here—"

"You're only here because ya want to see what ya can get out of the goddess," Meera cut off Carrig. "I know yer type, don't think—"

A silver pixie hovered in front of Finn. "Does the goddess really have four men? Are ya really one of them?"

This one had been at the cottage with them, Finn thought her name was Taire. Before he could answer or wave her away, she jumped in again.

"I wish I could figure out to handle four men. The closest I've gotten was three, but two of them didn't know about the others, and..."

Finn walked away only to be brought up by Ailis and Femi—one of the men of ba—squaring off. "Look," Ailis said, exasperation coloring her voice. "I'm telling ya, it's just dye. I'm no' a mermaid! I don't even know if mermaids have green hair." Ailis threw her hands in the air.

"I just want a scale for my collection. All I ask is that, if time permits while we are on the boat, you transform and let me have one." The man of ba's brow was furrowed and his lips were pulled back in a terrifying grimace.

Ailis's eyes widened and she twisted her head around, scanning over the assembled fae. No doubt looking for Saoirse to defend her innocence about being a mermaid.

Femi reached for Ailis's hair and she slapped his hand away. He hissed.

"Enough," Finn finally shouted. Everyone froze. He opened his mouth to say more when his phone rang. "Finally," he muttered as he fished it from his pocket.

"We got it," Dub said as soon as Finn answered, skipping the greetings. "The Blue Heron, up at the Keeley docks. It'll be ready in about an hour, but you might as well head up that way and get settled in. We'll be right behind you."

Then Dub hung up, not even waiting for Finn's acknowledgement.

Finn's fingers tightened around the phone. What had crawled up the Fomoiri's ass and died? *Did something happen to Bat, to my goddess?*

He froze as dread filled him. Possibilities flashed through his mind before he could get himself under control. No, whatever happened had nothing to do with Bat. Otherwise, the eldest O'Loinsigh would not have been so calm. He'd been curt and cold, but he'd been in control.

Finn shifted and turned away from the prying eyes of the now quiet group of ragtag fae. He needed a moment to gather his balance.

It had been happening more and more. Ever since he allowed Bat into his heart, ever since he acknowledged the possibility of loving again—of loving her. Ever since the conversation where he told her he didn't know if he loved her, or ever could.

He'd been lying—both to himself and to her. He just… wasn't ready to admit anything. Not until this was over, not until he knew she wouldn't be ripped away from him by fate.

He'd known that pain before. Not once, but twice. His first wife had been cursed into the form of a deer and forced to leave him. He'd searched for a cure for centuries before finally admitting defeat. Despite all this, he'd continued to visit her, but eventually she'd forgotten her former life and husband.

Then there had been Grainne. While he now knew that he hadn't fully loved her, it had certainly felt like it at the time. The pain of loosing her not just once, but twice still haunted him. He did not regret that day nearly three months ago, or what he'd done in the shadow of Benbulben. He'd worked long and hard to carve those emotions from himself.

If he lost Bat… he wouldn't survive. And he knew it.

Drawing one last deep breath, he turned back to the assembled fae.

A few dozen fae. A few dozen immortals who were used to being on their own. A few dozen allies whose very nature dictated their rivalries.

How in all creation was this even supposed to work?

He trusted Bat, he did. She claimed this was what needed to happen for them to finally take down Balor. That these were the people they needed, that these few would allow them the advantages necessary to prevail.

He trusted in Bat and her intuition and insight and visions.

He just didn't have to like being made to work with such amateurs. He was a trained soldier, once the leader of the Fianna, and currently a captain of the Guardi.

"So, where we off to now?" Meera snapped at him.

Finn sucked in a breath, this time out of frustration instead of apprehension. "Keeley Docks. They got a boat."

Saoirse stepped forward. "Do you know what kind?"

"No." He paused. "Can you operate it?" He knew she was a selkie, but that didn't necessarily mean she could operate a ship. The seal-shifters lived *in* the ocean, not on it.

She shrugged. "Possibly. Have to see what type it is."

Finn nodded, putting his attention back on the immediate task at hand. "Anyone else have experience sailing or operating a motor vessel?"

"Sailing, yes. Engines, no." That was Con.

Teagan stepped forward. "No boat experience, but I'm good with machines. Very good," the banshee said.

"Anyone else?" He had hoped for more, but wasn't surprised. Most of the fae they'd gathered were earthbound, taking their powers from the land in one way or another. The Fomoiri were the immortal race that had always dominated the waters around Ireland.

Dechtire, the silver haired goblin, raised her hand. "I have a small fishing vessel. It's only a six-meter, but I'm not lost aboard a boat." She gave Finn a wry smile. "I'll know what ya mean when ya say 'port', and I won't think ya mean wine."

Finn nodded. With these four, and the brothers, they would probably be able to manage. The immediate priority was to get away from the reach of the Wild Hunt while they strategized the next steps for when they reached Tir Hudi and the cauldron. "We'll finish this up once we're aboard. It'll take about an hour to have the boat ready and fueled, according to Dub, so that gives us time to sort things. You four," he continued, pointing at those who had spoken up, "will go to Dub as soon as we arrive and tell him exactly what you have experience with. The rest of you, stay alert and out of the way." He paused. "And *behave*."

They shouldered their packs once more. He gestured everyone closer, stretched his arm behind him to pat the harp hanging over his back, nodded, and then twisted his hands, taking them to the next leg of their journey.

He managed to land them in an empty parking lot designated for the owners of the boats moored at the Keeley Docks. It was a lesser-known marina, luckily, and mid-morning on a weekday didn't see many people in this area.

"Let's go." He headed for the walk that lead to the docks below, making sure that Old Mike and the human were close behind him. That man was a key piece to unraveling Balor's plans, and he couldn't get away.

"I'm staying behind, now that ya have yer boat," Finnegan said and didn't move.

Finn turned back to him, waving the others to continue. "Not an option."

The barkeep crossed his arms over his chest. "I got no business in this."

Finn pulled in a deep breath, analyzing the scent. He'd assumed Finnegan was at least part Fomoiri. Crisp apples and the scent of fresh grass after a rain filled his senses. Under it was... holly? "Druid?" he asked.

The man nodded.

Huh. Lone druids weren't that common these days. Most had found themselves in the employ of the Tribunal centuries ago, like Ruith, the seer. While powerful in the use of runes and other learned magics, they didn't have inherent powers like other immortals. Their longevity was due to the amount of energy they channeled through their body from the earth, as opposed to being born that way.

"Not a call I can make on my own," he finally told the druid.

The other man's lips thinned, but he shrugged and started forward.

They brought up the rear of the odd procession.

"We could use someone skilled in runes," Finn said, keeping his tone conversational.

"The boys know everything I do."

The boys? Finnegan made it sound like he was older than the O'Loinsigh brothers, and Dub was at least four millennia old. The druids officially landed in Ireland only twenty-five hundred years ago.

"How exactly do you know Dub and the others?"

Finnegan twisted his head to study Finn as they approached a set of stairs leading down to the quay. "Let's just say I helped them out a time or two, a while back. And let's just say that they've occasionally returned the favor."

Finn didn't reply. That was probably as much as he would get out of the man. Truthfully, it was all he needed. Immortals led extremely long lives. There was not one person or deity who knew the totality of what he himself had experienced. He did not need to know the whole of someone else's existence. Sometimes the best thing to do was to leave the past in the past.

As long as this man posed no threat to him or his goddess, he would let the past lie.

Just then five figures appeared on a pier about fifty

meters away next to a medium sized cruising trawler, maybe twenty-five meters long. It was older and a little beat up around the edges, but the deep blue paint-job was fresh, and not a speck of rust was in sight. There was a small observation tower above the bridge, and the upper cabin took up at least half the upper deck.

Finn wasn't too familiar with boats, just enough to know some basic terms, but he had to admit that it looked like it was going to be a tight fit to get everyone on there. There would definitely be more than a few bodies bunking under the stars and stretched out on the foredeck...

The other fae had spotted Bat and the O'Loinsighs, and headed toward the boat. Or was it ship? He honestly didn't know.

Finn was bringing up the rear with Finnegan, about halfway down the wharf running parallel to shore, when the attack came.

Chapter Nine

DUB

*W*hy *fucking me?*

That's the only thought that would stay in his head.

After dealing with the nightmare that was his father, and keeping Mell from exploding, Dub was ready to grab Bat and leave everything behind. And he meant *everything*.

He really didn't care about the cauldron, gods, or Balor and what the fucker was trying to do. He cared about his brothers, his pub, and Bat. Unfortunately, Bat cared about what Balor was up to and the repercussions of his return, so...

So, Dub was now busy mentally brushing up on his knowledge of sea-faring motor vessels. It had been a decade or so since he last had anything to do with the sea.

As he scanned over The Blue Heron, he decided that luck was falling on his side. His asshole father had actually given him a boat he knew a little something about; and it was old enough that unless it had had a major refit some time in the last couple of years, he would be able to helm the damned thing.

He waited impatiently for one of his father's men to come greet them. Bat, Shar, Mell, and Cuchi stood beside him on the pier. Bat shifted, restless. She looked as though she wanted to say something, but held it in.

What did she think of Da? He'd been focused on Mell and Da while in the office, but the few glimpses he'd caught of Bat's expression... her expressions weren't what he'd expected.

Not that he knew *what* he'd expected, but she'd *smiled* at the asshole.

Dub didn't like it.

From the corner of his eye he caught the group of people approaching from the walk above. The dull sound of their steps echoed once they hit the pier and soft murmurs from their conversation floated on the gentle breeze.

Aside from the occasional creak as a boat rubbed against the docks, it was the only sound in the marina.

That wasn't right.

Dub stiffened. "Mell," he said. He didn't need to say more.

Mell tilted his head. "There are blank spots."

"Fuck," Shar said, his voice low. He moved behind Bat once more, ready to grab her at the first hint of danger.

Cuchi was a second or two behind them in realizing what was going on. But he did catch on. "How many?" he asked.

Dub shoved aside the ever-present resentment that welled any time he had to acknowledge the warrior's presence. They would never be friends, they were barely allies, but he had enough maturity to push the past aside —at least for his goddess's sake.

"At least a dozen blank spots," Mell answered, keeping his voice low. "Three on the boat, the rest..."

The attack came from the water. A half dozen Fomoiri shot into the air with a spray of salt water. They headed directly for Bat, barely sparing a glance for the men surrounding her. Shar wrapped his arms around her and spun, running down the pier toward the wharf, and the additional fae who were only a dozen meters away by this time.

Dub blocked two of the men, pushing them back just enough to give him the room to pull his sword from its fold of space. He spun and attacked. He wouldn't be able to kill them, this wasn't that type of blade, but he needed to incapacitate them.

They needed to get on that boat and out to sea. He could only hope that whoever was waiting for them aboard hadn't had the time to sabotage anything vital.

He twisted his head to check on Bat. Shar still had her. Mell was beside them, his own sword out and held at the ready. Bright spots of color winked above them all—pink, red, silver, violet. The pixies were diving at the Fomoiri, causing just enough distraction to keep them off balance, for now.

Dub knew what he had to do, but it went against every instinct he had. He turned away from his goddess and back to the boat. The gangway was in place, a narrow bridge from the pier to the foredeck. He needed to get on board, take out the men Mell had sensed, and get the boat started.

"What are you waiting for?" Cuchi spat out, then headed up toward the boat.

Dub was a step behind him. "I'll head for the bridge. You find the engine room."

Cuchi nodded and stepped lightly over the gunwale and onto the deck, heading directly for a companionway at the rear of the cabin. Dub went the opposite direction, toward the bow of the boat and the door to the bridge.

There really was no time for him to stop and analyze the situation, but he took a few seconds nevertheless.

Who out of the clan would be the most likely to sympathize with Balor and side with Scath against their father? Which men could he expect to come against? He'd recognized a few of the faces that went after Bat in the half-second he'd had to recognize them. They were among the oldest and strongest of the clan.

Figures.

They were also the ones who best remember what it had been like with Balor running things—the wars, the battles, the blood and victory and spoils.

These were all things that were seductive to the Fomoiri—Dub admitted it. Hell, these were all things that called to him on a certain level. The Fomoiri thrived on conflict, and embraced and revered physical strength. They were a race that struggled to control themselves in this modern era of pseudo-peace.

Bracing himself, he shoved open the door to the

bridge. He took the room in, in a glance. Everything looked to be in place.

There. A shimmer in the far corner.

He didn't hesitate. Tucking his sword back in its fold of space, he dove at the shimmer. His body hit hardened muscle and armor. The two Fomoiri crashed to the deck of the small space.

Dub needed to finish this fast, or he needed to get them out of the small room. There were too many delicate controls and equipment here—equipment that wouldn't be able to handle a sustained battle between two immortals.

He grabbed the now visible man and rolled. There was a sharp pain in his side as the smell of copper filled the air. He didn't pause, just wrapped his arms tighter around the man, and squeezed. He put all his strength into it.

A sharp grunt and crunching bone were his rewards. The man still struggled in Dub's hold despite this. He pulled the dagger from the eldest O'Loinsigh's side before thrusting it in again, this time twisting the blade.

An all too familiar haze began to envelope Dub. The battle frenzy was coming on him. He needed to get out of the bridge before it took over, before all he could think about was destroying the enemy regardless of consequences.

Dub shifted his arms, wrapping one around the man's neck. Seconds. That was all he needed. If he could just get the correct hold, get the right pressure on the arteries in the neck, he could...

There. Dub flexed his arm, uncaring if his strength did

more than block the flow of blood. There was another crack as a few vertebrae gave way, and the man went limp.

Dub sucked in gulps of air as he struggled to push back his thirst for blood and destruction.

Not now, not now. Now is not the time. Need to get the boat started. Need to get it started for my goddess. For Bat. For Bat.

The haze began to recede. Dub grabbed up the limp Fomoiri from where he'd fallen to the deck. It was Eichil. The Fomoiri was a few centuries older than Dub, and very skilled with a knife. He had a bit of ability with charming the air around him, which was how he'd been able to hide so well. He was usually used for reconnaissance missions, or assassination.

Dub grabbed the back of his leather belt, dragged him from the bridge, and threw him over the side of the boat. Moments later Dub was at the helm, studying the controls.

He knew this set-up. Good. The keys were also there. Doubly good.

Vaguely he wondered what had happened to the men his father asked to prepare the boat. Someone had obviously begun complying with his father's orders if the keys were where they needed to be.

He powered up the boat. Lights lit up across the helm and gauges adjusted. They had a quarter tank of gas. Not good, but at least it wasn't empty.

The boat had power and basic capabilities. He pushed the button that would start the engines. A low rumble greeted him as faint vibrations made their way from the engine room and to the bridge deck. He kept the boat at a low idle and locked the controls.

Now that he knew the boat was secure and still operable, he crossed to the bridge door and threw it open. He needed to see how the rest were faring.

His heart stopped and his stomach dropped, but he didn't move. He couldn't. He wanted to charge down to the dock and jump into the fray, but he also knew that if he did, they risked losing the boat, and any chance of getting away.

Chapter Ten

Bastie,
Should I become a goddess of music?

- Bat, who has no particular title at this time

BAT

Shar refused to set her down. She pinched his arm and twisted the skin. All he did was grunt.

He was fighting against three men, two of them just as big as he was. Mell was there as well, but he had his own attackers to deal with. The pixies, faster than any of the other fae, had zipped forward and were diving at the attackers in semi-successful attempts to distract them.

There was a cry behind them and Shar twisted his head. It was only a half-second, but it was enough to allow one of the larger men past his defenses. A blade sliced through the air heading directly for Bat's face.

Shar spun at the last moment and grunted.

She knew he'd been hit.

"Let me down, now." He couldn't fight them like this.

He didn't answer her. Instead, he ran toward the group of fae that had huddled together in defense, crossing Ari and the other men of ba as they ran to assist Mell.

She and the brothers weren't the only ones under attack. Finn and Finnegan were battling three more immortals as a fourth dragged Daniel and Mike away from the main group.

"No!" she cried out. No, they needed Daniel. He was their ticket to controlling the confrontation with Balor.

Then her gaze caught on something else.

Her harp, the Uaithne, in its case. It was slung across Finn's back. They'd left it with him for safe keeping when they'd gone to visit Alatrom.

The three attackers were concentrating on Finn. He took the brunt of the assault, and Bat knew why. They were after the harp. Killer and the other hounds were doing what they could, snapping at the enemy's legs, but they never seemed to connect.

The fae had twisted toward her and Shar at her cry. Why were they just standing there? Neall and Faolan were slack-faced for a split second before their expressions transformed into determination. Shadows shot out of Faolan, wrapping themselves around one of the men. Neall... changed. His body grew taller, his face thinned, and fangs sprouted from his mouth. Unlike the men of ba, whose teeth were thin needles, Neall's were large and triangular, almost like a shark's.

They were teeth made to slice through flesh and tear it from the bone.

Neall dove for the man who had Daniel and Old Mike. He aimed for the legs, a fierce predator determined to cripple his prey.

The attacker screamed and released Old Mike, who then hung on to Daniel and attempted to pull him away. A sword came down on Neall's back, slicing deep enough to reveal bone through his clothing and bloody muscles.

More shadows stretched across the few feet separating them all as the other sluagh joined in a beat too late.

Ailis and the other trooping fae shook their heads and blinked. Her eyes widened then narrowed as she pulled a dagger and dove into the fight.

The rest remained where they were. The leprechauns, Con, Saoirse, Dechtire, the banshees... why did they not fight?

Flash. Bat, the harp in her hands. She stood alone on the pier as she plucked the strings. Melody poured forth, the soothing notes weaving through the air in a subtle dance. Those notes entered the ears and minds of all who listened and calmed them. They dropped their weapons and arms as they swayed where they stood. A few sat on the rough wood planks and stared out at the waves of the sea.

The battle ceased as Bat played. She spoke of the rest after a battle, of the time in the deep of the night when armies slept. She told them of the peace of coming home after the war. She painted pictures of restful nights beside a fire, laughing with comrades. She painted this picture, and she did it all with the harp.

"Ailis!" she cried out. "The harp. Get me the harp!"

Ailis didn't turn, but she must have heard Bat. She went straight for Finn. The sluagh had their shadows wrapped around all four of the enemy. Snarls and clashing metal still sounded behind her, drawing closer.

No time, they had no time. She needed the harp.

"Shar. Please."

No answer from her giant. They were surrounded by the rest of the fae now, who shifted restlessly on their feet.

Finn had been right. They were a ragtag bunch of misfits who didn't know how to work together. This was their first test, and they were failing.

"I need you to trust me," she said, reaching behind her to find his cheek. "Trust me, my giant."

There was a low growl, but his arm loosened.

"The harp, I need it." Bat pushed power behind those words.

It was Teagan who answered that power. The dark-haired banshee raced toward Ailis and Finn, then past them. She dove onto the back of one of the Fomoiri, opened her mouth, and screamed.

Blood erupted from the man's eyes, nose and ears. His mouth fell open and he dropped to his knees.

Teagan leapt away, but not before one of the enemy's blades found her side. She staggered away and fell to one knee at the edge of the dock. Swaying, she fell into the water.

"No!" Meera stepped forward, but Saoirse was faster. The brown-haired girl dove into the sea after the banshee.

Teagan's distraction provided Finn just enough time to

withdraw from the fight and shrug the harp case over his head. Ailis sprinted back to Bat and laid the precious treasure in her hands.

The Uaithne.

The Dagda's harp.

One of the four treasures of the Tuatha de Danaan.

Bat was about to learn exactly why it was considered as such, and why most armies surrendered in the face of it.

She opened the case and then let it drop to her feet, promising herself she would remember it after everything was over.

She cradled the smooth wood against her, placed her fingers over the strings, and began.

It was hard at first. Even with the vision, she struggled to find the correct tune, the melody that would speak of finished battles. Every time she'd played the harp before this, the songs were instinctive. She put into them what she felt. She simply... added to what was already being played.

Now she needed to create something new.

The song started out hesitant. A few notes plucked with no rhythm. Nevertheless, the warriors paused—on both sides.

She closed her eyes, needing to better concentrate on the song. Shar hovered over her, his heat reminding her that she wasn't alone. Metal crashed together around her, flesh struck flesh, and cries of pain called to her to finish this.

Bat imagined the scene from her vision. She envisioned the attacking Fomoiri laying down their weapons. She conjured up images of them resting together.

Her fingers moved of their own accord. The song picked up speed.

So this was how it worked. She did not need to know the song to play. She needed to tell the harp what she wanted—the instrument would do the rest.

Gradually, the sounds of battle faded, leaving behind harsh breathing amidst the gentle lap of waves against the shore and pilings of the dock. Shar's arm wrapped back around her as her fingers slowed. She opened her eyes.

Their enemies were laid out on the wood slats of the dock, sleeping. Of the fae who had come to help Bat, those who remained whole were helping the injured to stand.

It was over.

For now.

She twisted her head back and up so she could see Shar. His lapis-gaze met hers. "All right?" she asked. She didn't mean only him.

He picked her up, one arm around her back and the other under her legs, uncaring about his injury. "All right enough."

"Shar, you are injured. Put me down."

Her giant grimaced, but set her on her feet. Then he wrapped an arm around her shoulders and headed for the boat.

Mell came alongside them, his left arm hanging limp at his side. Ari and the men of ba strode ahead of them, leading the way. Small cuts marred their dark and wrinkled skin, and Adom left behind a small trail of blood from a deep cut on his thigh.

Meera and Neasa helped Saoirse pull Teagan from the water. Con helped Ailis as she limped beside Eoghan and Cliona. Ailbe and Casey—the leprechauns—trailed after Neall and the other sluagh who supported their friend, their short arms outstretched in case they needed to catch one of the shadow wielding immortals. The pixies darted above everyone, murmuring among themselves in worried tones. Finn and Finnegan brought up the rear along with the hounds.

Bat looked up from where she was cradled against Shar. Dub and Cuchi stood at the side of the boat. Each held a limp form. These were tossed over the rail and into the water. As Dub turned to head back to the bridge, she caught sight of his side. It was covered in a deep red stain.

Her heart pounded. She assured herself that the wounds couldn't be that bad, otherwise he wouldn't be moving so well. *Plus, Finn can heal him with a sip of water from his hands. Finn will be able to fix them all.* Bat held onto this thought as the beaten and injured group made its way up the gangway and onto the boat.

This was their first true test as a team, she realized. And they had failed—every single one of them.

We are going to have to do so much better when we reach Tir Hudi.

Chapter Eleven

SCATH

*H*e flinched as pain tore through his mind.

You dare.

Scath bowed his head.

If she had been harmed before it is time…

"Forgive me." Scath's lips tightened. Resentment filled him.

A whip of pain coursed up his spine. *I own you. Never forget this.*

"I have not forgotten. But, to have everything rely on one pitiful goddess…"

Soothing pressure replaced the pain in a heavy caress. *She is the one who can wield the harp.*

"Are you sure it has to be her?"

Yes.

Scath lifted his head. "She must be swayed."

One way or the other. If we cannot do it through words, we will do it through pain.

"Can I be the one...?"

I will tell you when it is time. For now, we must let them come to us. Do not interfere again.

Scath smiled as he envisioned a certain full-figured goddess spread before him as his shadows held her in place. He would drain her power, slaughter those she loved before her eyes, and make her scream in pain. Then he would claim her.

A broken and powerless goddess. A toy that would never die.

"Oh how I hope you do not succumb to the pretty words..." he whispered into the dark.

Chapter Twelve

SHAR

*S*har lay face down on the foredeck of the *Blue Heron*. The early June sun warmed his bare back and the boat rolled gently under him. While he would always prefer the verdant forests and his little garden by the pub, a part of him had missed the way the ocean could hold and rock a man in her arms.

The worst of the injured had stayed out here on the foredeck instead of moving into the salon or belowdecks. Easier to wash away the blood. If he concentrated hard enough, he could block the groans of the other injured immortals who lay around him being treated. He could even block out his own pain. And he could pretend he was out here for a leisurely day of play with his goddess, where the only thing they'd need to worry about was too much sun and the sea birds stealing their food...

A cool cloth stroked down his back.

"Mm-hmm." The slight grumble slipped from his lips before he could stop it.

"I am not hurting you am I?" Bat's voice was tense and low.

"No, *a stor*." She wasn't hurting him at all. The grumble had been an instinctive reaction to being pulled from his daze. For a minute he'd managed to forget the utterly fucked situation they were in.

A *week*—maybe. That was how long it had been since his life had been turned upside down, beginning with the arrival of that damned invitation. Everything after that was a blur. Well, other than a few very memorable moments.

Moments he hoped he had the chance to repeat soon.

"Finn will be here soon," Bat said as she continued to clean the skin around the slash across his back.

He didn't respond, didn't feel he needed to. He'd received the wound while protecting her, and in truth it was negligible compared to other injuries he'd sustained during the countless battles of his past. The little pain he felt was well worth enduring in order to keep his Bat out of harm's way.

Shar was more worried for Dub, Neall, and the banshee who'd fallen into the water. Mell had a dislocated shoulder, and one of the men of ba had sustained a fairly serious gash on his thigh. Other than that, their group was surprisingly unharmed.

Surprising because, though there had been a mere dozen attackers and their group had outnumbered them by more than twice their amount, some of the volunteer "militia" were so useless in battle they became more hindrance than help.

Yes, he was being ungenerous. This was a group of immortals who had come together just that morning, and had never had a chance to fight together, let alone train together. The fact remained, though, that if things continued this way he, his brother, Bat, and Finn would be better off without the entire lot, including the men of ba and Cuchi.

But that could be his frustration talking. *Maybe I should do what Dub sometimes grumbles about, and make off with the goddess. Just leave it all.*

A pair of heavy boots came into sight, stopping a meter away. "Finn is with Dub," Cuchi said.

Think of the devil... Shar tensed, which caused his skin to pull across his back. There was a burning pain and Bat hissed. "Be still."

Shar deliberately relaxed into the polished wood under him. Bat's hand, sans cloth, caressed his shoulder. He let his eyes fall closed, taking the moment for himself.

"He—" Bat's voice hitched.

Shar shifted just enough to find her calf with his hand and give her a reassuring squeeze.

"He's doing just fine," Cuchi said, a new note entering his voice.

Oh fuck no. That is not happening. Shar knew that tone. He'd heard it enough over the years. It was the same one his Da used when he wanted to coax a woman to his side. It was also the same one Mell used to use.

"Can you tell him I will come check on him once Shar and Mell have been seen to?"

"Of course." A rustle of cloth accompanied the words. "Is there anything else?"

Bat paused, her hand still rubbing Shar's shoulder. "Can you ask either Mell or Ailis to come over?"

"Dechtire is still working on music-boy's shoulder, but I'll ask the insane one to come see ya." Heavy steps moved away as Bat let out a snorting laugh.

Shar frowned. "So, Cuchi is making ya laugh now?" He was still getting used to the idea of her with his brothers and Finn—who he actually *liked*. Her becoming friendly with the asshole who stole his eye...

Jealousy burned in his gut.

Her hand never stopped its gentle caresses. "Hush. I will admit that I have found a few—very few—admirable things in the asshole."

She echoed his mental moniker for the guardi and an unbidden smirk twisted Shar's lips.

"He is a wanker, a shameless womanizer, condescendingly entitled, and too stubborn about all the wrong things, but... he does not dance around topics, nor does he hesitate to say if he feels something is not as it should be. Which are qualities we need in our *allies* in this situation." Cloth brushed across wood as she shifted, and her hair ticked his shoulders as soft lips pressed against the skin of his neck. "I do not like him, but he is not an evil man. I am also... at the last of my rope? I think it is this saying. And his assessment of Ailis was all too accurate. The laughter slipped out."

I am a jealous wanker. "Sorry, *a stor.*"

"There is nothing to apologize for. You did warn me that there would be times during this relationship that you would be difficult." Was that a teasing note in her voice? *I wish I could see her expression right now*.

Shar opened his mouth to continue to apologize, because he *was* at fault here, when another pair of boots appeared before him. The man crouched down and ducked his head until Shar could meet the hazel gaze of the guardi captain that Bat had decided to make hers. There was a bottle of water in one of Finn's hands and a spare t-shirt that smelled faintly of fish in the other.

Finn set the t-shirt aside and unscrewed the cap on the water bottle. "Just a small sip at first, to get the healing going. You're going to need to be able to sit up properly for me," he said, pouring a bare mouthful of water into the palm of his hand. Finn brought his fingers to Shar's lips and tilted his hand so the liquid trickled into Shar's mouth. Warmth and power flowed through him from that small taste, then settled into the skin around his wound.

It itched.

Finn had to feed him two more trickling mouthfuls of water before the skin on Shar's back had closed enough that sitting up wouldn't re-open the wound. It took three more palmfuls of healing water before the injury was gone, leaving only a pale pink scar behind.

Finn left them to check on the other injured. He wouldn't use his healing power on everyone since it drained him, but he could at least make an assessment of their general state.

Bat cleaned the last of the blood away from Shar's back, remaining silent the whole time. Then she handed him the shirt Finn had brought.

"Are ya all right, *a stor*? Ye're awful quiet." It didn't

worry Shar, exactly. She was often silent. But this silence had a weight to it, one he couldn't quite identify.

Was she disappointed in them? In him?

"Of course." There was no hesitation in her voice, and a tightness in Shar's belly eased.

He grabbed her wrist and pulled her in front of him, maneuvering her into his lap. Wrapping his arms around her, he rested his chin on her head. *Just a few moments. I am going to steal just a few more moments before we need to return to planning and worrying.*

"You know I will always protect you," he said as he rocked her softness against him.

She didn't answer right away and he tensed.

"I know," she finally said, laying a soothing hand over one of the arms around her. "But there will be times, my giant, when you will need to let me face my battles alone."

Her voice echoed with visions he couldn't see. He'd come to know that particular note, and all he could do was hold her a little tighter.

I will never let you face them alone. He made the promise to himself and to her.

Chapter Thirteen

Dear Bastie,

When is too much, too much?

When is it better to speak than hold your silence?

What is the line of betrayal?

I bet you never expected to have such questions coming from me, huh?

- Bat, the goddess who is realizing she has never lived in the real world

BAT

*H*er throat closed as Shar rocked her in his arms. She would need to move soon. She wanted to check on Dub and Mell, and on Teagan, Neall, and Adom.

She also needed to find a quiet hour or two to sort her

thoughts. So much had happened in just this one day that she had not had time to properly analyze the new visions, nor process both her fear for her not-men and her relief that they were alive and back with her. Not to mention that visit to the brothers' father...

A blue-grey expanse of water stretched out before her, the sun glinting off ripples and waves as the boat rocked under her. A salty breeze washed over her and the sun warmed her. Bat wanted to sink into these sensations, to ignore the responsibilities pressing down on her.

"Ya summoned me, oh goddess on high?" Ailis popped up in front of her. The trooping fae's green hair was a mess, her deep-blue t-shirt was worse for wear, and dried blood decorated her arms. But her smile was bright, and the usual mischief sparked in her eyes.

Shar's arms tightened around Bat once more.

"Uh. Giant of mine, I must have room to breath." Bat's voice was faint as she attempted to suck in oxygen.

Her pirate-giant grumbled but loosened his hold. Bat patted his arm again then turned her attention back to Ailis. "I was wondering if we could... talk." Bat had never understood why people used that one word to cover a multitude of hidden meanings—until now, that was. *Talk*. The innocent word could conjure both dread and secret meanings. Even to her own ears it sounded ominous, and she really hadn't meant it to be.

Ailis's brows rose and Shar's arms tightened, again.

"It is nothing bad," Bat hurried to interject. "I simply have too many thoughts to easily sort out on my own. The brothers are needed to handle the boat—" this she added for Shar's sake, "—and Finn is still helping the injured."

"So, I'm yer fifth choice."

"No!" Bat bit her lip. "Of course not..."

Ailis laughed again. "I'm just poking at ya. Come on, let's go." Ailis reached down and pulled her up. There was a brief tug-of-war before Shar finally released Bat.

Bat turned back to him for a moment. Using her free arm, she tugged his head to hers and planted a light kiss against his lips. "I would love to stay in your arms the rest of the day, but Dub no doubt needs your assistance with the boat, and I need to speak with Ailis."

Shar frowned but didn't protest further. She knew she had hurt him on some level by choosing Ailis to speak with, but she really couldn't talk over most of her concerns with him, or any of the brothers. Not until she got some clarity.

And Ailis was very good at telling her just the things she needed to hear to gain that clarity.

"Ya can just tell him it's 'girl talk' next time. Most men back away from that phrase like it's gonna tear chunks of flesh from their hides," Ailis said as she led Bat around the upper cabin and salon toward a narrow ladder leading up to a small observation platform.

"I've been exploring. This is as much privacy as we're going to get on this boat," the fae told her.

When they were settled, Bat stared at her friend. *Where do I start?*

Ailis waited.

"I met Alatrom." Bat decided to begin with the one thing she had a clear question about.

"Ah."

"He... was not what I expected him to be." Bat

fingered the hem of her light sweater. "He kicked them out of the clan, which some may call cruel, but…"

"It's what they've always wanted, to be on their own," Ailis said, her tone even. Gone was the teasing humor.

"I think he knew that. I think he… I think this invitation he sent was a last effort to connect with them. I do not believe he meant it as a threat, or as anything other than one last chance to see his sons gathered together and with him. I… saw some things when I met him." Bat took the time to choose her words. She wouldn't reveal the details of the vision, for that was something private between the brothers and their father.

"A vision."

"Yes."

Silence fell between the two women. Voices filtered to them from below. Someone slammed a door, and heavy steps carried on the air.

A dark head appeared at the top of the ladder. Dub's hair was wild and his jaw was shadowed with scruff. He wore his concerned frown. "Ya all right, *storeen?*"

Bat swayed, drawn toward this not-man. "Yes," she finally answered. "Ailis and I needed girl talk."

Dub's eyes narrowed, but the magical words worked. He nodded. "You'll tell us if it's something we need to know." It was not a request.

It was Bat's turn to frown. "Of course I will tell you. Do you not trust me?"

Dub snorted. "Of course I trust you," he shot back, echoing her words. "But ye're keeping secrets again. I know you well enough now to be able to know that much."

Bat's eyes widened. She'd been keeping secrets for not even a full day. *How...?*

Dub raised his brows. "See? Secrets."

Ailis came to her rescue. "A woman is entitled to her secrets, Dub O'Loinsigh. If you take all the mystery from a relationship, you take most of the fun." The green-haired fae waved a hand. "Now, go away. We're not done with our girl talk."

Dub's frown turned to a scowl and he took a step down.

"Wait!" Bat called out.

He paused.

She hurried to lean forward and press a kiss to his lips. "I am glad you are well, now." She studied his face as his expression eased. "The injury was not too bad?"

He grunted. "It was manageable."

"I will come see you when I finish with Ailis? There are many things to discuss and plan, once I have my thoughts gathered."

He gave her a kiss of his own, deeper than the quick peck she'd given him. "The boat only has a quarter tank of fuel, and no provisions. Saoirse knows of a town with a small marina about an hour from here where we can stock up. Ye've got time. I'll be down in the pilot house."

Bat gave him a confused look.

"The bridge," he clarified. "Where the boat's controls are."

She nodded and watched as he disappeared from view.

Ailis cleared her throat. "Ya handle them verra well."

Bat's cheeks flushed with heat. "I've been meaning to ask, but there never seems to be time, who is Saoirse?"

she asked in a nonchalant tone, or what she hoped was nonchalant. She buried the small tendril of jealousy that had formed at the sound of the woman's name coming from Dub's lips.

Ailis flashed her a look that let Bat know she wasn't fooled. "She's a selkie, a daughter of Lir. And she's no threat to ya, so don't be pulling out yer claws just yet."

Bat's cheeks heated further. "I am easy to read, am I not?"

Ailis reached out and gave her shoulder a playful shove. "Maybe. But it's not a bad thing." The fae sobered. "Saoirse is a good ally to have. I'm not sure why she decided to help us, but having a daughter of Manannan mac Lir on our side is a true advantage."

"So, she's the seal from my vision," Bat said.

"Probably. We may have the men of ba to track the cauldron, but Saoirse will be able to lead us through any ocean pitfalls as we make our way there. And... she probably knows more than she's saying. Most fae do. I think we need to trust her, for now."

Bat nodded. "I need to make the time to finish scanning everyone."

"Can't the men of ba do that?"

Bat paused. They could, and she trusted them. "Yes," she finally said.

"Ya need to remember we're all a team now."

Bat lay on her back, her head butting up against the low bulwark. There was just enough room with her knees drawn up. "I know. I suppose I... need the reminder." She'd been alone for millennia. Those habits would not change in a matter of days, or even weeks. She'd done well over the last couple of days with utilizing the skills and strengths of the people around her. She just needed to remember that this was a war—even if there were only a few players—and that she had allies and fighters waiting for her to direct them. "That is yet another thing. I need to finish meeting everyone. I need to know all their strengths and weaknesses in order to properly strategize, and I—"

"Bat, stop." Ailis appeared over her, leaning in on one arm. "Again, rely on those around you. I happen to know the answers to every single thing you just mentioned. Finn and Dub and the rest know it all too. They are experienced warriors and battle leaders, they can handle that side of things." Ailis's gaze softened. "I don't mean to belittle your purpose here, but from what I see, the main thing we need from you is information. Your visions, your intuitions, your guidance. And maybe a song and a smile or two to keep everyone in line." Ailis's tone was matter of fact as she said all this, and she never broke eye contact with Bat.

The words hurt, but at the same time brought a sense of relief. A part of her felt she was letting everyone down by not being able to take on all of these tasks. She was the one they were looking to for guidance, to lead them, and she did not know how. She did not know anything about boats, and held only the smallest knowledge of strategy from those brief sessions with Narmer and Seth during the war to unite Egypt. Other than their favorite drinks, and who preferred a reel over a ballad, she knew *so little* about the fae that now accompanied her, and even less about the best way to utilize them.

It was all a reminder of how removed she'd been from the world for most of her existence. And as much as she'd broken out of the shell of isolation she'd built around herself, that confidence was new and all too fragile sometimes.

"Thank you," she said to Ailis.

The fae sucked in a breath and blushed. "Now, no need to be going and making this awkward."

Bat chuckled. "I mean it. Somehow, you always know just what to say to me." She reached over and poked her green-haired friend's side. "Even if your words *are* sometimes harsh."

Ailis stuck out her tongue then sobered. "I'm not saying you shouldn't meet everyone and learn about them. You should. They're only here because of you. I'm saying not to worry about it, we got this. Also, *we* need to feel useful too." The last was said in her usual playful tone. "Got it?"

"Got it."

Silence fell once more as they let their minds wander. Bat's thoughts eventually returned to their original discussion.

"I don't know what to tell them about Alatrom," she said.

"The O'Loinsighs?"

Bat nodded, her head shifting against the wood of the platform.

"I'm not sure you need to say anything."

"But…" Bat searched for the right words. "I saw pieces of them in him. There was so much of Dub and Mell and Shar mixed together in Alatrom, it was impossible for me to hate him, even if I wanted to for their sakes."

"You want to mend that rift."

"No. I do not think so. I just want them to stop hurting. Maybe if they realize he held some care for them…"

"Or it could make everything worse. Would you rather be hurt by someone who hated you, or someone who loved you?"

The simple question silenced Bat. The answer was easy.

Pain was so much worse when inflicted by the ones who were supposed to love you.

Ailis sighed. "If they ask, tell them the truth of what you saw, what you think. But wait for them to bring it up."

Bat smiled up at the blue sky. "What would I do without you?"

"Probably flounder in confusion and make a mess of things."

"I'm glad you found me on the street that night."

Ailis was silent for a long moment. "Me too," she finally said.

With that, Bat allowed her mind to turn to the next problem. As Dub had said, she was keeping secrets.

"Ailis?" She waited until the fae grunted at her. "Do you believe there are some secrets that must be kept?"

"Yes." There was no hesitation in the short answer.

"Even from those you love and trust?"

This time Ailis didn't answer right away. "Yes. Trust doesn't mean you tell everyone everything you know. Trust goes both ways. If you are holding something secret, I trust you are doing it because you must." Then she whispered, "Some things are not meant to be known."

Ailis's words played around in Bat's mind and resonated deep inside her. They firmed Bat's resolve to keep the secret of Osiris's re-birth just that—secret. Part of her resented the Egyptian god of the Underworld for telling her this truth, for giving her the burden of something that must remain unspoken. The other part of her realized just how much of a burden it had been for the god to carry.

Once more a comfortable silence enveloped them, broken only by the creaking of the boat, the lapping of waves against the hull, and the trickle of conversation from below. Bat took the opportunity to sort through everything that had happened that day, everything that she had been through, every change that had occurred since one cream and gold invitation had been delivered to The Dubros pub.

Ailis was right, she needed to concentrate on figuring out what her visions meant and what path they needed to take so that Dub and the others could figure out the strategies needed to follow that path.

Bat conjured up each vision she had received since this quest began. There were the visions of the past that gave her clues to who the players were and what they were after, there were the flashes that showed her the direction her actions should take, and then there were the ones that hinted at futures to avoid, such as the one of Shar and Ari in the alley behind the pub.

Was the one of her playing her harp for the cauldron one to avoid, or one to follow? On the surface, it was obviously a future eventuality that should be avoided, but something in her urged her not to dismiss that future so readily.

A narrow path to take. The Morrigan's words came back to her. Just how narrow could the path to taking down Balor be?

Flash. Daniel-Balor and Ailis lay lifeless amongst the shards of a destroyed cauldron.

Bat let out an involuntary whimper. Surely this was not the ending they were headed toward? Could there be another way? Her eyes burned as a pale and limp Ailis haunted her, overlaying the sight of the clear blue sky above her.

"Bat?"

She swallowed, her throat thick. "Yes?"

"Ya all right?"

She remained silent for a long moment. Then she uttered what may have been the hardest words she had ever needed to say. "Some things are not meant to be known," she whispered.

Clothing rustled as Ailis shifted. Then she let out a sardonic laugh. "Guess I deserved that." Ailis's hand found Bat's and gave it a squeeze. "Ya do what ya gotta do, goddess."

The words were full of trust. Bat gripped her friend's

hand as her throat tightened and tears threatened once more.

She *would* find a way to change at least one part of this latest vision. She would not lose this person, nor disappoint the trust given to her.

Chapter Fourteen

Bastie,

I like silence.

Never thought I'd say that. I spent all too much of my existence in silence.

Now, I am growing to appreciate it. Especially when that silence is spent in good companionship.

I really do believe you would like Ailis. Maybe one day I'll be able to introduce you two.

- Bat

BAT

She and Ailis stayed like this for another ten minutes before one last thing occurred to Bat.

"Ailis?"

"Hmmm."

"Why did you hesitate this afternoon?"

"When we were attacked? Not sure. There was something… almost like a glamour, but not. If it were a glamour we would have sensed it right away. Whatever it was, it clouded my mind, and I couldn't move. I was seeing what was happening, but not, all in the same moment."

"It didn't affect everyone."

"No. I suspect it's some kind of battle magic. I was going to bring it up to Dub and Finn during the next huddle." Ailis sat up. "Which is probably soon. Any more girl talk we need to engage in?"

Bat pulled herself up as well. "No. I think that was mostly it." She tilted her head. "Is there any girl talk we need to engage in for you?"

Ailis laughed. "Unfortunately, no. My life's a bit barren of company of the male persuasion. But I'll let ya know if that changes." Ailis sent her a wink and stood. She peered over the edge of the lookout and laughed. "I was wondering why no one was bothering us."

A red streak shot into the air above Ailis's head. "Goddess are ya done broodin'? The grumpy one said it was 'girl talk' but I know that just means ye're broodin' but I also know it's best to let a female brood or—"

A pink spot appeared next to the male pixie. "Ya stop it, Daire. I told ya it's no' broodin'. Just because ye're a male and a fool does no' mean ya can—"

"I'm after thinking ya should both stop now and let them down." This last was from Taire, her silver glow nearly invisible against the bright sky.

"Oh!" the two other pixies exclaimed before zipping away from the top of the ladder.

Bat grinned at them as she approached the low rail. Peering over the side, her grin widened. Killer and the two other pups whose names she had yet to learn had stationed themselves at the foot of the ladder, preventing anyone from approaching.

She climbed down and gave her baby a good scratch behind his ears. "You are such a good pup, my Killer." His tail waved in gentle agreement to her compliments. The other two pups pressed against her, begging for attention, and she gave it to them.

Once all the heads were scratched and puppy-love had been given, she headed for the place the boat was steered from—the *bridge*, she reminded herself. "I really need to learn about boats and ships," she muttered.

Glass and windows surrounded the bridge. Dub, Finn, Con, Mell, and Saoirse were crowded inside. Five people did not seem like many, but the space was tight, filled with equipment and controls housed in panels and cases ranged around the perimeter.

Dub and Saoirse stood close, their heads bent together. Mell, Finn and Con were in a conversation of their own.

Saoirse grinned up at *her* grumpy not-man, who smiled and shook his head, and the single seed of jealousy that had been planted earlier pushed to the surface.

Mell's head came up and he frowned. He twisted to partially face her, and waved a hand, gesturing Bat to come in. Dub looked up at the movement and their gazes locked. His frown returned, but this was his concerned one, again. When Bat hesitated to enter the bridge, he crossed to the door. As he grasped the handle, Mell caught his arm and whispered something to him. Dub's frown melted away and a wicked grin formed. He gave Mell a short nod then pulled open the door and stepped out. Joining Bat in the narrow strip of deck that ran alongside the boat, he crossed his arms and squinted down at her.

The silence stretched. Bat wanted to simultaneously throw herself into his arms and hit him for *smiling* at another woman. He never smiled. For the gods' sake, she'd only ever gotten a few of those precious gestures, and here he was handing them out like candy to some random woman who turned into a seal, and…

And she was being an insecure wanker. Bat sagged, her shoulders rounding as she looked away.

Dub's finger caught her chin and he lifted her head to face him. "Mell said he sensed jealousy from you."

Her lips thinned and her hand crept to her necklace. His eyes flicked down, taking in the gesture.

"*Storeen?*"

His deep voice wrapped around her and she shivered. The finger under her chin was a point of heat. She recalled his other touches, the strength of his hands on her flesh. And she thought of those hands moving on to another woman…

Pressure built behind her eyes and she blinked it away.

He didn't say anything, didn't try to reassure her, or press her into speaking. He waited there for her to pull herself together. And he didn't walk away.

She blinked again and her grip on that necklace became hard enough to leave an impression of the pendant in the flesh of her palm.

Still he waited.

"I was," she finally said. "Jealous. You said her name,

earlier. You smiled at her. You never smile. You have eighteen different kinds of frown, but only a few smiles, and you gave one to a woman we have known for not even a day." The pressure built and her eyes burned. *A woman we have not known a day, and who is very attractive, a woman who has the curves most men crave, a woman whose sensuality burns through her every moment.* Bat could see it in the selkie. This was a woman who liked men, and pleasures, and was used to getting what she wanted...

Bat blinked again, but this time it was not in an effort to clear her eyes, but in surprise at herself. Where were these thoughts coming from? She went over every interaction she'd witnessed between her not-man and the selkie. Two conversations and one smile. *That was it.* Two conversations and a smile.

She blinked once more and Dub's face came into focus. His expression had eased into his thoughtful frown, the one that barely pulled the corners of his mouth down and left his brows faintly furrowed. It was one of her favorites of his frowns, making him look like a boy in need of comfort.

It was... cute, if such a word could be applied to the Fomoiri warrior and smith.

"Are ya being reminded of the gobshite god?" he finally asked.

That startled a sharp laugh from her. "I... suppose so. I must have healing still to do."

"It has only been a few days since we came together. I would not expect you to heal from such a deep wound so quickly."

"This is amazingly... perceptive of you." *When did he get*

so wise? This was Dub. He was supposed to scowl and yell and hit something before grabbing her and kissing the thoughts from her mind.

His eyes darkened and he swallowed. Did he somehow learn to read her emotions just as Mell could?

Dub's finger left her chin and his hand slid around to the back of her neck. He tugged her up with that hand until she balance on her toes, and kissed her. It started as a simple press of his lips but it took no time for Dub to deepen it. He spun them around until he could press her against the wall of the cabin beside the bridge.

Teeth nipped, tongues tangled, and lips meshed. When he pulled away, they were both breathing heavily. Bat's cheeks were filled with heat, and her breasts had swollen with the need to be touched. She let out a faint whimper and pressed her body against his muscled heat.

What was going on with her? Why were her emotions so all over the place today, even after she'd had some quiet time to sort her thoughts?

Flash. Bat stood in the middle a field, early morning light falling around her. Fae gathered around her. Her hand was on Finn's chest, fingers and power pressed into him, threatening him unless he took her back to the cottage.

Oh. The answer was so simple she could not believe how imperceptive she was. She had nearly lost her grumpy not-man, and her giant-pirate, not two days after making them hers. She had yet to heal the fresh tear that had left in her soul.

She wrapped her hands around Dub's waist and buried

her head in his chest. "I need to hold you for a little while. Maybe a minute. Maybe a little more. I do not believe I am over the attack this morning. Or the one we experienced an hour ago." As she said the words the little ball of jealousy, anxiety and fear began to unravel.

He smelled of heat, spice, and faintly of fish. "Finn healed you? There was… a lot of blood, from what I could see." Her voice was muffled and small.

His hands ran up and down her sides, soothing her. "He healed me up just fine, *storeen*." A faint rumble radiated from his chest. It sounded like a cross between a growl and a purr, if that was possible for someone with a human throat. "Finn is useful. I suppose it is all right if he sticks around."

Bat burrowed into him even more. Her grumpy not-man was attempting to tease her. She appreciated the effort, but she was not quite ready for that yet.

Feet shuffled somewhere to the right. Voices murmured to her left. Dub stiffened and raised a hand, waving off whoever it was. Bat did not bother lifting her head.

She needed this. She needed the time with her not-man.

Ten minutes must have passed with the two of them holding each other, when he pulled back. "*Storeen*, as much as I would love to remain with you like this for the next month, there are things I must deal with. Mell and Shar can handle the boat well enough on the open waters, but neither bothered to maintain their mariner licenses, and both were always fucking useless when it came to docking."

"And we are supposed to stop somewhere to get fuel and food and all the things that were supposed to be supplied by your father."

The muscles of Dub's back tensed under her hands at the mention of his father. Should she say something? Ailis had warned against it, but it didn't seem right to remain silent.

She decided to take a middle road. "I do not think he sent those men. I believe he was sincere in his anger at Scath's betrayal." When he didn't say anything, she added one more thing. "I do not think he wants harm to come to *any* of you."

He did not answer her, but he also did not pull away. Her mood lightened at this. It may not seem like much to anyone who did not know Dub, but *she* knew better. She gave him one more squeeze, then let her arms drop. "You are very good at putting up with insecure goddesses," she said with a thoughtful tone. "Have you had much practice?"

"You are my only goddess," he said, then stepped back so his calves met the gunwale. It only put a half-meter between them, there wasn't much room on this stretch of deck.

His words warmed her from the inside. They were a simple declaration, and exactly what she needed to hear. "Should we have a meeting now?"

Dub's frown returned. "No. We're only a half hour from the town Saoirse knows, it's not enough time. We'll do it once we're back out on open waters." His frown deepened and a grunt of frustration slipped out. "That selkie is more frustrating than Ailis. She keeps saying she can't tell us anything until she talks to you." He slid a glance to Bat. "I do think ya'd like her. She's been coming up with some pretty interesting insults for Balor and those who decided to side with him."

Was he… "Are you testing the waters?"

His lips twitched. "Are you practicing sea related slang now?"

Bat shrugged, keeping her grin off her face. "I have been meaning to officially meet everyone. Each time I try, we are interrupted by people attacking us, or needing to transport somewhere."

"Now is a good time. We'll need a few people to go ashore and deal with the locals, but other than that you now have a captive audience." He reached out and ran a hand down her hair. "I'll send Finn and Mell out to show you around, they're just taking up space in there anyway."

Bat thought of Dub alone on the bridge with just Saoirse and Con, and waited for the twinge of jealousy to hit her.

It didn't. Whatever Dub had done had healed that small hurt for her. He seemed to understand her better than she understood herself.

She only hoped it would be the last time this insecurity reared its head, but she also feared it wasn't.

"Yes, please," she said. She would also go to find Shar again, and see once more with her own eyes that he was still healed.

Expecting Dub to pull away and return to the bridge, she was surprised when he hesitated. "I'll ask Saoirse and whoever else goes ashore to see about getting some tea, and strawberries."

Delighted with his thoughtfulness, she smiled. While there had been tea at the cottage, the strawberries had quickly run out. Bat was aware she did not need them in order to function, but the small comforts helped. She had another thought. "How long did you say it would be before we are at this new place?"

"About half and hour."

She gave one decisive nod. "Then I shall be done by then. Please do not send anyone off the boat until I return."

He eyed her suspiciously. "You are not leaving the boat."

"Of course I will not, my grumpy one. I simply thought that if I was so comforted by the thought of strawberries and tea, then others must have things they miss, and that would help them through the trials of the next few days."

Dub narrowed his eyes. "Not too much. And I know tastes of the sluagh. We will not be bringing livestock on board so they can have fresh meat."

Bat stilled. She had never considered that possibility. Though, from what she'd seen of their nature, a liking of meat that fresh was not out of character…

She shook off her wandering thoughts. "No. No livestock. I will ask them to choose something small."

"And already dead."

"And already dead," she readily agreed.

He nodded, ran his hand down her hair once more, then retreated back to the bridge. Not long after, Finn and Mell emerged. Finn held a small notebook in his right hand.

There was no room on the side deck for two people to

walk side by side, and Mell was first. Bat wrapped her arms around him, much as she'd done with Dub, and listened to his heart. He'd had a dislocated shoulder. It wasn't a bad injury, not for a Fomoiri who had Finn to help him heal. Nevertheless, she did not like the idea of him hurt. Not to mention the injury was at the hands of his old clan.

Why did I not consider this when I was with Dub? His injury had been more severe. He must have known the man who stabbed him.

Maybe it was because Mell seemed to be so much more affected by the encounter with Alatrom.

"You are better now?" she asked, tilting her head back to peer up at him.

"I am better now. Finn's a handy one to have around."

She hadn't been inquiring only about his physical injury, but she let the moment slide. One hug from her would not heal centuries of wounds, and now was not the time to dig into that mound of dung beetles. "Will you help me with something?"

"That's why we're here, *realta*. Finn's going to play secretary and write everyone's requests down."

"What about you?" she asked as she stepped back and grabbed his hand, carefully making her way along the side of the boat until they'd reached the foredeck. They may as well start here.

"I am here to lend you my beautiful face and charming ways."

"Dub wanted him out from under foot," Finn added from behind them.

"And that," Mell admitted cheerfully. A mixture of calm and excitement flowed from him.

"I am glad you are accompanying me."

They stepped onto the foredeck and Finn came to her side. He wrapped an arm around her shoulders and squeezed. Mell still held her hand. The physical contact was soothing to her, and more of her tension melted away. She would concentrate on the small tasks in front of her for now, and think about the rest when it was time.

"Shall we begin?" Finn steered her toward the three banshees, who were huddle in a group at the bow of the boat looking out over the waves.

Twenty minutes later Finn, Bat and Mell returned to the bridge bearing a short list of requests from the passengers. Most had been surprised when Bat came to them and asked if there was anything that could be purchased that would ease the hardship of the next few days.

Bat had, in turn, been surprised by many of their answers.

Ari, Nour, and the other men of ba had asked for various types of crisps. Ari had enjoyed the barbecue flavor Bat had given him at the pub. The others had been able to try them while at the cottage, sharing a small plateful between them. They all agreed these were one of the better human inventions.

The pixies had requested some potted plants. Bat nodded. She had already planned to ask Dub for these. "Is there anything else?" The plants were necessary for their survival, after all. They were not the sort of item she had meant. "Something you would enjoy?"

The five of them—her three cottage pixies plus Ciara and Siobhan, the violet pixie that had come with Old Mike and Daniel—exchanged a look. Ciara's cheeks flushed. "Marshmallows," she muttered.

"And cocoa," Daire added.

All the pixies were flushed, their colors shining brighter. Were they embarrassed by the request?

"I like those as well. It is a good request," Bat said. They gifted her with smiles.

The trooping fae, including Ailis, had asked for fleece blankets if they could be found, and the leprechauns requested jerky, a type of dried meat strips. It was apparently hard to find, so they didn't know if it would be available in a small town.

They found Neall, Faolan, and the other sluagh tucked into a shadowed storage room next to the engines. After a longer hesitation than the pixies, they gave Bat their request—jelly beans.

Cuchi had been in the middle of an inventory of the boat's existing supplies. He'd refused to tell them anything he may want, said true warriors didn't need that sort of consolation. Bat left him to his stubborn misery.

The banshees' request was still her favorite, though. They'd asked for earplugs. Something about not being able to sleep with so many people around making noise.

The irony had not been lost on the goddess, but she had saved her chuckles until she was well away from the small group of destructive and deadly women.

This small quest was a very effective way to get to know these immortals of Ireland, Bat realized. No, she did not learn their powers, or how they could be of the most use in battle, but she learned about them simply as… people, if she could use that word. Their requests gave her glimpses into their lives. She could only appreciate the small gift.

Her one worry was Daniel. They'd finally located him and Old Mike in a corner of the secondary salon that was tucked next to the galley. Finnegan was there as well, sitting across a small table from them, his gaze sharp and trained on the human. Daniel had been laid out on the cushions, asleep. He was paler than he'd been in the morning. His eyes flicked behind his lids, faster than they would have if he'd been in a normal sleep.

"He still has the dream guardian amulet?" she'd asked. Femi and Mell had spent hours making them for most of the group, and Bat had insisted the human receive one.

"He does," Old Mike answered. His gray eyes were faded and distant. "Goddess, I do no' think he has much more time. I'm no' like the Hunt, I do no' track the lost souls. But this man, he is lost." Gray eyes fixed on her. "Will ya be able to help him?"

Bat was left speechless. This was a side of Old Mike she'd never seen. The wisp was usually mischievous, maybe a little cruel if pushed, but he had never shown compassion for a human. "I will try," she finally said, unable to promise more.

Old Mike blinked a few times, then nodded. "Apple juice," was all he said next.

Bat had nodded then silently risen, Mell and Finn on

her heals and just as quiet. As they neared the door, she'd paused and asked Finnegan if he required anything. He'd just waved them off before returning his attention to Daniel. "He'll fall soon," the pub owner said as she and the others left.

What was Finnegan, exactly?

"That is not good," Finn said once they'd left the salon.

Bat nodded in agreement. "After we have acquired provisions, there are some things I need to brief everyone on."

"New visions?" Mell said, a tight note in his voice.

"Yes," was all she'd said. "We still need Con, Saoirse, and Dechtire's requests."

"I think they're all up at the bridge, I saw the goblin headed that way," Finn said. "I'll take the list and get their items as well."

"Come, *realta*. Let's go find Shar and your pack." Mell took her hand and dragged her along the narrow passageways until they came to a door at the end on a longer hall. It seemed he knew exactly where he was going. "I do," he said, answering her thoughts. "I had Shar bring your pack to the only decently sized cabin on the whole boat. Everyone else is going to have to double-bunk, or sleep in the salons or on deck."

Pushing open the door, he revealed a room about half the size of the one she had back at the pub. Against one wall was a twin-sized bunk, and along the other was a small desk, cabinets built-into the wall, and a dresser, also built-in. Along the far wall was another door, and she could just make out a small shower, toilet, and sink.

Near the foot of the bunk was a small chest. Her pack and the harp case were nestled on top. Bat had passed the harp to Finn for safe keeping once they'd reached the boat, he must have stashed it in here before going on to heal everyone.

She finally turned her attention to the figure on her bed. Shar was crammed into the bunk. His giant frame left only a small sliver of mattress for her to squeeze onto. That is, if she was supposed to share...

Not that she minded. She supposed she could use him as her mattress...

"Guess he got tired of waiting." Mell shook his head in mock-disapproval. "*Tsk.* And here we are working our asses off."

Seeing the sleeping giant, Bat swayed. The brief rest she'd gotten while up on the observation deck with Ailis wasn't really rest. It was more like a... respite. Everything that happened that day, the attacks, the running, scanning new people—it all caught up to her.

She yawned.

Mell smiled and nudged her toward the bunk. "Get some rest. We'll be docked for a few hours at least, and nothing's going ta happen in that time."

"All right." Bat stumbled her way to the bunk. There was one last thing she needed to make sure of. "Ask Ari and the others to finish scanning everyone?" she asked as she laid herself over the solid bulk of her giant. He... was... so... warm...

Caught in the haze of sleep, she felt tugs on her feet as someone removed her boots and a light blanket was spread over her.

Little goddess. Little goddess, will you play me a tune?

Melody wound through her mind. The song was beautiful. It called to mind the stars above and the earth below her feet. It spoke of the red lands of her original home, and the green fields of her new one.

You see, little goddess? This is the song of creation.

The voice hummed.

Did you know the power you have at your fingertips? Literally?

Her fingers twitched. She tried to stop it, but this voice was clever. It didn't try to temp, or to twist. It simply showed her what could be.

Only, it left out a few vital pieces of the picture.

Listen, goddess. Listen.

The notes wound through her, grafting onto her very being. The voice was... teaching her the melody. She would never be able to forget this...

Energy zipped through her veins. Vitality and life filled her. There was nothing dark about it, nothing wicked or twisted. It was pure...

Enjoy.

Bat blinked her eyes open. Her heart raced and her fingertips tingled. She sprawled over Shar, her legs open around his waist and her hands tucked under his back. He slept on, his breaths deep and even. The lashes of his good eye lay against his cheek in a soft fan, and she wanted to run a finger along the tips. His lips were parted, allowing her a glimpse of even, white teeth. Scruff shadowed his jaw, and a loose strand of hair fell over his cheek.

Had she ever had a chance to just study him like this?

She lay like that for a good ten minutes before pulling her limbs away and attempting to get out of the bunk without waking her sleeping giant.

It didn't work very well.

"*A stor*? What...?"

She bent and pressed a quick kiss to his lips. *I love being able to do that.* It was very freeing, finally confessing her feelings to these not-men, and having them accept her. It meant she could touch them, kiss them, and hold them as much as she wanted.

The boat rolled under her with wide and deep movements, not the small ones she'd been feeling when they were close to shore. They must be in deeper waters.

"We must get up. I am not sure of the time, but we have slept enough, and it is time to plan. I have things that must be conveyed, and have yet to speak with Saoirse." The brown-haired woman's first words returned to Bat. "Apparently there were messages for her to convey. With everything that has happened this day, they never were, at least not to me."

Shar rubbed his eyes and scooted from the bed. Bat found her boots near the chest at the foot of the bunk and pulled them on. Then she grabbed the harp and slung it over her shoulder. This was not leaving her sight again.

Chapter Fifteen

Bastie,
Bastie, Bastie, Bastie.
Sigh.
I learned more secrets tonight…
You are all dead the next time I see you. Just to give you fair
warning.

- Bat

P.s. Or maybe not. Because now I have secrets of my own.
What is that phrase? Something about casting stones?

BAT

*N*ight had fallen. The stars winked overhead as Bat made her way along the narrow side deck and toward the main salon where Mell said the others were gathered.

Not everyone, she noted. Saoirse and whoever accompanied her must have done a very effective job with the shopping, because there were signs of it everywhere. Potted plants sat in stands that were secured to the deck. Hammocks with sleeping figures were strung between posts. The scent of stew and bread mixed the with sea salt aroma of the ocean, and sent her stomach to growling.

Killer and the other two pups lifted their heads and sniffed, then bounded over to her from where they'd been laying on a pile of lifejackets someone had dumped in a corner. She generously doled out scratches and pets before telling them to stay.

Pushing open the door, she took in the salon turned strategy room. Dub and Finn were already seated at the bench-type seat that wrapped around three sides of a small table. Saoirse sat in a chair that had been pulled up to the other end. There were two more chairs shoved in close to each other. Cuchi occupied one, and Ari the other.

Bat pushed into the room, Mell and Shar right behind her. As she slid into the bench-seat beside Dub, Ciara entered from another narrow doorway. She held two off-white bowls from which rose steam and that tantalizing scent of stew. She set one in front of Bat and the other was presented to Saoirse. "I'll be back with more. Bread's just about done."

"You are wonderful, Ciara," Bat said. She bent over the bowl and drew in a deep breath. Her stomach rumbled again.

Ciara flushed. "Everyone's been running all day. There's lots of hungry fae on this boat. The first meal needed to be hearty."

"Don't forget to eat your self," Bat told the pixie.

Her blush deepened. "I won't, goddess." She hurried back to the galley and soon the sound of silverware and clanging pots could be heard. Ciara was back in moments, three bowls in her hands this time. In mere minutes the pixie had everyone served.

Ailis burst through the door. "I'm not late, am I?"

Ciara appeared as if by magic with one more serving of stew. Ailis took it and scanned the room for a place to sit. She finally settled on propping herself against the wall. Dipping her spoon into the thick stew, the green haired fae shoveled the food into her mouth.

Once everyone slowed down, Ciara appeared in the doorway again, a smaller bowl in hand. Setting it down in front of Bat, she gave the goddess a small smile and disappeared once more.

This bowl held red-pink goodness smothered in a bit of cream.

Bat licked her lips, the rest of the room fading away.

Mell laughed.

A small fork appeared in front of her. "We won't ask you to share this time, *a stor.*"

She barely noted the deep bass of her giant's voice as she took the utensil from his hand and speared one of the berries.

When half the bowl was gone, Bat came out of her strawberry induced haze. The others in the room stared at her with a range of emotions, from indulgence to puzzlement to mirth.

"Ready now?" That was Cuchi, barely-suppressed appalled laughter in his voice.

Bat licked a smear of cream from her lower lip. "Yes." With a look of longing, she set the fork beside the bowl, promising herself she would return to the treat as soon as she'd told them what she could.

"I think I should go first," Saoirse said. "My messages have waited all day, I am not sure they can wait much longer."

"I agree," Bat said, before anyone could speak. It would give her additional time to decide how to avoid saying anything she shouldn't without leaving out the vital pieces. She was also curious as to what this selkie would tell them.

"As ya may know by now, I'm a selkie. I'm also a daughter of mac Lir. When the goblin came to me, asking me to set up a meeting with Da, I was... intrigued. Not much catches my interest these days." The selkie shrugged. "I reached out to Da, he basically gave me permission to play, as long as no one broke the treaty."

Dub, Mell, and Shar stiffened so suddenly they nearly jumped from their seats.

"Treaty?"

Saoirse hummed and tapped her lips, no doubt deciding what she could say.

It was Mell who finally answered. "When Balor first crossed the oceans and headed for Ireland, he struck a deal with the sea god for safe passage. It's a treaty that has existed since that time, and the reason the Fomoiri prefer to operate from the sea—we have the advantage."

"That is basically correct, but there is more to it than that," Saoirse admitted. "It's not only a deal between mac

Lir and the Fomoiri, but also includes Apep, Ma'at, and humans."

Dread filled Bat at the mention of the Egyptian god of chaos and destruction. Apep was the exact opposite of the balance and justice she had aligned herself with at the beginning of her existence. He was the serpent that slept in the deepest trenches of the ocean and waited for the time he would waken and devour the world.

He had apparently attempted to do so once, six thousand years before. He was the whole reason Seth had sent the Egg of Creation—the original vessel—away from Egypt, in the care of the Fomoiri.

Bat had never heard of this treaty.

She tilted her head, all her attention focusing on the daughter of mac Lir. "I admit there is much of the Egyptian gods' history I am unfamiliar with. It is strange to think I had to come to a foreign land for answers. Explain. Please." She added the last out of courtesy. This was the daughter of a god, after all. Though Saoirse herself was not a deity, there was no reason not to offer her respect.

"Balor thinks he made the treaty. He didn't. That Seth did. He struck a deal with Da to gain his help in subduing Apep and protecting the ships he sent north and their cargo. In exchange, there would be... sacrifices. A certain number of human souls would be used to keep Apep content in his sleep. To maintain the balance, only those souls would be taken, no more, no less. The Fomoiri would provide gifts of their own to mac Lir. Usually treasure, sometimes women." Saoirse shrugged. "Da's a lusty man."

"How does this affect the current situation?" Cuchi growled out. Something in Saoirse's little speech had rubbed him wrong.

"There was an additional stipulation, insisted upon by Da. Mac Lir likes... loopholes. The treaty would be broken if one of two things happen: if a child of the sea is killed by a Fomoiri, or a Fomoiri is killed by a child of the sea." The selkie rolled her eyes. "Da pays lip service to maintaining the treaty, mostly because Apep is a pain in the ass to deal with and he's too lazy to do it again. However, he also didn't expect the Fomoiri to restrain themselves so well when it came to not harming the children of the sea."

"Probably because Balor didn't want to share power with a giant serpent bent on world destruction," Ailis said, cutting to the heart of things like she always did.

Bat absorbed everything the selkie had told them. She shoved aside the dull hurt at finding even more secrets that had been kept from her. It truly didn't matter at this point.

Meeting the deep brown gaze of the selkie with her own dark eyes, she peered into the soul of the woman. No doubt the men of ba had already scanned her, but Bat was curious as to what she'd find.

Saoirse was different. Instead of being shadowed with shades of gray or black, she was a swirl of colors. Was it because her father was a god? What would happen if Bat ever tried to see into another deity this way?

And she was distracting herself again.

"So," Bat said to the selkie. "What you are saying is

that you cannot kill Balor or his allies. And if you are killed, then Apep is freed from his… sleep." Could the fate of the world be held up on such a delicate balance?

"Yup." Saoirse popped the "p" of that one word, and sent a grin at the slack faces around her. "Guess none of ya knew the whole truth of the treaty, did ya?"

"Some of us didn't even know there was a treaty," Ailis shot back. But her face, too, held traces of shock.

Maybe Bat had become inured to the shock of universe-shaking information being dumped on her. Maybe she'd gotten to the point where the large things barely moved her, but the little things like a bowl of strawberries or a nap in the arms of someone she loved were able to break her down in little pieces.

"You'll also need me to lead you into Tir Hudi. It's… less of an island and more of a… state of existence in its own space?" She shook her head. "I don't know how to describe it. You can only find it if you've been there before. I've been there." She sucked in a deep breath. "And Balor has been there. I'm no' sure how he convinced Da ta take him, but it's no coincidence that he was able to escape the full power of Nuada's blade."

"You know why he's headed there," Finn said, his voice emotionless. He'd gone into full guardi-mode.

Beside Bat, Dub trembled and his hands were curled into hard fists. She laid one of her hands over his, letting him know she was there. On her other side, Mell did not look like he was about to come out of his skin, but he had locked down. As he did when he was deeply affected, he'd pulled into himself and locked all his emotions away. The usual eddies and tendrils of emotion she could sense from him were gone.

Bat leaned forward and craned her neck to take a peek at Shar. Her giant's eye was closed, his lips tight. He showed no other reaction, though.

They would need time to process all of this. A spark of vindictive satisfaction flared in her. *Now they know how I felt. Hah.*

"I am not sure how much Da would want me to tell you. Let's just say that there's something in the western caves of the island that Balor needs to make everything work." Saoirse's gaze met Bat's and it held a promise to tell her more later.

Flash. A cave. In the center of the cave was a spring that flowed in a slow stream into the dark recesses of that cave. A man knelt beside the stream and dipped his hands in. When he drank, his silver hair grew dark and thick, his hunched shoulders pulled back, his spine grew straight.

Balor needed the waters of that spring. She wasn't sure if the liquid merely healed whoever drank it, or if it offered more. But what was clear to her was that it held life in it. This spring, plus the vessel of creation, could pull together the pieces of his soul and mend them.

"And there are the stars," Shar said.

"I believe the goddess should be the next to talk." That was Cuchi, his words slow and careful. It was the most subdued she'd ever heard the man, even when she'd laid the curse on him. "Unless you have more to add?" he asked Saoirse.

She shook her head.

Everyone turned to Bat. Dub turned his hand over and threaded his fingers though hers. Mell's hand slipped behind her and settled on her lower back, rubbing in small circles.

Where should she begin? "The Morrigan once mentioned to me that there was a very narrow path to tread in order to attain victory over Balor. She was right." Bat closed her eyes, unable to look at the faces of the people around her. "He will have five ships, and they will be lead by a dark-haired man holding a golden spear. They will anchor in a small bay at the east side of the island. There are cliffs and hills on the west end. Saoirse will help monitor the enemy's boats. There will be at least one giant, and Finn will be the one facing it. Mell will hold our spear, and he will face down a white-haired man with the golden spear. Later, Old Mike will hold our spear. Dub, Finn, Cuchi, Ailis and I will restore the cauldron with our blood. Daniel will—" she swallowed, not wanting to say the next part, but knowing she needed to. "Daniel will be the house of Balor's soul. Nuada's blade will pierce his heart and he will be cast into the cauldron." Here she hesitated, but not because she didn't want to say the words. She had to find the right ones. "When he resurrects, only at this point will we be able to send the entirety of his soul to Anubis for judgment. Our spear, the one embedded with the shard of the Egg, will pierce his back, and he will fall." Nothing she had just said was untrue. They didn't need to know the last part of her visions, or how the harp played a part in them.

Bat opened her eyes and snuck a look at Ailis. Her

friend gazed back at her, brows scrunched together. Bat tired to send her a smile, but she must have failed. *I am no good at subterfuge.*

Silence fell over the group as they all digested the information. There were not that many new pieces, she realized, only details.

"Is that all?" Finn asked.

Bat swallowed and nodded.

His hazel eyes pierced into hers. "All right." He turned to Saoirse. "How long until we reach the island?"

"We will arrive the day after tomorrow. Probably mid-day."

"Can you sketch the layout of the land for us?"

The selkie nodded. Finn handed over his small notebook.

Moments later the men were bent over the small drawing, talking in quiet murmurs. Bat followed their conversation with one ear. Ailis had been correct. They knew the strengths and weaknesses of each of the fae with them: the trooping fae, the sidhe, the pixies, the banshees, the leprechauns, all of them. Ari filled in what was needed regarding the men of ba. It took barely twenty minutes, and they had the outline of a strategy.

The first step would be reconnaissance. When they were still a few kilometers out from the island, Finnegan and Dub would cast a cloaking spell over the boat—and she now knew what Finnegan was, a Druid. They were the ones who learned to cultivate magic from their environment. Bat wondered if Finnegan was familiar with Heka, the Egyptian god of magic...

It was truly amazing how much she had learned since she'd come to Ireland, both of this new land and of her homeland. Maybe she should write an Idiot's Guide of her own? One specifically for immortals and gods? *An Idiot God's Guide to The Immortals of Ireland.* She could write it, and have copies printed up to be sent back to Egypt. She could also keep a few on hand to give to any of the Irish deities she ran across. Though she had only met The Morrigan, her general impression was they were arrogant, hypocritical and selfish—at least, that's what she'd gathered from snippets of overheard conversation and the fae's general reaction to any mention of their gods…

"Goddess?"

"Hmmm?"

"Goddess!"

Bat blinked and focused on Finn.

"We're done," he said.

"We are?"

"Yes."

"Oh." She frowned. She really should have been more active in this meeting, just as she had been in the others. Ailis had said to leave the military strategies to those who had experience with them, but that was no excuse for her not to participate in the meeting, or suggestions and opinions on the plan.

Finn frowned. "Are you all right?"

Bat shrugged. Finn exchanged a look with Mell and the middle brother nodded.

"We'll regroup when we get closer to the island," Dub said. "If anyone thinks of something that must be added, or comes across additional information, please let Finn or Bat know."

Her eyes widened that he'd included her in that instruction, what with how passive she'd been though the whole meeting.

"In the meantime, get rest. Shar, you'll take the con since you've already gotten some rest. Saoirse will relieve you, then Mell will be next. I'll take back over in the early afternoon." Dub grabbed the back of her neck, pulled her to him, and kissed her forehead. "Get some rest, *storeen*."

His phone rang. Glancing at the ID of the caller, his expression hardened. "Fuck." He swiped to take the call. "What?"

As he listened to the person on the other end of the line his face flushed a deep red and his lips drew into a tight line. Without a word to the person who called him, he hung up.

Other than Dub, only Bat, Mell, Shar, and Finn remained in the salon. The rest had left to find places to bunk down.

"Dub?" she asked.

"That was Da. Scath is gone, along with a good twenty members of the clan."

"That's... not good," Finn said.

"Twenty," Mell breathed out. "That's nearly half the clan."

"And he has no way of knowing if the ones remaining with him are there out of loyalty, or as spies," Shar added.

The brothers exchanged a look. It was one she'd seen before—they were keeping secrets among themselves. "What?" she asked.

"We could… give it to him," Mell said.

Dub's expression went from hard to terrifying. Bat had never seen her not-man like this.

"Give what…? Oh." As soon as she started to ask, she realized what Mell referred to. The brooch. The talisman every clan leader bore to prove his leadership. The one Dub had in his possession, and had intended to use to bargain for their freedom.

"We don't need it," Mell said. "Not anymore."

Dub's shudders hunched and he placed his hands on the small table. His movements were deliberate and oh-so careful.

The table creaked then collapsed.

Bat squeaked and jerked her knees to the side, hitting Mell. Shar reached over and plucked her from between the two brothers.

"I'm after thinking she needs to go to him," Finn said, gesturing to Dub.

"No," the eldest brother growled out. "Not right now. I might…"

"You wouldn't hurt her, Dub. And we need you to not punch a hole in the hull and sink the boat," Finn said.

Bat reached for Dub, then paused. Why was he reacting so strongly? She backed away a few steps and really studied the scene before her.

Dub was angry. Not just angry—he was *enraged*. Finn stood near the door, his feet spread and weight balanced, arms easy at his sides. But Bat knew he would be ready to move at a moment's notice.

Mell stared at Dub. The middle brother's face was blank and his emotions were locked down, but some still leaked through. There was fear, regret, sorrow, pain, anger, and… longing. Mell was a seething mass of negative emotion, but his attention wasn't on that. It was on this brother.

Shar… Shar was not looking at Dub. No, Shar's gaze was locked on Mell, and in his expression was sorrow and… resignation?

Flash. Dub sat at a wood plank table, Shar beside him. Alatrom was a few meters away in a large wooden chair carved with swirling designs that sat atop a dais.
"You did what?" Dub asked his father, his fingers digging into the wood table.
"I sent him off." Alatrom rubbed his eyes. "He'll never be a proper Fomoiri, and I can't have such weakness in my clan."
Wood splintered under Dub's fingers. "Where did he go?"
Alatrom shrugged.
"You are a fool, old man." Loathing seethed in Dub's voice. "You will lose more than one son today." Dub carefully released the table and rose to his feet. Without another glance at the man on the dais, he spun on his heel and left the stone room that acted as a receiving and dining hall.
Shar was a beat behind him. He said not a word, but he bowed to his father and followed his brother, leaving the older man alone.
Neither brother noticed the sheen of moisture in the old man's eyes.

Dub wasn't simply angry at his father, he was angry *for* his brother.

Both brothers were on their feet now. Dub faced Mell, his lapis-blue gaze clashing with his brother's chocolate brown. "I will not allow him to gain what he wants so easily. He has to pay."

Mell's hands curled into fists at his sides. "He has."

"Why do you always do this? I know how much he hurt you. I know the pain he's put you through. Yet you always end up defending him. I feel your loathing, no matter how hard you try to hide it. I found this brooch for *you*. So we could have our vengeance, so we could be free. *And you want to throw that away!*" Dub's hands gripped his hair and pulled.

Dub was ready to give up that very brooch to their father this morning in exchange for a boat, but Bat did not think now was a good time to point this out.

"We are free! He set us free today! *He let us go!*" Mell's shouted words cut through Bat with all the pain and longing he'd buried since the day his father cast him out. Except Alatrom had not officially severed the brothers' ties to the clan. No, he had simply left them in a limbo they could not escape without his permission.

Mell knows exactly what his father did today. She had thought none of the brothers realized, or they would have been happier. Their father had handed them exactly what they'd been longing for. *Except, freedom from their clan isn't what Mell really longed for, it's simply a way for him to move forward. And his brothers know it*.

Moisture gathered in her eyes and Bat opened them wide, trying to keep the tears from falling.

Bat stepped forward, but she didn't head for Dub. Instead, she wrapped her arms around Mell's waist and laid her head against his back. Her breasts were pressed to the firmness of those muscles, and she knew of one thing she could do.

She'd been wanting to claim Mell anyway. His pain was not her motivation, not really. It was merely an... impetus? Not even that. It was barely an excuse. She was just glad she was here for him, that their night together could help him heal in some way.

She also may have gotten ahead of herself, considering Mell did not yet know they were going to have their night together...

Mell's tensed muscles relaxed a fraction. "*Realta*? What are you thinking exactly?" His voice held a cautious note.

"That you all need to calm down before this boat sinks. That you are the reason your brother is about to punch holes in metal. That you are in pain." Her hands stroked over his front, never going farther then the hem of his jeans. "That I know a way to help with that pain."

"Are you thinking of using sex as therapy?"

She couldn't read that tone. "Yes?"

His chest shook. He spun in her arms and pulled her to him. "Damn, you make me laugh."

"Are you feeling better now?"

"Nope. You promised sex as therapy. No backing out now." His arms fell from her and he grabbed her hand. "Come on, let's go rumple the sheets in that all too small bunk of yours, and leave these three in their misery."

Bat peeked around Mell and blushed at the heated looks all three men were giving her. Passion was warring with anger in Dub, and the others... well, they looked vaguely envious.

Her hand crept up to her necklace as her gaze locked

with Shar's. Would he be angry? He had agreed to this after all, though he warned her it would not be easy for him. Now that they had been together, would he change his mind…?

Shar waved his hand. "Go. We'll clean up here." Then he offered her a small smile, and she returned it.

Without another word, Mell dragged her from the salon and to the hatch that led belowdecks.

Chapter Sixteen

Bastie,

Damn, these O'Loinsigh brothers...

You will be sooooo envious when you meet them.

- Bat, the satisfied goddess that you should be jealous of right now

BAT

*M*ell pulled her along the narrow passageway just as he had once before. Only this time, she was not headed in there for a nap.

Her blood rushed through her. She'd been attracted to this flirting fae since her first night in Ireland. If she was honest with herself—and she always *tried* to be—she had been attracted to all of them that night.

Mell pushed open the door to her cabin and tugged her inside. Without a word he shut and locked the door, then pulled her to him. He captured her mouth with his in a hungry kiss.

His control over his emotions was wearing away. He was a maelstrom of raw emotions. Passion had come to the forefront, pushing aside the others that had been raging in the salon.

Mell's hands were on her, never stilling. They gripped her waist, then worked over her ass and slid to her hips. A moment later those hands were on the move again, skimming up and over her rounded belly. They gripped her breasts and squeezed their fullness before one dove into her hair and the other slid up her back.

The whole time he never broke the kiss.

He walked them to the edge of the bunk. Bat's knees hit it and buckled, finally separating her from Mell.

His emotions continued to assault her. His passion caressed her skin, and need bit at her flesh. It was like a thousand lips covered every inch of her skin, and a thousand tongues teased her nerve endings.

They hadn't even gotten their clothes off.

She gripped her sweater and worked it up her body and off her arms. She pulled away from him long enough to rip it over her head, then went back to his lips for more. He found the hook on her bra, and a second later that was gone as well.

She found the buttons of his shirt and worked them out one by one. He shrugged the cloth off as soon as the last button was undone. Her hands found his chest and she dug her nails into him, before sliding her arms around his shoulders and holding on.

Neither spoke. They didn't need to. Mell was

completely open to her. He hid nothing from her. Not the pain and sorrow that hid in the corners of his soul. Not his passion for her body or how much he reveled in her curves. Not the need he felt to be with her, possess her in some way, to see her smile, to hear her laugh. He showed her every layer of himself, and every contradiction.

He bared himself to her like he never had before.

In answer, she fed him every bit of her love.

"Fuck." He sucked in a breath, then moved down to her chest. Gathering one breast in his hand, he kissed his way around it until he found her nipple and gave it one hard pull with his mouth. Then another.

Just as his hands had been, his mouth was restless. He could not stay in one spot. It was as though he wanted to devour every inch of her, but didn't have the patience to savor it.

Bat didn't mind. His urgency had become hers. Her hips moved on a rhythm of their own, seeking relief.

"More," she breathed out. "Need more, now."

His hands found the top of her jeans just as his mouth found her belly button. He undid the button and pulled the zipper down as his tongue laved the small indentation.

He reared back, gripped the top of her jeans, and pulled them down her legs, only to be stopped by her boots.

"Stupid boots," he grumbled to himself. They were off her in seconds and the jeans followed.

Then he was back on her. Vaguely she heard a dull thud, and wood crashing into wood, but she paid it no mind. She had more important things to concentrate on.

She gripped his hips and pulled him into her, pressing his bulge right... where... she... needed it.

There.

She ground against him, no longer caring if they were moving too fast, or that he still had his pants on, or even if they were making so much noise the entire boat could hear them.

All she could think of was the growing sensation between her legs, the pressure that was building, the pleasure that was ready to burst over her if she could just get the right angle...

Mell jumped off of her, taking the pressure and heat with him. She whimpered. He fumbled with the snap on his own pants as the toed off his shoes.

Lucky those are not lace-up boots. Gods, I might have to tackle him and mount him if he takes much longer. The thought was barely there, more her mind's attempt to calm her than anything else.

Then Mell was back in her arms and between her legs, nothing separating them this time. His hips pulled back and he grasped his cock, placing it at her entrance. He was thick, thicker than Shar, and he had to work himself in with short thrusts. Finally he was fully seated within her.

They paused for a bare second. Bat to savor the sensation of being so full. Mell to revel in the tight warmth wrapped around him. He pulled back and thrust forward, generating a delicious friction.

Fucking heaven.

Bat didn't know if it was his thought or hers. Somewhere she'd lost all sense of herself, and of Mell. There was only them, together.

She wrapped her legs around him to add her own power to each surge inside her. Her hips rose to meet each of his thrusts. He shifted and angled his hips up a bit more until he managed to hit a spot inside her that had her channel rippling around him.

Mell bent over her and his mouth found her shoulder. He licked up it until he hovered over the tender muscle connecting to her neck, then he bit down.

Bat screamed as her core tightened once more. She was almost there, so close.

So close, so close, so close. The words echoed around her.

Mell slammed into her over and over, hitting that spot each time.

Then the pleasure, the sensation and the pressure, all came together and exploded, sending waves of power though her. Mell stiffened over her and groaned as he came, filling her with more warmth.

As he sagged over her, darkness crowded her vision.

As she drifted off, she had one thought. *I'm glad I could help him work off his pain and anger... Wonder if that is what make-up sex is like...*

Bat woke to the sound of running water and an empty space next to her on the bunk. Well, not an empty space, really, because just one person filled up the space of the bunk. But there was definitely a missing *body*.

"Hey," Mell said, coming out of the small washroom. He no longer radiated the wild passion of earlier. Instead all she sensed coming from him was... embarrassment.

"Why are you embarrassed?"

He sat beside her, his butt half off the mattress. Running a hand up her leg, he tugged it until she was once more exposed to him. In his free hand he held a small cloth he'd dampened. Mell laid the cloth against her center and cleaned her.

No one had ever cleaned her before. She'd either bathed when the sex was done, or when her partner had left.

She did not think she'd have wanted this treatment from any of her past lovers. There was something so intimate about it, and she was left vulnerable before the man caring for her.

Something as simple as this took a great deal of trust.

Bat waited for him to answer her question. He took his time, his attention on wiping their fluids from each fold and dip of her flesh. When he was done he closed her legs and returned to the washroom. The faucet ran for a few seconds before being shut off. Returning to her he left the door open a crack so there was just enough light to see by.

Mell slipped into the bunk, effectively crowding her against the wall. Bat half lay over him, her head on his chest and one leg thrown over his. Her fingers traced random patterns over his chest as she continued to wait for his answer.

"I don't usually do that," he finally said.

"Do what?"

"Lose control."

She planted a quick kiss just under his collarbone. "I enjoyed it. As I am sure you know." She paused. "Are you fishing for compliments?"

Mell let out a bark of laughter. "No, *realta*. But you may compliment me if you like," he teased.

"Should I call you Mell the Mighty, who slays all with his prodigious sword?"

His chest shook. "Please do. Tomorrow at breakfast, I dare you to say those exact words in front of my brothers and Finn. Oh, I can see their faces now." He reached over and traced a finger down her arm.

This was one of her favorite parts of lovemaking. The cuddling and touching that came after.

"Maybe we save that kind of teasing until we can be sure Dub won't tear a hole in the hull of the boat."

Mell stiffened then sighed. Regret rose up and fought the contentment that had replaced his embarrassment as they talked.

I can feel so much from him. Bat marveled at how open Mell was being with her. He'd brought down all his barriers during their bout of sex, and had yet to pull them back up.

"They were just worried about me," Mell said.

"I know." She hesitated, uncertain if she should delve into what happened. *If he shows any signs of withdrawing, I will sto*p, she promised herself. "I do think you were right."

His fingers continued the gentle dance along her arm. "About what?"

"About sending it to him." There was no need for her to specify what "*it*" was and which "*him*" she referred to. "It would... end things. Properly end them, so all of you could move on. If Dub keeps it, he's still hanging onto the past."

Mell's hand closed over her arm, so he was rubbing his palm over her skin instead of just his fingers. "I know that to. It hurts to cut that last tie, though. I think part of me —and them—always thought Da would welcome us back with open arms." He let out a dark chuckle. "Even though I *know* that would never happen. Da couldn't make himself do it. Because of me."

They were heading into dangerous territory. She'd say one more thing, and then let the conversation lie. "I don't think he ever hated you."

He tugged on her arm until she was laying on him fully, her breasts pressed to his chest, her legs parted over his upper groin and her head nestled in the curve of his shoulder. Both his arms wrapped around her as though she was a giant stuffed animal he needed to hold in order to sleep. "He did. It lasted for a little over three hours. After that he was... changed. I was eight. It took me a long time to figure out what happened."

He was silent for a long while. Bat was dozing off when he spoke again.

"I know he cared for me, in his own manner. I mean, I could always *feel* it. His actions just never matched those emotions I felt from him. I think it makes it worse that way, to hear the care he has for us, only to feel the pain of his treatment a moment later. It was tearing me apart." He hummed a snatch of melody.

There were flickers of the pain he mentioned, and anger, but they were overshadowed by his contentment.

"I was the one who made the decision to leave, he simply... gave his blessing in a twisted kind of way," Mell continued. He had opened the gates to these memories and feelings, and was determined to get them out. She understood this. "It's the same as what he did today. He cares, but he doesn't know how to show it in any but a cruel way." One hand stroked over her back. "You're right, we need to truly let it all go. If we keep the brooch we are hanging onto a future that was never going to exist from the moment Da found out I wasn't his."

Relief surged out from Mell. Had he never admitted that piece of his pain out loud? Had he maybe never admitted it to himself? Was he following his own words and letting the past go? She didn't know, but she did know that something in him shifted with those words. A tear deep in his soul started to close.

Mell sighed. "I'll talk Dub around eventually, I always do. I wouldn't mention this to either of them, though. Not about Da kicking us out for our own good, or him loving us in his sick and twisted soul. That... would no' go over well."

Visions of Dub tearing his father's boat, The Golden Crane, to pieces one strip of metal at a time entered her mind. It wasn't a true vision, but she could see it so clearly it may as well have been.

"Agreed," she said. "Can I ask you a question?"

"Is it a naughty question?"

"No."

"Oh. Well, if you must," he said with mock-disappointment.

"If you had not been born as Alatrom's son and a Fomoiri, what would you have wanted to become?"

"A bard."

She hadn't expected him to answer so quickly. "You have thought about it."

"Yes. I love my music. Da let me learn how to play, but he refused to let me try my own songs, or take lessons for them. Claimed a proper Fomoiri took up the sword and fought for his clan. Part of him wanted to let me do as I wished, but..."

She knew what that but was. They did not need to revisit it. "What about when you left home? I'm sure you could have found someone to teach you? As Dub found someone to teach him smithing?"

Mell shrugged under her. The contentment was fading away. "Maybe I'll look for someone when we're done with this."

"Really?"

Flash. Mell bent over his guitar, scraps of paper with melodies and lyrics scribbled over them littered the table in front of him.

"Well, I have to survive this first."

"You will," she said, determined. *I will make sure of it.*

"So fierce. Go to sleep, little warrior. My *realta.*"

"Okay. Love you."

He didn't answer, but a glow of warmth radiated from him. Bat fell asleep with that feeling wrapped around her.

Chapter Seventeen

FINN

*I*t was their second day on the boat, and they were nearly halfway to their destination, at least according to Saoirse. Ari had informed them the cauldron had stopped moving some time the day before, and Bat and this rag-tag group were definitely heading in the correct direction.

Finn wasn't sure he trusted the selkie. They were like cats, scheming and sly. Finn also didn't like the woman's choice of words. She had wanted to come "play." The fae of Ireland hadn't been up against a foe like this in far too long. They had forgotten just how ruthless and cunning Balor could be, if words like "play" were being thrown around.

Then again, she *was* a selkie—and a daughter of mac Lir. And considering they faced Balor of the Evil Eye, Finn knew full well he couldn't be picky about his allies. He *should* be weeding out the weak and incompetent—and that was at least *half* of what they were currently dragging around with them—but no matter how he thought about it, they needed the sheer number of *bodies* to make their plan work.

If only The Morrigan wasn't being a fickle bitch. If only the Tribunal hadn't washed their hands of the whole thing. *If only an Egyptian goddess hadn't decided that Ireland would be her new home...*

No. He didn't really believe that, and he wouldn't think like that. He was well aware he was being a grumpy asshole-wanker that should be dipped in tar and then skinned alive. He even knew the real reason he currently acted like more of a shit-spittle than Dub...

It was because of Bat, his goddess. She was keeping secrets from them, something he'd never thought she would do. She'd always been so *different* from all the other deities he'd ever known in his too-long life. But Finn was familiar with that distant look, that smile that wasn't a smile, and he knew what it meant when evasive and cryptic words were used. Like the ones she'd used last night.

Either she didn't know the answer and was trying to maintain some air of authority and mysteriousness, or she was keeping secrets. As much as he hated to admit it, the latter was more likely than the first. Oh, his goddess could be mysterious, but she never did it deliberately. Of course, he didn't think she'd be keeping secrets either...

He twisted his head to where Bat sat on a low bench-seat running along one end of the foredeck. Her harp, the

Uaithne, was in its case and cradled in her arms. After yesterday, she'd not let it leave her sight.

Finn didn't blame her for that one.

There was an invisible circle around her. Despite the lack of space on a boat not really meant to carry over thirty people, no one sat next to her; not even Ailis or the brothers. Not Finn.

A soft breeze danced around her, playing with the strands of her dark hair, then shifted, bringing him her scent—heat, crisp air, the subtle bite of pepper and the light fragrance of cornflowers. Then the breeze carried it away once more.

He recalled the first time he'd scented that particular combination, the day Mell had called him to the pub to take charge of Dano's body and the murder investigation. The day The Morrigan showed up in his office in Sligo.

He sighed. That was the beginning...

Bat sat alone, gazing into the horizon of where sea met sky, her lips tipped up. He wouldn't call it a smile, it was more a quirk of her lips, and held nothing of joy or happiness.

No, it was the smile someone used to mask loneliness.

What had happened?

His earlier anger was gone, washed away by the look on her face. Concern replaced it. He only wanted her to smile like she used to, like she had just two days ago as they sat at the cottage's small breakfast table and plotted what they would need to take Balor down...

Then she had called someone, one of the gods in Egypt. After that call was when she changed, he realized. She'd withdrawn. It was so gradual; he hadn't noted it at the time. Then yesterday, during the meeting, she'd barely participated. After she'd summarized her visions in a flat voice, she'd sat between Dub and Mell, her eyes distant. True, they hadn't settled much, mostly due to the fact they couldn't until they had done a proper reconnaissance of the island, but it had been extremely out of character for her.

Ailis stood on the opposite end of the small deck, Meera and Teagan next to her, and they too casted worried looks at the Egyptian goddess. Bat had spent a while with the trooping fae yesterday. Killer and the pixies had guarded the ladder, keeping everyone away, and Ailis must have cast some type of "don't listen" glamour, because even Finn had found it hard to keep his attention on the two figures in the lookout over the bridge.

Ailis knew something...

Finn shook off his thoughts. No, if he was going to find out what was troubling his goddess, he needed to speak with her directly, not go behind her back to dig out the information from her best friend.

I guess a guardi's need to interrogate has become ingrained. His lips quirked up in a self-deprecating smile.

He needed to talk to Bat. With any other deity he would have left it alone. They operated on a different plane than the rest of the mere mortals—or immortals as the case may be—but Bat was different. She lived *with* the brothers and those she met at the pub, not just among them.

How was he going to approach this?

His gaze fell once more to the harp. Maybe...

His phone rang. *Of course.* He glanced at the caller ID. Criedne. "Yes?"

"Finn. We kept them as busy as we could. We've been trading off with Cu Chulainn's team as well as macMorna's. Then they suddenly broke off, and we haven't been able to locate a single hint of shadow."

The Hunt. "When did they disengage?"

"Three hours ago."

"Hmmmm." Even if you disregarded the fact that The Wild Hunt had come after them in the first place, their behavior was strange. He'd assumed they were sent to capture Bat, the human, and the harp, then get them to Balor's allies. The Hunt couldn't follow them onto to seas, though. They would have sensed it as soon as their prey hit the water, and gone back to whatever plane of existence or dank corner they occupied in between chases. "Tell me exactly what they've been doing."

"They stayed around Sligo for a bit. At first they headed north, but after an hour or so they circled back around to Sligo."

Around the time of the attack at Finnegan's.

"A few times they entered the edges of the towns, but we blocked them. Early this morning they began fighting their way east."

Finn's blood went cold. "Where, *exactly*, east?"

"It... We thought Dublin, and the Tribunal."

"Criedne," he ground out. It wasn't like her to be so evasive. She usually just spit out whatever she needed to, uncaring of the reactions her words would generate. It was one of the best things about having her on his team.

"They disappeared a few kilometers outside Tara."

What new hell was this? If Balor took Tara... They

wouldn't just have a potential war on their hands, they would have chaos. The humans' legends of Tara only scratched the surface. It was not just the seat of the kings of Ireland. Whoever held Tara very literally held Ireland. There was a very real reason the solitary fae and other more rebellious immortals did not attempt rebellions and uprisings every few decades. No, they left that to the humans. "Criedne..."

"We know. I've alerted the Tribunal, though they didn't sound concerned. The Chief is coordinating with the guardi units in Meath and Leinster," she said, referring to the two districts nearest to Tara.

"And how much do *they* know?" *Fuck. Fuck. Fuck.* Yes, his team and Cuchi's knew most of what was going on—he'd planned to use them to fight Balor, after all. They'd told the Chief of Connaught district even less, simply stating that there was unusual activity among the solitary fae that needed to be investigated. Having a sluagh or Fir Bolg in the interrogation rooms wasn't all that uncommon, nor was calling in a Druid to help with that interrogation... The chief had given them leave to run with their investigation.

If the Chiefs got involved, they would attempt to take over the operation. The Morrigan could step in and put them in their place, of course; but with the fickle nature of their gods, the likelihood of that happening was fifty-fifty, even with her sending Cuchi to help them. Oh, and the raven that was as fickle as its master and only bothered to show its beak when The Morrigan had something to say.

No, if the higher-ups in the Guardi knew what was happening then Bat, her visions, and her intuitions would be relegated to the side, even if she *was* a goddess. She wasn't powerful enough, and she was Egyptian—an intruder. Respect would be outwardly shown, then her opinions would be lost in the booming voices of arguing generals. And that was only if some asshat didn't decide she was somehow behind it all and took everything in the wrong direction...

As frustrated as he was, he agreed with The Morrigan and the Tribunal on one thing—Bat was the key to unraveling Balor's plans.

All of this went through his mind in the time it took him to blink.

"Just that the Wild Hunt has been acting peculiarly, and was last seen headed for Tara." Criedne said. *"The Wild Hunt acting out of character was alarming enough, I didn't need to tell them more."*

"And what did you tell them about me?"

"That you were using some of your more unsavory connections and had gone undercover to infiltrate the solitary fae and find what you could that way."

Finn had to stifle a sudden laugh at the note of derision in his lieutenant's voice. He knew it wasn't directed at the "unsavory" connections he had, but at the gullibility of the upper echelons of the guardi. She'd pandered to their conceit and she knew it.

"You are all too clever to be just a lieutenant."

"I know."

He did laugh at that. "Keep tracking The Hunt, and make sure no one, and I do mean *no one*, gets into Tara. The only people I trust at this point are the ones I am with on this too crowded boat, Oisin, you and the rest of the team."

"*Got it.*"

Criedne didn't hang up. "Anything else?"

"*How is she?*"

Finn knew who he meant. Criedne had met Bat once on one of the guardi lieutenant's rare visits to the pub. Bat had worked her charm on Criedne. "She's Bat."

"*She's good for you.*"

Finn nearly choked on his own spit. He and Criedne never talked about personal matters. Never.

"*Don't fuck this up,*" she said and hung up.

Once he'd recovered he tucked his phone in his pocket and stared out at the open water, not seeing the gray-blue expanse or clouded horizon. There was nothing he could do at the moment about what was happening on the mainland. No, he needed to concentrate on the situation on this boat, and on what was going on with Bat.

He had also just gotten an extremely important piece of information.

Which he was not going to share unless it became absolutely necessary, he realized. There was no reason to worry about Tara unless they failed in killing Balor. If he told Bat or the others, it would only add another layer of pressure and stress, but would change nothing about their strategy.

Secrets…

Finn snorted and mentally slapped his own head. The last of whatever resentment and anger he might have held towards his little goddess drained away. He was a lot of things, but he was no hypocrite.

There was still a day until they reached Tir Hudi and could actually *do* anything.

He pushed away from the railing and headed for Bat. Finn had a new mission in mind, a very personal one. He was going to do what he could to see his goddess smile for him…

Chapter Eighteen

Bastie,

Have you ever wondered just what *it means to be a goddess?*

- The Goddess Bat

BAT

A shadow fell over her and Bat looked up. Finn stood there, the sun outlining his imposing profile.

"Goddess," he said as he sat beside her.

She'd been here for an hour or so, trying to enjoy the rocking of the boat under her and the gentle breeze that carried the scents of salt and foreign lands. Mell was taking his turn on the bridge, Dub and Shar were sleeping, and...

And everyone else seemed to sense that Bat needed some time to herself.

Or they were embarrassed by all the, um, moaning and groaning and banging that she and Mell had generated last night.

It had been a good night.

But the day had come, and her worries pushed in on her. The worst part was that there was nothing for her to do. She didn't know anything about boats, Ciara had kicked her out of the galley, and there was no planning to do until they'd reached the island.

Not that I would actually contribute to that. She knew she was being unfair to herself and everyone else. But she'd woken this morning to an empty bunk and a surge of self-recrimination about her performance in yesterday's meeting. For Seth's sake, she didn't even know what had been decided.

And she was too embarrassed to ask.

She was supposed to be the one leading them, the one pulling them all together, the one they looked up to.

Bat hugged the harp closer to her as Finn put an arm around her shoulders and tugged her into his side.

That was... new.

"I've told ya before, *acushla*. I am here for you, no matter what you need." The red-gold-haired sidhe kept his gaze on the horizon, presenting her with the clean lines of his profile.

"I do not need that right now. I mean, I would surely welcome it, but after last night I do not think the others would appreciate me making so much noise again. Well, not so soon." Although she *did* want to make Finn hers before they reached the island.

It might be her last chance. He may not want her after…

After he saw how weak she was. After she was unable to keep her friends alive.

Bat shivered.

"I did no' mean *that*." He paused. "At least not right now."

"What do you mean, then?"

He responded with a question of his own. "Why are you sitting here alone?"

"I…"

He waited. When she didn't continue, he nodded, as though coming to some sort of conclusion. "I know a thing or two about secrets."

She jerked under the comforting weight of his arm and tried to pull away. He didn't let her. "Were you listening in on my and Ailis's girl talk yesterday?"

He chuckled and leaned into her. "Girl talk? I would never. I've heard it's a sacred time for women that must never be trespassed upon." He finally turned his head and peered down at her, his golden-hazel eyes gentle. "Like I said, I know a thing or two about secrets. I know how to spot someone who is keeping them, and I know how they can make someone feel, especially someone who is not used to keeping them."

Or, someone who is not used to keeping them from those who trust and care for her, Bat amended. But she did not say the words aloud.

"Most gods and goddesses I have interacted with keep

secrets only because they can," he continued. "I know that if there is something you are not telling us, then you have a very good reason." He leaned down and placed a gentle kiss on her forehead.

What should she say? Should she admit there were pieces of her visions she was holding back from everyone? But then he would ask her what those were, and she would need to outright lie, and she did not want to do that with him.

She stayed silent.

But she did take his words to heart. There *was* a very good reason she did not share all she knew. And it had not been any easy decision to come to. It was just that...

She felt as though she'd betrayed them in some way. She'd promised no secrets after her night with Dub. This was a betrayal of that promise. Then there was Ailis. How could Bat possibly withhold the vision of her best friend's lifeless body? Shouldn't she be doing everything she could to ensure her survival? Bat should be refusing to allow her onto the island, or sending her back to Sligo and the guardi headquarters with strict orders that the green-haired fae not leave the premises.

But Ailis was a puzzle piece on the very narrow path she had to tread to see Balor defeated.

Bat had chosen the fate of thousands, if not millions, of people over that of her friend.

And what about the immortals who had accompanied them to Tir Hudi? Everyone said they were here because of her, because she had shown them warmth, had treated them with equality and with care.

Now here she sat, acting just like every other deity

they had ever known. She was no different from the beings despised by her new friends.

How could they possibly trust her?

Bat sighed.

Finn's phone beeped. He pulled it out and frowned down at the screen. "It seems you are projecting, *acushla*."

"What?"

"Mell just messaged me, asking what I was doing to you and why you were spiraling into 'a farking mass of despair.'" His words were easy, conversational. His arm remained firm over her shoulder. "So, tell me, why the despair? Is it Balor?"

Bat let out a humorless laugh. The fae around them cast her concerned looks. Killer made his way to her and laid over her feet, pressing his side into her legs with a faint whine.

"How about I tell you a little story?" Finn said, ignoring her non-response. "Once upon a time, there was a little Egyptian goddess. Everyone who ever knew her had forgotten her. One day, she decided to go find a new home, and traveled the lands searching."

Bat snuck a look at him. *Where is he going with this?*

"One damp and rainy night, she came upon a pub. It was a special place, one filled with magical beings, both beautiful and dangerous."

He should have been a storyteller instead of a warrior. The tales he spins...

"This goddess knew nothing about the land she was in, or the people she had found. Nevertheless, she decided to help them where she could. These people welcomed

165

her in their own way, giving her gifts and treating her with song and drink."

Bat couldn't hold back her smile at his rendition of her coming to Ireland. It sounded like a fairy tale.

"The goddess remained distant, though, for she did no' trust these new friends. The goddess had no' fully trusted *anyone* for millennia, for she had once been hurt by the people she cared for the most. She was not yet ready to hand over the last part of herself into the care of her new friends."

"Over time she revealed herself bit by bit. She shared her past, and her worries and fears. She lived among these new people, not as a goddess, but as one of them. And they loved her for it."

Tears gathered in Bat's eyes as emotion welled. It was not sorrow, nor was it happiness. It was just... a big ball of *emotion*.

"One day, a new danger came to this land. It came in the guise of an ancient enemy, someone who was also connected to that goddess's past. Old secrets were revealed, and these secrets threatened the new trust the goddess had built piece by piece.

"She overcame this trial, though. She was determined to guide her new friends though this troubling time, for she could see the path they would need to take to defeat this evil. She gathered them together, and gave them a purpose.

"Now, these friends were not warriors. Well, most of them were not. The goddess worried for their safety during the coming battle. What she did not realize was, they worried just as much about her."

His words were low, meant for her ears only. Bat fell into the rhythm of them as pictures formed in her mind. The way he told it, she could imagine this goddess was not her, but someone else. The story unfolded before her.

"One day, the goddess received word from her old home. Whatever she had been told changed her. She once more grew distant, and distracted. Her friends wondered what she had been told that would change her back into the distant goddess who first set foot on their land. They missed her laughter, the smiles she would freely share, and the songs she would sing them.

"One of her new friends, a very *close* friend, saw what was happening. He had come to know this goddess very well, and knew she longed to share with someone what her old family told her. But he also knew she could not. It was perhaps not her secret to tell."

Bat swallowed. "No," she whispered. "It was not her secret to tell." How could he cut to the quick of the situation so accurately? The way he stated the situation also gave her a new perspective. What had happened to Osiris, the fact the Egg of Creation could birth seeds of godhood. These were *not* her secrets.

"This goddess also received visions that she used to guide her companions," Finn said, his words coming slower now. Not hesitant, but as though he was testing each word on his tongue before speaking it aloud. "One day she saw something that made her blood run cold. And she had a new decision to make. She could tell her friends what she saw and attempt to alter it, or she could keep it to herself and continue to guide them on the path she knew they needed to take to defeat this evil."

"The goddess must have been so sad," she murmured, fully caught up in the tale.

"She was," Finn agreed. "You see, she was no longer a distant goddess. She had formed bonds with those she lived with, had begun to care for them more than a deity should. For, she had forgotten something in her happiness and joy at finding her new family. She had forgotten that gods and goddesses remain distant from the lives of their followers and supplicants for a reason." His hand ran up and down her arm. "Sometimes, those gods and goddesses must make sacrifices of their own, as much as it pains them, in order to protect the world around them."

"It would not be *her* sacrifice." The words slipped from Bat before she could stop them.

Finn ignored her. "This close friend of hers was not worried, though, for he remembered that she *was* still a goddess—and he had learned something about her while she lived among them. He had learned just how much this goddess valued their friendship and loyalty, and he knew she would do everything in her power to save her friends —even if she could not tell them, even if she pulled away from them, even if they did not understand."

"She would," Bat told him. "She would do everything she possibly could to alter what she had seen." A tear slipped down her cheek and she reached up to wipe it away.

"I know." The confidence in his voice settled Bat. Everything he had said was true. She had hated needing to keep things from everyone. It had felt as though she betrayed them, and she had withdrawn, the guilt piling up on her.

She wiped her eyes again and looked around her, truly *looked* at the mellow wood of the deck, the white painted bulwarks and rails, the brass trim and fittings. She looked at the hazy blue sky, and the blue-gray waves that swelled under the boat. She looked at the fae gathered around her, and the sneaking looks they sent her. She looked at Killer sprawled over her feet.

Then she looked at the man beside her. "When did you get to be such a wise man?"

Finn shrugged, his hand rubbing small circles over her upper arm. "It is always easier to see a situation when you are not the one in it." The corners of his eyes pinched as something dark moved through them. "And as much as I dislike it, I really do know that sometimes there are things you cannot share, even with allies and lovers."

I wonder what secrets he holds? Bat did not ask, though.

His words echoed Ailis's from yesterday. Everyone has secrets, and some things were not meant to be known. She understood that, of course. But somehow Finn's story let her *know* the truth of it.

Determination filled her. She may not be able to share the entirety of what she knew, but she would find a way to amend that last vision. She would find a way to prevent the end of Ailis's and Daniel's lives as she'd been shown.

"How about a song?" Finn suggested after a few more minutes of silence.

Yes, Finn somehow always knows what to say. Bat smiled up at him and he flushed.

"There it is," he whispered, almost to himself.

Bat stretched up and laid a light kiss on his lips. *A promise for later.*

Then she pulled the harp from its pack. She fingered the strings for a few beats, searching for the song this moment needed.

She found it. Bat played them a song that spoke of losing and finding home. The fae listened, some tapping their feet, others dancing a few measures. But most of them simply listened as the goddess, their friend, let them know exactly how she felt about them.

"Goddess?" Ari stopped beside her, his needle teeth showing and claws tapping against each other.

"Yes?"

"We have finished searching the souls of those on the boat. I apologize that it took us so long. We needed to rest properly and regain our strength to ensure nothing was missed."

"That is perfectly understandable, Ari." Bat sat back in the chair she'd claimed as her own during dinner. It had been lively, bodies coming and going from the salon— Ciara trying to keep everyone from the galley, laughter from the pixies as they tampered with people's food then flitted out of reach of swinging hands and fists.

The atmosphere had been very much like a night at the pub, only with less space and no way to kick anyone out. Or so Dub had grumbled when he left the bridge to gulp down his own meal.

"Did you find anything?" Bat asked Ari.

"No, goddess. We even checked twice, just to be sure. The human is deteriorating, though the portion of Balor's soul housed within him has not fully taken over." Ari's lips pulled back in an instinctive snarl.

"Is the dream-guardian amulet helping?"

"I believe so. But, I do not think it is wholly effective. The human has not woken, and he continues to speak nonsense words in his sleep. I suspect Balor has some ability to see through him. I sense the faintest connection, similar to what we have with the cauldron, but much darker." Ari's gaze drifted to the half full bowl of crisps in the middle of the table.

Bat handed it to the man of ba who gripped it tight within his too-many-knuckled fingers.

The conversation of the few fae still gathered in the salon faded away.

"I am not worried about this. He has been removed from any conversations regarding our strategies, and will continue to be so. There are certain things both sides need to have happen, and one of them is arriving at Tir Hudi. We will simply need to move very quickly in our first few steps of surveillance." Bat sent a smile toward the pink and red glows that hovered within one of the potted plants that had been placed in the main salon.

"Of course, goddess," Daire declared, his red glow flaring. "We Smalls are *much* better than the Bigs at spying." His little voice swelled with pride.

Bat's smile stayed firmly in place, and it wasn't forced. Or, mostly. After her conversation with Finn, and her song, something had clicked into place within her. She was a goddess, she could not change that. She was also a friend and a lover to the beings on this boat. She *wouldn't* change that. The responsibilities inherent to each aspect of her would just need to learn to get along.

She may not be able to share everything she knew, but she would no longer distance herself from her companions, and she *would* find a way to alter the final outcome she had seen.

She yawned.

"Bat, ye're still worn." Ailis reached over the table and gave her a gentle shove. "Go sleep." The green-haired fae slid a sly glance at Finn, who could just be seen though the windows of the salon. "Or, do something else to gain energy. Didn't you once mention how... effective certain types of sacrifice were?" The wicked woman sent her brows up and down in a comically suggestive gesture.

It was too silly, and it should have made her laugh. Instead, it sent Bat's mind in a direction it had been skirting around all day. She did want to make Finn hers, and tonight would be her last chance before the confrontation with Balor.

She rose from her seat. *One last chance to live in the moment.* It was time for her to grab another piece of happiness.

Chapter Nineteen

*D*arkness. It surrounded him, cradled him, soothed him to sleep. He had been lost in it for centuries, he learned.

Even now it called to him.

He had to ignore it.

He stretched out his senses. Flashes and snippets greeted him, coming from each soul he'd reached out to in his slumber—each soul that had pledged itself to him.

One in particular shone brighter than the others. He followed the strand and found himself in a darkened room, swaying with the motion of a ship.

Ah, there it was, hidden in the crannies of a puny human's mind. It was the piece of his soul that he had already embedded in an effigy even before Nuada's blade had pierced his belly and stolen his life. This little bit of himself had been his tie to the world, and was what had finally allowed him to escape the darkness.

Soon, he whispered to that fragment of himself. *We will be together soon.*

The enemy was less than a day away. He would play with them, allow them to believe they were the ones in control. That little goddess would not be able to thwart him.

After all, he'd had millennia to prepare for this day. Millennia since he overheard a whispered conversation between Osiris and Isis, and the seeds of his plan had been planted.

It was coming together. He'd needed the original vessel of creation out from under the watchful eye of Seth. He'd needed to die. He'd needed to gather his forces in secret, and what better way to do that than if everyone thought you were no longer there. He had needed someone who could speak with the vessel, who could persuade it into an act of creation one last time.

And she had come. A goddess from the homeland. A goddess who was no more than an ignorant girl, abused and alone. A goddess too innocent to ignore his whispers.

A goddess too in love with life to be able to ignore the seduction of The Final Melody. The song that would herald the end of the Egg of Creation, and the beginning of the world's destruction.

She would play it, if only to save those around her.

Yes, all the pieces were coming together...

Chapter Twenty

Bastie,
If you were me, you would be purring…
Damn it is good to be a worshipped goddess.

- Bat, the very satisfied goddess

BAT

*B*at faced Finn. Up on deck, he'd allowed her to take his hand. He'd allowed her to lead him belowdecks and down the passageway. He'd allowed her to take him inside her cabin.

Now he stood, feet apart and arms crossed, a stubborn look on his face.

What had happened to the tender man of that afternoon?

"Finn. Please. I… despite my visions, I do not know what will happen tomorrow, or the day after. I do not know if we will have this moment again. And..." She disliked the pleading note in her voice. Stopping, she firmed her resolve and met his hazel gaze. "And I am not interested in having regrets. I will regret it if we do not come together, if I do not grab this bit of happiness for myself, and for you."

He stepped back, his expression unreadable. "You really are being selfish, aren't you?"

Where is this coming from? It was as though a stranger had invaded his body.

Then the conversation they had had in his apartment came back to her. "Is that so bad? Do you not want this?" She supposed she would leave him be if he asked her to let him go. She was not such a monster as to force this moment on him. Yes, she had decided to grab her happiness and hold on with both hands, but she would not *force* it.

Shadows moved in his eyes. "Are you doing this for the power? I didn't miss the boost you got after your nights with the brothers."

Had he overheard Ailis? Bat opened her mouth to protest, and stopped. Could she honestly say that the thought hadn't occurred to her? No. Was it the reason she wanted Finn tonight? *Also no.*

"I see." He took another step back, but there wasn't anywhere for him to go. The cabins on this boat were *small.*

Bat shook her head, her dark hair flying. "You don't see, Finn." Heat built within her, part arousal and part anger. "And stop assuming things. I haven't answered your question."

His lips thinned. "Answer me then."

She had to remember that the question of romantic entanglements was a different matter from dealing with Balor. She also had to remember that he had been hurt too, and recently. Someone wanting him for his power was a jab that hit all to close to the wounds Grainne had inflicted upon him.

Trust. He trusts me to guide the way to Balor's defeat. We have to build the trust between us for this type of relationship too. What they had was all too new, and all to fragile, despite all the pretty words that had been exchanged up to this point. *He has pinpricks in his soul as well.*

Finn had been the calm one through this whole thing. He'd been the one to come to her and offer his body that day in the garden. In his apartment, he'd been the one to first admit that what he felt was more than the physical, even if the admission was couched in hints and subtle words. He'd been the one to keep her company after the brothers ran amok through her heart after her night with Dub.

He'd done it all for her. And inside him, under that oh so calm exterior, he hid the holes and tears of his own soul.

He needed to heal, just like she did. And Bat knew all too well that in order to heal, you needed to uncover the wounds.

These were his wounds, and he was finally beginning to show them to her. She, more than anyone, knew the pain a calm exterior could hide.

She grasped her necklace and pulled her shoulders back. "I cannot say the thought of a power boost did not cross my mind. I would be an idiot if I was not thinking of ways to prepare for what will come tomorrow."

He scowled.

"*But*—" she held up a hand, "I could have gone to any of the brothers if that was all I wanted. I didn't. I came to *you*. You already know how I feel about you. You *know* it. I understand you have pain in you, just as we all do, but I will not play this particular game with you. I will not allow you to push me away because of imagined slights." She dropped her hand. "If you truly do not want this, I will not stop you from leaving." Bat shuffled along the side of the bunk and toward the door.

He caught her arm. "No." His teeth dug into his lower lip and his brows pulled together low over his eyes. His red-gold hair was soft in the low lamplight. "No, not like this."

The heat and anger in her faded away in the face of his obvious confusion.

"I—" He ran his free hand through his hair. "I didn't want my first time with you to be on a boat, anchored off of a mythical island, while evil waits for us," he continued. "But you are right. We don't know what's going to happen tomorrow or the next day. I hate that the circumstances are forcing us together like this. I admit that originally I thought I'd be satisfied with your body. Gods, when I went to you in the garden that day, I fully intended to use you, and allow you to use me. But you..." He let go of her arm and scrubbed both hands into his hair. "I said I would be there, whatever you needed. I did not question when you wanted all four of us. I even understand it, to a degree. You are a goddess, I would never presume to tell you what your needs should be." His arms dropped and his shoulders slumped. "I don't know how to say this."

Bat reached up and laid her palm against his cheek. There was so much pain and confusion reflected in this not-man's eyes. She only knew pieces of his history, but this was a man who'd been alive for millennia. Maybe even as long as her. "You can tell me when you are ready."

His eyes slid closed and he pressed his cheek into her hand.

"I want you," he said. "So badly. I want this to be more than flesh and desires and sacrifices."

Bat slid her hand to his neck and pulled him down her. She laid a soft kiss against his lips. "It already is." She did not try to tell him again that she loved him. She did not attempt to give him grand declarations or reassurances. She kept her words simple, and she put the entirety of her sincerity behind them.

He bent to her, and their lips met once more. Again it was soft, almost chaste.

He straightened. "If we are doing this tonight, then grant me one thing."

Her gaze focused on his lips. Their color had deepened, inviting her to explore. "What is this request?"

His eyes dilated, the hazel becoming a slim ring around the pupil. "Allow me to worship you."

The heat that had become a banked fire during their earlier conversation flamed once more. Her lips curled up into a soft smile and she glanced up at him through her lashes. "I could allow that," she teased. Her hand

179

skimmed over his shoulder, down one well-muscled arm and back up, then settled over his chest.

His heart was pounding.

She'd done that to him. Her lower belly tightened as moisture gathered at her core, readying her for what this man would do.

Stepping forward, He pressed his chest to her breasts. He widened his stance and brought his hands to her waist, holding her against him. One slid around to her back and pressed her into his groin. He was already aroused, the length of him pressing hard against her belly through their clothes.

Finn stepped forward, and she was forced to move back. Her knees hit the edge of the bunk. He lowered her to the narrow mattress, angling them both to avoid the bulkhead.

He pulled away, and hit his head. "Dammit."

Bat giggled.

"This is the other reason I wanted to wait. No damn room on this boat."

And everyone will hear us, Bat silently added. She didn't say it aloud, scared that would be the last straw for Finn and he'd leave.

She reached out for him, skimming her fingers along his thigh and over his hip before running them across his lower abdomen just over his groin. She pushed a trickle of her power into the touch.

He shivered. "Well now, and why are you wasting such hard earned power?"

"With a reaction like that, I do not believe I would call it wasted," she replied.

He caught her wrist, forcing her hand to her side. "I said that I would be the one worshipping you, goddess."

Her lips pulled down. Did that mean she was supposed to lie there without participating? She wasn't sure she wanted to do that. Not if it meant having to keep her hands to herself.

Finn came over her, his body slotting between her legs. "Sshhh." He kissed her forehead, then over each eye. His lips skimmed over her cheeks before settling over her own. They kissed, the movements slow and easy, almost lazy. They tasted each other, taking their time.

He moved to her jaw and worked his way to her ear. "Let me do this." His teeth closed over the tender flesh of her earlobe and tugged. "Please," he added.

It was the 'please' that got her. A 'please' from this not-man swayed her every time.

He didn't wait for her answer, only kissed down her neck, leaving a trail of warmth. He propped himself up on one elbow, freeing his other hand, and studied her face.

Slipping that free hand under the helm of her sweater, he rested his calloused palm over her belly, pressing his fingers in and kneading her. "I adore how soft you are." He worked the sweater up her torso and over her breasts, revealing her crimson bra.

She *may* have worn it hoping this very thing would happen...

He paused, staring at the bright fabric against her dusky skin. "Your skin is amazing." Finn ran a finger along the swell of each breast, right where her bra ended.

Her nipples puckered under the thin fabric. His lips

parted and for long seconds he only stared, that one finger idly stroking her.

He looked... enraptured. As though he had anticipated this moment for longer than a few months and was determined to savor it.

At that moment she truly did feel worshipped.

Finn rolled to his feet, and she nearly followed him, not wanting to loose the contact with him.

"Sshhh..." He placed a hand to the middle of her chest and pushed her back against the mattress. "I'm just getting rid of a few pesky pieces of cloth. The bunks too narrow for the both of us."

He grabbed the bottom of his sweater and stripped it away in one movement. The white t-shirt underneath was gone a moment later. Two moments later he stood before her in nothing but his skin.

He'd stripped down as though his clothes were poisonous—or cursed. Just like the other three of her not-men. Bat bit her lip in an effort to keep in the laugh that wanted to bubble to the surface.

The golden lamplight outlined every plane of his body. It cast shadows that she wanted to explore with her hands and mouth, and highlighted intriguing swells of muscle. This was her first chance to examine Finn, and she took her time.

A light trace of hair covered his chest before narrowing down to his belly and lower. His manhood was framed in the same red-gold that graced his head. Right now it was a standing proudly erect, flushed a dusky red. His thighs were as muscular as his arms and shoulders, though not overly thick, and his calves were graceful.

She finished her inspection with his feet. Her hips rolled. She'd never been aroused by a man's feet before, but somehow Finn's were… entrancing. They were large but not overly wide, nor did they have extra flesh. The nails were trim and clean, and his toes were slender.

Those toes flexed, as though Finn knew just what she was thinking, and had decided to tease her.

Bat lifted her gaze back to his. His face still held the same flushed and serious expression.

"Now," he said. "It's time we got you out of your own clothes."

Bat sat up to finish pulling off her sweater, and Finn stopped her, kneeling beside the bunk. "No. Let me."

She let her sweater go. Finn grabbed it and slid the thin cotton knit over her head and off her arm. Then he reached around and unhooked her bra, only fumbling a little as his big fingers struggled with the small hooks. When he peeled the thin fabric away from her, he again paused and stared.

She straightened her back, forcing her breasts forward. She sat there proudly, allowing her lover to gaze upon her.

He raised a hand and hesitated just before it would have made contact with the round flesh of her left breast. "May I?"

She nodded, the movement a single dip of her head.

His heated palm settled over her. She sucked in a deep breath, forcing the soft flesh into his hand. She flushed and her nipples drew tighter, the areoles darkening to a deep pink. He switched his hold to her other breast, lifting and kneading it. Then he abandoned that one as well, skimming his palm down her arm and then back up, before repeating the motion on the other side.

"Lay down, please." She complied, and he continued his exploration of her body, still using just the one hand.

When he made it to her jeans, Bat was flushed all over, and more than ready for additional stimulation—for his lips and tongue to follow the path of his fingers, for his touch to deepen, for his body to cover hers and press her into the mattress.

She rolled her hips, asking silently for what she wanted. He had said he wanted to worship her, but she suspected he was the one to cast a spell over her. Why else would she, Bat—a once fertility goddess—lie silently waiting and yearning for the slightest touch of this man?

His hand remained between her breasts, the touch warm and just heavy enough she knew he meant it when he said he wanted to lie there without moving. Then that hand skimmed down her body until it reached the button on her jeans. He teased the sensitive skin there before finally slipping the button open and pulling the zipper down.

Bat shifted her hips again. She was willing to play this game with him, but she was not above doing what she could to urge him along. Shifting her hips in a little circle, she let out a pleading moan and lifted her rib cage, thrusting her breasts high.

Finn's hand froze and Bat took a peek at his face. He still wore that worshipful expression, lips parted and eyes soft. His tongue darted out to moisten his lips and then he lowered his head. He placed soft kisses against her collarbone, working his way lower until his mouth hovered over the peaked tip of her left breast. She couldn't help the small sliver of pride she felt at the fact that while her flesh was abundant, it was firm enough that her breasts didn't sag to the side.

The golden-red-haired not-man licked along the underside of that breast then took her straining nipple into his mouth, biting it lightly before sucking. He continued his attentions in this manner until Bat couldn't hold it in.

"Finn…" she breathed out.

He switched to the other side, giving that mound the same treatment.

The heat at Bat's core increased until she was moving her hips in small circles, anything to relieve the sudden need to move. "More," she said, her voice husky. There was power behind the order, a goddess ordering her supplicant.

The low vibrations of his chuckle traveled through her. He didn't answer, but he did move, shifting down her body. His warm breaths puffed against her sensitive skin, and his tongue darted out in teasing licks as he made his way south.

Then he finally removed the rest of her clothing. Bat lifted her hips to assist in getting the denim off of her. As he worked the material over her legs, she continued the dance she'd begun with her hips, the movements wholly instinctive by this time.

When Finn had stripped the last of her clothing away, he threw it into a shadowed corner of the cabin and returned to the place he'd left off, his mouth directly over her mound.

"Spread for me goddess," he ordered.

By this time, Bat was beyond caring about orders and pleas and who was worshipping who. She pulled her legs wide. Finn settled between them, his wide shoulders and pale skin beautiful between her thighs. His hands settled in the curve where thigh met groin, his thumbs perfectly positioned to pull apart the lips of flesh that guarded her core.

His lips lowered and settled over her. He licked up her slit then found the button of pleasure every goddess knew, even those dedicated to celibacy. He played with her there, nipping and licking the sensitive flesh until Bat could no longer hold back, and she came with an intense moan and jerk of her hips.

He lifted his head, and Bat moaned again at the sight. Mussed red-gold hair over glowing hazel eyes. His mouth was stretched in a fierce grin, and her juices glistened around his mouth.

Finn licked his lips. "And that is how to worship a goddess properly."

Bat, her muscles now limp with satisfaction, chuckled. "I would say that was an acceptable offering." Sensing the game was over, she finally moved. She half sat, grabbed his head, and pulled him up for a passionate kiss. She could taste herself on him.

That kiss had the heat within her building once again. Breaking the kiss, she whispered, "And I would say that sacrifice deserves a reward." She flipped him over so their positions were reversed. This time it was her turn to play. She repeated every thing he had done, teasing him with nipping kisses and licks, until she reached his straining cock.

"While I appreciate the attentions, my Finn, there are many ways to worship a goddess, and many offerings you may present." She wrapped her hand around his engorged manhood. "And this is a very fine offering."

Then she bent her head and took him into her mouth, sucking in a slow and teasing rhythm. The hot flesh was silky against her tongue.

Bat wasn't sure just what had come over her. With each of the brothers their love had been passion filled, yes, but the acts themselves had been fairly straightforward. There'd not been a lot of... play.

What Finn had done had called to a part of her long buried. A part of her that hadn't seen light since before the uniting of Upper and Lower Egypt, since before she'd stood between Seth and Horus.

With the brothers, this intimate act had been more that between a man and a woman.

With Finn, he had treated her as the goddess she used to be—as the goddess she still was. And now that goddess wanted to play, at least for a little bit.

Bat opened her senses and continued her ministrations. One of her hands held the base of his cock steady, and the other slipped down to cradle his balls. Both hands set up a rhythm of steady squeezes.

When she had things exactly as she wanted them, she raised her eyes and met Finn's gaze.

The wondering look was gone, and in its place was pure need. His face had flushed and his lips pulled back in a snarl. His fingers had dug into the sheets and his muscles were locked. Not a sound escaped his mouth, not a movement was made by his body.

He was a warrior holding onto the edge of his control. He was a man on the verge of breaking. He was a sacrifice laid out just for her.

And he was beautiful.

Bat gave one last hard pull on the flesh in her mouth before pulling away. His eyes followed her like a cornered animal.

"This is a very fine offering, indeed," she purred, her hands still on him. "Do you want me?" When he didn't answer right away she tightened her hold on him.

That got the reaction she wanted. A groan was forced from his throat and he jerked his hips.

"Do you want me?" she asked again.

"Yes," he ground out.

Bat released him and crawled back over his body. Her lips took his and she lay flush against him. After a long moment she pulled away once more. "Then take me." She licked along his neck then bit down on a straining tendon. "Worship me."

And that was Finn's breaking point. His arms came around her and he flipped them once more. His head met the bulkhead with a thud, but he didn't pause or notice, far beyond being deterred by a few pesky bumps or bruises.

He pressed between her thighs and Bat opened for him. Reaching down, he aligned his shaft with her opening and thrust. He was large, but Bat was more than ready for him.

He paused over her, muscles straining, and their gazes locked.

"You are mine, are you not?" It wasn't only Bat who spoke those words. Or, it was, but it wasn't only the Bat who had come to Ireland a broken and abandoned goddess. At this moment, power was flowing through her, her being opened to the sky above and the earth below. She channeled the very essence of herself into that question.

"I am yours," Finn growled out. He pulled back and thrust into her again, pulling groans from both of them. "I am yours." The last was a mere whisper, as tenderness broke though the passion for a brief moment.

Then the heat overwhelmed them both. Finn's hips worked in long thrusts and Bat met each and every one. As they neared completion, their movements shortened until Finn barely pulled out, only jerking into her. Bat clenched around him, keeping him within her, not wanting him to escape from her hold for even those small shifts, no matter how she craved the friction.

They were together in this, as the goddess took in the man who had pledged himself to her.

Finn's lips took hers in a biting kiss as he pulled away one last time only to slam back into her. They groaned together as the building sensations finally burst. Power flowed between them then surged into Bat and she threw her head back. Her mouth opened but her throat was too tight for any sound to escape.

Finn collapsed over her, heavy breaths hitting her neck. After a few seconds he groaned and rolled, only to slam into the bulkhead. Bat followed him, nestling into his chest as they both lay on their sides.

He shifted again, hitting his elbow on the curved wall behind him. "Fuck this," he growled.

Bat giggled. The power was fading away. Well, not fading, exactly. It shifted between them as she gradually siphoned it away. She was coming back to herself.

And she realized that that other woman Finn had pulled from her, that goddess hungry for physical sacrifices of passion, was not her. It was a part of her, yes, an aspect of the Egyptian deity Bat—but it was not *her*.

Bat cuddled into Finn's sweaty chest. The air of the cabin shifted over their exposed skin, cooling her. The boat rocked on gentle waves, lulling her now that passion was spent.

Her eyes closed as she drew in the scent of Finn.

This. More than the sharing of their bodies, this was what she craved. *These are moments I need*. The moments of intimacy after passion, the moments when all defenses are down, the moments when it is just a man and a woman with nothing between them.

"Love you," she whispered as she drifted off to sleep.

Finn pressed his lips to her forehead. He did not return the words, and she did not expect them, not yet. It could be decades before he gave them back to her. She didn't mind, for he was already hers. If they overcame Balor, they would have those decades together.

She could wait. Because this not-man was already hers, and she would not allow him to be taken away.

Chapter Twenty-One

Dear Bastet,
I do believe I have been going through what humans call
growing pangs. Or is it growing pains?
Never mind.
Who knew a five-thousand year old goddess still had
growing up to do?

- Bat, the goddess who is a bit more mature now.

BAT

"Here," Saoirse said from where she stood next to Dub at the front of the bridge, staring out the observation windows.

Dub throttled the boat back and set it to idle. "Do we need to set an anchor?"

"No, this shouldn't take long. We just need to set the wards, then I can lead us in."

Bat had spent the morning with Saoirse. The selkie was actually nearly as entertaining as Ailis, once Bat could see past her own unfounded jealousy. It also helped that Bat was able to spend the morning on the bridge with Dub, Con, Finnegan, Finn, Saoirse, and Mell.

Yes, she was squeezed into a corner and not very comfortable, but she was participating again. Mostly in the form of questions because she didn't understand most of what they were referring to, but she was done with taking the backseat, even if she had put herself there in the first place.

"How far out are we now?" Bat asked.

Saoirse twisted back to look at her. "Maybe two hours."

Bat nodded. "From what Ari told me of what he sensed on Daniel, Balor and his allies are no doubt also aware of this. Can the wards disrupt his sense of where we are?"

Finnegan opened his mouth to respond, then paused. He frowned. "I want to say yes, but I don't know exactly what this connection is."

Bat thought for a moment. She should have brought this up earlier. Well, what she should have done was taken her head out of her ass and participated in the first meeting.

She shook the stray thought off.

"How long were you allowing for the reconnaissance?" she asked.

Dub and Finn exchanged a glance. No doubt asking each other why Bat was suddenly so vocal when she'd held her words for the last two days. "A few hours," Finn finally said.

"But that assumed the wards and cloaking runes wouldn't allow Balor to find us, or to know we were already there."

"Yes," Dub said. He frowned his thoughtful frown. He was starting to get it. Then he sighed. "If Finnegan can't guarantee that his wards will block Balor and Daniel's connection then we can't rely on surprise as an element."

"So we concentrate on what we *can* control," Finn said.

"And we play into Balor's hands," Bat said.

Everyone twisted to stare at her.

"There are certain things we *all* need to have happen. Where the struggle begins is *after* Balor emerges from the cauldron." She left the rest unsaid. They assumed she meant he would try to get away after he'd returned to life, and avoid the spear they'd created to ensure his death. She would allow them to believe this. When the time came, the final battle would be between her and Balor, and it would not be fought with swords or spears.

Bat had picked up a lot of what she'd missed in the earlier meeting. Certain roles had already been decided on, no matter what the pixies found on the island. Con would be in the air. The banshees would find a vantage point somewhere near the bay and take out the enemy ships, if for no other reason than to cause chaos. Certain people, such as Ciara and Finnegan, would be left on the boat to guard it. And then there was the group who would be going after the cauldron.

"What if we... circumvent the time needed for that step of the plan?"

Finn's brows rose. "How?"

"Saoirse was already set to do surveillance of the bay,

so there is no need to adjust that, of course. Con goes into the air as soon as we cross the barrier into Tir Hudi. He is a dragon, after all. I am sure he can figure out the best ways to inflict pain and chaos on his enemies."

Con let out a bark of laughter then bowed to her. "You are a perceptive goddess."

Bat gifted him with a smile. "I am, aren't I? I will share my strawberries with you later. The banshees can also get into place. The question was always where to place everyone based on the distribution of the enemy, correct?" She didn't wait for them to agree. "So, we skip that step, and play to our strengths."

A very narrow path of success that you must travel...

The Morrigan didn't say it was a narrow path that *they* must travel. The narrow path was Bat's to navigate.

She thought about the fae that had joined them. Other than the brothers and the two guardi, there were no trained warriors.

These fae do not work well together. Finn had told her that just two days ago. Even the time spent in close quarters on the boat hadn't changed that. They still stuck to their own groups, with a few floaters like Ailis chatting with everyone.

Play to our strengths...

"We are a rag-tag bunch of misfits who do not play well with others," said, thinking it through. No one interrupted her. "Misfits who, from the stories I have heard, are very good at causing their own particular forms of chaos when provoked."

Mell laughed and Finn snorted. "No argument on that."

She was getting excited now. Everything was coming together in her mind. Bat bounced on her toes. "We are trying to treat them like warriors and trained soldiers. As you all have already noted, they are not. What if we just... give them a goal and let them figure out how to reach it? What is the main thing we need to achieve?"

"Balor's death as soon as he is restored."

"Yes. What if he is able to slip away from us?"

"Then we can't let him get off the island." That was Dub. He stared at her with wide eyes.

"So we make that impossible!" Bat clapped her hands, thoroughly pleased with herself. They did need to plan for all eventualities. What if Balor decided to slip away and use the cauldron later to gain his godhood? What if his soldiers overpowered her own small force after the cauldron was restored but before Balor came back?

They needed to prevent any possibility but the narrow path Bat needed to walk to victory.

Saoirse was grinning at her. "I knew you were my kind of goddess."

"Cause enough chaos and destruction to keep Balor and his men distracted," Finn said, nodding slowly.

"This is not a battle where we must win against the enemy soldiers," Bat said. "This is a battle we must win against *Balor*. And the way we win is we do not allow him to reach his goal. That is the *only* thing we are fighting here." It did not matter that they did not understand his true goal. Her statement was truth.

Dub smiled at her. It was fierce, the smile of a warrior who scented blood. "We will need to leave some things in place. Finnegan and the others designated to stay on the boat will remain. And I do not think it smart to have Daniel accompany us for the first part."

"We can use the pixies as messengers instead of recon," Finn said. His gaze was distant, his brows drawn as he no doubt ran through the various scenarios in his mind. "And we will need to agree upon a signal that allows the others to know when to begin. If we can manage a concentrated attack, it will be more effective."

"Leave the goblin and at least one of the fae aboard the boat. They can assist Ciara in guarding it. I can transport Daniel to the island when it's time." Finnegan began mumbling to himself, and Bat could only make out part of it. "… communicators… fire? No… wind… back…"

Shar shook his head and patted Finnegan's back. Not for the first time Bat wondered what the brothers' relationship was with the Druid.

Everyone began talking, discussing timing, signals, transportation, finalizing who would stay behind, which pixies would go with who, and just how many people needed to be with Bat and her group. Bat listened to it all, ready to jump in with an opinion.

She had nothing more to add, though. She'd said everything she needed to. She was a little astonished that they had listened to her so readily, that they had taken her ideas and run with them without protest. But she also knew this was the right thing.

Mell sidled around the edge of the room and to her side, nudging Finnegan from beside her in the process. He leaned over and whispered, "Don't be so surprised, *realta*. You were right, this isn't the usual dog and pony show. Dub, Shar, and I know better, but even we were still treating the solitary fae as though they were something they are not." He pressed a kiss to her cheek. "Ye're one of a kind, goddess." Warmth and affection wrapped around her.

"No time for that now," Finnegan interrupted them. "I'm going to set the wards, then work on a way you can communicate back to me." The Druid marched from the bridge, a determined glint in his eye.

"And that's my signal too," Saoirse said. "Time for me to strip down and jump in the ocean." She sent a wink to Bat before sashaying out the door.

Oh. Bat's cheeks colored as she realized *just* how much she'd misinterpreted Saoirse.

"Hmmm… Not that I want to add anyone else to our little nest of love, but if you want her, who am I to object?" Mell's words sent even more heat into Bat's cheeks.

She sent a hard elbow into his gut. He coughed but that was it.

Stupid giant warrior Fomoiri brothers. And he was the smallest. She did not even put a dent in him.

Dub reached out and grabbed her wrist, dragging her to his side. "Mell, stop being a wanker and go tell the others the new plan."

Bat shot a smug look at the middle brother and stuck out her tongue. *Hah!* She had the grumpy one on her side.

Mell grumbled and left the bridge.

"I'm going to put together a few small packs of equipment and provisions. Don't know what we'll find in those cliffs," Finn said. He cupped the back of Bat's head, turned her to him, and gave her a hard but quick kiss before leaving the bridge as well.

Then it was just her and Dub. They didn't speak, but the silence was not uncomfortable.

She was finally on the right path, she *knew* it.

Chapter Twenty-Two

Bastie,

TODAY I SAW THE DRAGON AS A DRAGON!!!!
He was so pretty...

- Bat, the goddess who has seen a dragon!

BAT

The island matched her vision perfectly, down to the five boats anchored in a small bay. She'd caught sight of them briefly before sheer gray cliffs that fell directly into the ocean blocked the view.

"The cauldron is close, goddess." Ari stood beside her, his round red eyes trained on those cliffs.

"Good." She looked down at the man of ba. "Are you ready?"

"Yes, goddess." The two words echoed with blood and fury. The tone perfectly conveyed his need to avenge those of his clan who had been slaughtered by Balor's men—and the ones who'd been persuaded to betray their own. Bat had not forgotten the scene that had met her eyes in that clearing, nor the number of souls she'd helped send on their way to the afterlife in the Land of Reeds. Ari had held back that need for justice as he helped her, but now he and the other men of ba would get their chance.

Finnegan approached her. "Here." He held out a flat stone, a small rune painted on one side. "You just press your thumb to the rune and say 'now.' It's a bit simple, but anything more complicated would take time we don't have, especially if it needs to get through the wards I set on the boat."

Bat tucked the stone into her pocket and nodded to the man. She'd learned this morning that the brothers had once stayed with the Druid about nine hundred years before. He was also the one to teach them what rune-magic they knew. "You should come visit them."

He didn't ask who she meant. "No. There is no need."

She shrugged. "The invitation will stay open."

Finnegan stared at her a moment longer then turned on his heel and headed for the bridge. A few minutes later Dub emerged. He shrugged on one of the small packs Finn had put together. There were bandages, water, rope, and a small axe that had been dug up from the emergency fire kit in the engine room.

Bat herself had the Uaithne. She adjusted the strap again, making sure the precious instrument sat securely against her back.

With the arrival of Dub, everyone who would be seeking the cauldron was gathered on the deck. Well, everyone except the guardi. Finn and Cuchi were still transporting the small units of fae to the island.

Bat grinned as she recalled the expressions on the faces of her new friends as they'd stood on the deck earlier. Bloodthirsty glee was the only way she could think to describe it. Even the pixies had looked eager to cause bloodshed.

They hadn't quite believed the plan at first. Carrig, one of the sluagh, had even asked her if it was true.

"Yes," she'd replied. "Think of this as permission to do whatever you want, as long as it is toward the goal of distracting Balor's men from what is happening in the hills. Destroy the ships, their supplies, their weapons. Incapacitate them however you like." She'd felt no compunction on uttering those words. As she now knew, the only way the men with Balor would die would be through the use of soul blades or the new shard-spear. Since none of the misfit fae whose mission it was to torment the enemy possessed those things, there would be no murder.

She was okay with anything up to that point, especially considering the circumstances.

"Remember, if you see the golden spear or the sword with the green gem in the pommel you do not have to engage directly. See if you can find another way to distract them," she had added. She did not think they would encounter Nuada's sword, as that would be needed to kill Daniel and revive Balor, but the golden spear was another matter. It was said whoever held it could not be defeated, and it would be best if her new friends avoided it.

Teagan had given Bat a mock salute. "Yes, General

Goddess, sir. We will create mayhem, sir." The banshee had then rubbed her hands together in glee.

Now, Finn appeared before her, his usually neat hair wind-blown. "They are in position," he said, referring to the banshees. They had all agreed that a high hill to the south of the bay would afford them the best vantage to hit the boats and men on shore with their voices.

Cuchi appeared a few seconds later. "The sluagh are stationed to the North. They'll work their way south. The leprechauns decided to stay with them, something about using their shadows until it was time." The guardi shook his head. "I didn't ask."

"The trooping fae?" Dub asked.

Finn shrugged. "Somewhere at the base of the hills leading to the cliffs. We may even run across them." Then he smiled. "It's kind of nice not worrying about each movement of every soldier. Though I wouldn't use this strategy in every battle."

"That's it then," Dub said.

Dechtire, Finnegan, Ciara, Daniel, Old Mike and Odion were staying behind on the boat. The man of ba, Odion, had protested being left behind until Bat pointed out that it was only until she called for Daniel. They needed someone who could sense the different souls in him to stay and monitor the human. He'd still been a bit resentful until Bat further pointed out that it was unlikely there would be much fighting until Daniel was near the cauldron.

Saoirse had slipped off as soon as the island came into sight. She didn't need to guide them anymore, and she wanted to get in position as soon as possible.

As planned, Con had transformed and taken off even before that, just after they crossed the border of Tir Hudi's space. The barrier had felt much like the brothers' wards the first time Bat had crossed them, only a hundred times stronger. Everyone but Dub had cringed against the pressure until it finally gave with a pop.

Bat had been entranced by the dragon's sinuous form. He was not like the depictions of English dragons she had seen. Instead, he more resembled the Eastern dragons, his body thinner and snake-like, though he still bore broad wings. When they were folded, they fit so well against his sides he could have been a serpent.

He was a pale gray in color, and even curled in on himself he'd taken up the entirety of the foredeck. Bat had been skeptical of his ability to take to the air. At first. Then he'd slid over the side of the boat into the water. She'd rushed to peer over the rail, but couldn't see anything. The gray of his hide blended too well with the blue-gray of the water.

Then he'd burst from a wave, his snout leading the way in an amazing leap that had his entire body hanging above the water like and arrow aimed at the sun. He'd unfurled his wings before the leap lost its momentum and beat them in great strokes that took him into the hazy blue sky.

She'd stared after him open-mouthed until Ailis had pulled out her phone and snapped a picture. "I'm going ta need ta show this one to Con when we get home."

Mell came to her other side and nudged her. "Thinking of dragons again?"

"He was so pretty," Bat said, then shook her head.

There would be no more distractions from this point. She needed to be completely in the here and now. She knew an opportunity would come for her to alter her vision of Ailis, she just had to spot it...

Mell looked over at this brother. "You have it?"

Dub growled. "One time. One time I left my sword behind."

Mell laughed and Shar chuckled. It was obviously what they called an "inside joke."

Cuchi rolled his eyes. "Okay, kids, let's go."

Bat was too excited to take offense at his words. Energy and power poured through her. Her fingers tingled and her stomach jumped.

The group pressed together, Bat in the middle. Cuchi twisted his hands, and they were off.

Chapter Twenty-Three

SAOIRSE

*S*he dove in and out of the water, spinning and flipping a few times. Even three days without being in her seal form was three days too many.

Her current task was to scout the small bay that most of Balor's ships were anchored in.

Five boats, most a mere ten meters in length, but two were larger. One matched the Blue Heron for size, and the other was even larger, nearly thirty-five meters. She swam close enough to read the name painted on the hull. *Angel's Roar*.

Saoirse snorted, the honking cough drowned out by the shouts of the unruly Fomoiri and Fir Bolg crawling all over the boats and ranging across the shore. Diving back below the surface, she came up once more on the other side of the bay. The distance should keep her masked from prying eyes.

Observing from her new vantage point, she counted. Fifteen men on shore, another twenty that she could see on the smaller boats, five from the medium boat, and... one, two, ten, eleven on the larger boat.

She calculated. Fifty-one that she could see. Didn't mean there weren't even more belowdecks.

She'd watch a while more.

And in the meantime, she'd rehearse what she wanted to say to The mac Lir when this was over.

She had a few choice things to convey to dear old dad.

The fucking idiot.

CON

Con wrapped air and moisture around himself in a cloak of illusion, bending the light away from his form as he flew. He sliced though the air, wings spread to catch an uplifting thermal. He needed to get high enough that the sharp eyes of the Fomoiri on the island below wouldn't be able to spot him.

He wasn't so worried about the Fir Bolg or the sluagh. Neither of those races possessed powers to contest his. The Fir Bolg were too tied to the earth. No doubt right now they were retching over the side of the boats, or kissing the gravel on the narrow beach. The sluagh depended on their shadows, and there were no shadows where Con now flew.

The Fomoiri, however, had always been formidable foes. Some possessed senses so keen even the best cloaking spells couldn't fool them. Others were in tune with wind and water to the point a tiny shift would alert them to Con's presence.

Con flapped his great wings and struggled higher. He much preferred the water—he *was* a lake dragon after all—but they had Saoirse for that. The Egyptian goddess needed him in the sky for this round.

He liked that one. She was a little spitfire, handling those O'Loinsigh brothers like a pro. And from what Ailis hinted at, and he'd seen so far himself, the girl had decided to take on Finn Cumhaill of all men.

She was going to have her work cut out for her.

That assumed everyone survived this. There were bound to be body parts littering the island at the end of this particular battle. Oh, he'd wanted to stay snug in his lair when Ailis had first contacted him, but he had to admit that this was going to be fun. And this particular dragon hadn't had this kind of fun in far too long.

Would the little goddess or the greedy Fomoiri win this battle? Con was curious as to what the outcome would be. Though dragons were creatures of neutrality by nature, in truth Con hoped it would be the girl he'd met one memorable St. Paddy's day as she shivered on a chaotic and mist-filled street. He wouldn't have allied himself with her otherwise.

Plus, he'd always had a soft spot for round women and big eyes.

A rumbling chuckle spread through his chest. Con reached the desired altitude and leveled out, chasing the thermals as he glided and hovered over the island.

He would wait up here until the signal came. Then he

would show the world once more what dragons were capable of.

MEERA

Meera turned to Neasa and Teagan. Her fellow banshees stared back with eager grins. Even the once reluctant Teagan. Getting stabbed by an asshole and thrown into the water will do that to you.

It wasn't just about helping out Bat and the O'Loinsigh brothers anymore. Now it was about payback.

And banshees were very good at vengeance.

"The boats will need to go first," Neasa mused.

That was their primary goal, take out any possible way the enemy could leave the island.

"And after that we can rip into them." Old feelings rose up in Meera. Resentment, pain, the need to draw screams from her enemy, the thirst for blood, the desire to hold wet flesh in her hands and see the shattered pieces of civilization scattered around her.

She shook it off. That was not who she was anymore.

From their vantage point, the figures on the beach and in the clearing below were no more than ants scurrying along in paths determined by their master.

"Do you really believe it's Balor behind all this?" Neasa's quiet question pulled Meera's attention back to her friend.

Balor. Balor of the Evil-Eye. She shuddered as half-forgotten memories threatened to press in on her. Meera pushed them away. She refused to fall back into that nightmare. She had moved on from that time in her life the moment she'd left her old name behind. And Teagan and Neasa had been right behind her.

"Does it matter?" Meera finally asked.

It didn't matter to her, other than making the destruction she was about to wreak all the sweeter.

"No," Teagan answered. "No, it doesn't matter at all." The dark-haired banshee paused as wind whipped over the hilltop. "Do you think she can beat him?"

"I think that innocent little Egyptian goddess may be the only one who can," Meera murmured.

OLD MIKE

The human tourist tossed and turned on the narrow bunk he'd only left in order to occasionally piss and eat.

"Seed of godhood... Yes... The final melody will play... I will have the power... right... Tara..."

Old Mike's eyes closed in sorrow. He had become attached to the tourist, though the entire time they'd spent together the human had been either unconscious or lost in strange ramblings.

Maybe that was the attraction. This human was just so lost...

"Cauldron... creation... Osiris... death to rise..."

Osiris. Old Mike knew that name, it was the Egyptian god of the land of the dead. Kind of like Hades. Mike liked to spend time in the library when he wasn't roaming his bog. It was almost as much fun getting lost in the stacks himself as it was leading hikers astray.

Wasn't he the god that died and came back? But gods didn't die...

Old Mike's entire body locked down. He didn't even dare breath. If what he suspected was true...? It wasn't possible.... There was no way...

Daniel's eyes shot open. There was a green glow under the faded gray of his iris. He bared his teeth in a crazy grin.

Old Mike couldn't move. It was not shock, nor was it fear.

Somehow, Balor had managed to channel a bit of his power through the human and his gaze. It was just enough to trap Old Mike in his own body.

Daniel rolled from the bunk and stumbled to his feet. Then he staggered to the door and out into the passageway, disappearing from view.

It was a full fifteen minutes before Balor's magic wore off and Old Mike was able to go after the human tourist.

But when he emerged from below deck, he was too late...

FINNEGAN

Something was off.

Finnegan double-checked the boat's settings and controls. The engine was off, the wheel locked, the anchor set.

He checked his wards. They were intact.

He glanced at the stone that matched the one he gave Bat. It was quiet, she was not calling for them.

He scanned the horizon. Gentle gray swells met blue sky and whips clouds. Nothing out of the ordinary.

He turned to the island. Gray cliffs fell into the water and sea birds rode the winds. Nothing was out of place.

So where did this sense of *wrong* come from?

Two thuds came from the stern, followed by clanking.

What the…?

He rushed from the bridge. Daniel stood at the stern, guiding the life raft into the water. Finnegan was half way to him, when the human twisted his head to stare at Finnegan.

Grey eyes swirling with green lights found Finnegan's gaze. The Druid froze, one foot in mid-air, and toppled onto his side.

Fuck. Fuck. Fuck. Fuck.

The word was a chant in his mind. He concentrated on his fingers, on getting a twitch or a tick out of them. If he could just free his fingers from Balor's power he could sketch a rune and access his power. If he could just…

The life raft inflated with a whoosh and water splashed. The deck bobbed under Finnegan as Daniel disappeared from view.

Finnegan needed to get up. He needed to warn the others.

Even with the small bit of Balor's soul that resided in Daniel, his power was breaking through. There was a reason He of the Evil Eye was feared from Ireland to Iceland and across the North Sea all the way to

Scandinavia. At full power the once Fomoiri king could stop a man's heart with a single glance, could burst his veins and boil blood.

Finnegan had been assessing their chances of success at about thirty percent. He decided to downgrade that to fifteen percent. The flimsy forces Bat and the O'Loinsigh brothers had gathered would be defeated with one sweep of Balor's gaze. He still wasn't sure why he'd been going along with their imbecilic plans.

Light steps headed his way and Old Mike, the wisp, crouched down in front of him. Pastel lights flickered under the fae's skin as he bit his lip. "It'll pass in a bit," he finally said. "Only took me about fifteen minutes."

Old Mike rocked on his feet. About five more minutes passed and Dechtire stumbled into view. "What...?"

Ciara and her hound Fina were next. She sat beside the druid and hummed. "At least we're still alive," she finally said.

Old Mike's lights dimmed then flared. "Yes. We are still alive."

Finnegan tried to speak, but his body was still caught. There was something the wisp wasn't saying.

Siobhan, the lavender pixie, popped into view.

Finnegan tried once more and his lips moved. "Tell..."

"Oh." The pixie bobbed. "Yes, of course. I'll find them, warn them." She zipped out of view.

Finnegan's eyes slid closed. This was as much as he could do for them. The rest would be up to the Egyptian goddess.

FAOLAN

Faolan loosened the leash on his shadows and allowed them to play among the dapples of light and dark among the trees.

The other sluagh—Carrig and Dalaigh—watched him with their trademark smirks. Those two were only here out of curiosity. Faolan knew they were humoring him in his "obsession" with the Egyptian goddess.

They'd see. They were already beginning to. When Bat had played the harp during the attack on the dock, they'd been entranced, just as Faolan had. When she sought them out and asked if there were any treats they'd particularly enjoy, they'd been confused and befuddled that a goddess would care to ask after them.

Then, when she'd essentially given them free rein to do what they liked, as long as it was against the asshole Fomoiri, they had finally fallen, just a little.

Faolan knew she'd done that because she understood the sluagh, she could see into them, she knew what they were and what they craved. She was allowing them to be exactly who they were.

The sluagh sought cold-hard judgment. They held no mercy in their souls. And what the men who had set up camp in a clearing beyond the trees had done definitely deserved judgment.

There were other sluagh among Balor's forces. They would be the most difficult. Part of Faolan wanted to take them on, but he also knew he'd be most affective against those who didn't possess shadows themselves.

No, the sluagh on Balor's side had been convinced

they served justice, just as The Wild Hunt must have been convinced. He didn't want to harm them if it could be avoided.

But the Fomoiri and the Fir Bolg?

They were fair game. And this time there was no harp he needed to protect.

He grinned at Carrig and Dalaigh, revealing sharp teeth.

This would be fun.

Chapter Twenty-Four

Bastie,

I... have no words. None. I cannot possibly say aloud what I have wrought, what I have witnessed.

I... feel I should apologize, though I know not for or what.

I am not sure what my life will be from this point, but know this.

I have always genuinely cared for you. And I hope we do see each other again, even if I am not the same Bat you once knew.

- Bat, the goddess of...

BAT

They had been trekking through the lower hills below the cliffs for an hour. There had been no sign of the enemy, no indication that anyone other than their small band had been through there in centuries. Tree branches had swayed in the breeze, and the sweet scent of grass had risen from below their feet.

It had been peaceful.

The others had grown antsy, but Bat remained calm. Balor had no reason to *keep* her from the cauldron. In fact, she half expected a guide to pop up in front of them and lead the rest of the way.

Now, they stood just inside the wide mouth of a cave.

"This is it, goddess," Ari said as he waved his too-many knuckled fingers toward the depths.

Warm sunlight filtered in through the cave mouth as motes of dust danced in the air. The small spring burbled as it flowed in a thin stream farther into the dark recesses of the cave. Her eyes narrowed. Was this *that* spring?

Before them, nestled in a shallow hollow of stone, sat the cauldron. No, not the *cauldron*—the Egg of Creation, the vessel of life. She stared. She couldn't help it. Here it was, in front of her. She still didn't know the truth of the creation of other pantheons, or if this curve of stone and metal was responsible for more than just the Egyptian deities, but it was the beginning of everything she'd known for the majority of her life. From this, the start of Egyptian life and divinity had been born. It was...

It was beautiful. The stone glimmered with a faint pearlescent sheen and the bands of iron along the edge and bottom stood out all the more.

"I sense ten blank spots," Mell whispered, referring to immortals who had cloaked and hidden themselves using either their won magic or runes. While he couldn't sense anything from them, he'd once described it as a bubble that the usual emotional eddies slid around as though there was something there.

It was a skill he'd practiced frequently a few centuries before, and had had to quickly dust off in the last week.

Dub flicked his fingers to the side, signaling everyone to be alert.

Twelve of them had gone into the mountains to track the cauldron—fifteen if you counted the three pups. Bat, Dub, Ailis, Finn and Cuchi needed to be there to awaken the ancient artifact. Shar had refused to be left behind, and Mell was the keeper of the spear that would send Balor to his true death. Ari was tracking the cauldron, and Adom and Nour accompanied the group to provide extra protection. Maire and Daire were there to act as scouts and messengers. As soon as the cauldron was located, Daire would zip off to the banshees to inform them to begin the attack, which would signal the others around the island to begin their own, thus providing the much-needed distraction. Maire would remain with them until it was time to send for Daniel. Then she would go and guide the Druid and human to the cave.

Bat's chest tightened at the reminder that she was basically stealing the human tourist's life. Some might call it a sacrifice, but not her. A sacrifice was only that if the one laying down their life was willing—otherwise it was murder.

She still hadn't found a way around the final vision she'd received, but she hadn't given up hope. There had to be a way to save both Ailis and the human.

Once again, Bat wondered if she should have shared the full truth with at least her men. But, she had to trust her instincts, and everything in her screamed that it would be a mistake. Maybe not now, but in future years it would be something that would... bite her in the butt.

Bat moved farther into the cave, the cool shadows enveloping her. Ari stepped up next to her and the other men of ba flanked them. Killer pressed into her thigh as the other pups spread out, ears back and noses up. They eyed the ever changing shadows that danced through the cave and let out low growls, though they didn't attack.

They were such smart pups. *I wonder if Ciara would let us keep them...*

Mell and Shar took the lead, weapons in hand. The axe in Shar's hand glinted within the shadows and Mell's sword cast a shadow that stretched into the unseen depths of the cave. Dub, Finn, Cuchi, and Ailis formed a tight circle around Bat, pushing Ari and the other men of ba to the side. The pixies hovered over her head, waiting for the signal to carry out their assigned tasks.

Everyone knew what needed to happen—or most of what needed to happen. Both sides needed the cauldron restored, and both sides needed Balor to take over Daniel's body.

Lavender streaked into the cave and hovered in front of her. "Goddess," Siobhan panted. "The human—"

A low chuckle echoed through the cave. The air shimmered and the cloaked men came into view. Bat's gaze caught on one in particular, and she swallowed.

Daniel stood between a dark haired man wearing a crazy grin, and a silver-haired man clad in leather and dripping with blades.

"The human is here with us," hissed the dark-haired man.

"Scath," Dub spit out.

Scath tipped his head to the side as he laughed again. "Surprise."

Mell shrugged. "Not really."

Scath focused on the middle brother. "Oh-oh. If it isn't the sidhe masquerading as a Fomoiri. You were your father's downfall, you know. Does that give you comfort from your pain?"

This man was pure evil. Bat shuddered. It radiated from him in waves, more than any other she had encountered yet.

Mell ignored the man and turned to Bat, one brow raised as if to ask, what now?

She shrugged. This actually changed nothing, except to save a bit of time. "Daire," she whispered.

The red pixie zipped toward the cave entrance. Just as he was about to clear it he froze then dropped to the ground. Not a half second later Siobhan's violet light escaped into the afternoon light. Maire's pink was a beat behind her, moving so fast she was no more than a wink of shadowed sunlight.

Pixies were clever. They'd get the word out.

She scanned the men ranged on the other side of the Egg of Creation. There were ten, just as Mell had sensed. In addition to Daniel, Scath, and the silver-haired man, there were two sluagh surrounded in shadows, and five other warriors all nearly the size of Shar. Fomoiri, or maybe the Fir Bolg she kept hearing about.

The silver-haired man gestured to the cauldron. "We may as well get to it. We all know how this plays out."

Bat didn't move. Yes, they all knew how this went, up to a certain point.

She scanned the men once more, looking for the golden spear, or Nuada's blade. She spotted neither. *What are they up to? Where are the other pieces of my visions?* This wouldn't work without them all here, though she was still unclear as to the purpose of the golden spear.

Scath twisted his hand and Nuada's blade appeared. "Looking for this?" He licked his lips then swept his eyes over her form. "Oh, how I wish you'd picked the hard way. Maybe you still will…" Though the words were whispered, they floated through the silent cave.

Bat ignored him. The piece they needed was here. She stepped forward and rounded the cauldron, taking a spot nearest Daniel. Mell followed behind her and planted himself a meter away, forming a loose triangle. Ailis took the place to her right, and Cuchi stood to her left. Finn and Dub were across the cauldron from her, in the places closest to the cave mouth.

The men of ba and Shar placed themselves in a line facing Balor's Fomoiri, and the pups crouched in front of the sluagh with raised hackles.

Bat nodded to Dub, who drew a small blade. From this point forward, she could not become distracted. She knew there would be one opportunity for her, one decision she would make that would lead her away from that last vision of Ailis dead among shards of the Egg of Creation.

Dub drew the blade over his left palm and placed it against the rounded side of the vessel. It vibrated. Dub's mouth dropped open and a low moan emerged as his eyes slid closed. "Fuck," he breathed out. "The fuck was that."

Ailis's lips thinned. Taking a small switchblade from her front pocket, a determined look came over her. In one swift move she bloodied her palm and placed it against the vessel.

A wide smile pulled her lips apart and she laughed. She gave the vessel a small caress and pulled her hand away with a light chuckle. "Definitely female."

In succession, Finn and Cuchi repeated the small ritual, each with their own reactions to the cauldron. Finn remained stoic, but Cuchi nearly buckled to the ground.

Then it was Bat's turn. Scath and the other of Balor's men had yet to move a muscle. In fact, they stood nonchalant, not even drawing their weapons.

It was the strangest battle she'd ever witnessed, or heard of. One where both sides worked together as allies until up until the very end.

Ailis held out her blade. "Here."

Bat took it with her right hand. She swept her gaze over the strange assemblage around her, then pressed the blade to the meat of her palm just under the thumb. A thin line of blood welled. She let it gather, then pressed her hand to the side of vessel, just as the other four had done.

It hummed in pleasure. Energy and power ran over the surface of the vessel. The five smears of blood were absorbed into the shimmering surface. Bat's ears popped as pressure built.

The power burst and she swayed. Around her others

stumbled, some fell to their knees. Every single face was turned to the vessel.

The shimmer that was so faint it could have been easily overlooked was now a swirl of color under the hard surface. The cave was painted in ever shifting pastel light.

"It's like some kind of weird pastel disco," Ailis whispered, but the awe was evident in her voice.

"Was it ever like this?" Bat asked no one in particular.

"No," Ari answered her.

There was a buzzing in the back of her mind, too faint for her to decipher. It was asking her for something...

"And now for the next step." Scath turned to Daniel. Nuada's blade firmly grasped in his right hand, he shoved it into the human tourist's belly then twisted it. Daniel's eyes glowed with green light that quickly faded as Scath lifted the smaller man above his head and tossed him over the lip of the vessel.

The silver haired man ran to the spring, scooped a handful of the clear water into his palms, and crossed back to the vessel. He poured the water into the cauldron and stepped back.

Nothing.

Bat nearly snorted as Balor's men shifted. A few scowled at the vessel. One grabbed for his sword, growling. "What did you do?" he asked as he advanced on Bat.

The silver-haired man stepped into his path. "Stop. You know we need her for this to work."

"Get out of my way, Quinn. We know jack shit, and you know *that*. The shadow bastard likes to keep everything to himself." The man jabbed his sword in Scath's direction.

For his part, Scath stood beside the cauldron between Bat and Ailis, Nuada's blade hanging from his hand. He stared at the cauldron with an intent look, his dark eyes burning.

Bat flicked her gaze to Ailis, then tipped her head a few degrees toward the cave entrance. She needed to get her friend out of here now.

Ailis took a step and Scath raised Nuada's blade, placing the tip against the green-haired woman's neck.

"Ah, ah. No one moves. This could take some time."

With the threat to Ailis, Bat froze. She flicked her gaze to Mell, then the other men around the cauldron. Each stood with hands held slightly out from their bodies, ready to act at any moment.

Tension thickened the air. She itched to pull the harp from its pack and play something similar to what she did on the dock. Her hands rose.

A line of blood appeared on Ailis's neck. Bat froze once more.

"No. Not yet, goddess. You'll know when it's time to play." Scath bared his sharp teeth at her in a snarl.

The vessel's vibration went from the faintest tremor to a shudder that ran along the surface.

A pale hand reached up and grasped the rim.

Chapter Twenty-Five

BAT

*I*f everything before happened as though the universe held its breath, the moment Daniel's hand hit the lip of the cauldron, the universe exploded.

Screaming roar after screaming roar rolled over the island. Explosions, muffled by distance and rock, sounded. A lower roar, more like a destructive wind, built under the screams.

The banshees. Con. And probably the others.

Balor's men jumped then stepped toward the mouth of the cave, only to be blocked by the pups, Shar, and the men of ba. Dub and Finn backed away from the cauldron and their weapons materialized in their hands. Shar held his axe at the ready.

Another hand grasped the lip of the vessel.

Bat, Ailis, Scath, Mell and Quinn stood frozen.

Daniel heaved himself over the side of the vessel and rolled.

Ailis leaned back and spun.

Mell materialized the spear that had been made from the shard of the vessel. He pulled his arm back and aimed for Daniel.

Then Quinn was there, the golden spear in his hands. He blocked Mell's thrust and shoved him back.

"Fuck," Cuchi muttered. "Fucking spear of Lugh. I was hoping the goddess saw that one wrong." He dove between Quinn and Mell, engaging the silver-haired Fomoiri. Pushing his opponent back against the cave wall, Cuchi twisted to glare at Bat. "Whatever you're going to do, you better do now. No one can hold out long against the one who hold Lugh's spear."

As though his words were prophecy in themselves, the warrior was shoved back and he stumbled before falling to the ground.

Daniel-Balor had backed away until his back was against the cave wall, a smile playing around the corners of his mouth. Mell advanced on him, the spear held ready.

Bat still stood beside the vessel of creation. She was not in shock, nor was she undecided.

She was waiting for that opportunity.

Except she waited too long.

Daniel-Balor's eyes flashed green in the dim light and Mell froze. Blood dripped from his ears, his nose, his eyes. His mouth dropped open in a silent scream as his face turned a deep red.

Quinn thrust the golden spear through his side and plucked the shard-spear from Mell's now limp hand.

Bat's heart stuttered. This could not... she had not seen... what...

Mell hung there, suspended, a macabre figure. Then he collapsed as though someone cut his strings.

Daniel-Balor turned his attention to Bat.

The enemy now had the shard-spear. Their window of opportunity to kill Balor had been open for a measly few seconds, and was now closed.

But her men had not given up. The fight continued around her. Blades flashed and clanged, men grunted. The scent of blood and sweat filled her nostrils.

From the corner of her eye she caught Ari's dash to Mell's side. The man of ba bent over him, muttering low words she could not catch.

Daniel-Balor cocked his head. "Your young man may yet live. Wouldn't that be nice for you, goddess? I could make sure of Ari's success if you like?"

The voice was Daniel's but the cadence, the tone, was just like the one from her dreams.

"What now?" she asked.

"Will you play me a song?"

At his question both the harp and the vessel vibrated. The buzz in the back of her mind increased.

"No." The word slipped out before she'd thought about it. Something in her told her now was not the time. *Not yet, not quite.* She needed to hold out for just a few seconds longer...

"No?" Daniel-Balor's eyes narrowed. He swept his gaze around the cave. Abruptly the sounds of fighting faded.

Bat spun and her eyes widened in horror. Everyone

was frozen, even Daniel-Balor's allies. As she watched blood seeped from Shar's eyes and nose, and the veins in Dub's face swelled.

"I could keep going?"

Bat spun back to him.

"Or I could release just my men. They could take this opportunity to carve pieces from the men you love, bit by bit, until they are no more than piles of blood and flesh on the cave floor?" He waved a hand and Scath, Quinn and another of the Fomoiri staggered before regaining their balance. "Or…" Daniel-Balor pointed at a frozen Ailis, and Scath dragged the green-haired fae to his master's side.

"Or, I could play with this one." Daniel-Balor wrapped his hand around Ailis's neck. His gaze bore into hers and Ailis's eyes rolled back into her head as the small blood vessels there burst.

"Stop." Tears seeped from Bat's eyes. "Stop."

Balor twisted his head to face her. "Will you play?"

"Y-yes." Bat fumbled with the harp case, exaggerating her sloppy movements. She was horrified with what Balor had done, what he had been able to do with just a look from his eyes. She had wanted to give in right away, had wanted to do what he asked from the moment that golden spear had entered Mell.

Oh, Mell.

"You know what to play," Balor whispered. He spun Ailis until the fae's back was pressed to his front. "Play for me, goddess."

Bat swallowed. Her chance was coming, she knew it. She couldn't allow herself to be distracted, not by anything. She blocked out the sight of a fallen Mell and a tortured Dub and turned her attention to the harp now in her hands.

She plucked a string and a shudder ran though Balor, the vessel, and the harp all at once. She struck the next note, then the next.

With each note she pulled from the instrument the melody grew. And with it, magic built. The buzz in her head built in tandem with the vibrations of the vessel.

Yes. That was *not* Balor. *Life*.

It was the vessel, she realized. It had slumbered for so long before she and the men of ba had managed to awaken her a few days ago. She had been waiting for them to arrive.

She had been waiting for Bat.

Life? I do long to create one last time…

Wait, Bat sent her.

Her fingers danced over the strings. Power swirled within the vessel, both in the physical embodiment and the nebulous consciousness that existed somewhere outside the physical. That power began to condense, pulling in on itself.

This was it, Bat realized. This was the seed of godhood that Balor sought. The vessel wanted to give birth once more before the end of its existence. It put all of itself into that bubble of power, that seed. It was not considering who would receive the gift, it simply wanted to give it.

Maybe…

Quinn moved behind Balor, the shard-spear clutched in his hands. Balor held up one hand in a motion to wait. His head remained cocked as though listening for something.

Bat's fingers continued to dance over the strings.

"Now," Balor whispered.

Quinn thrust the spear through Balor's back, skewering his heart—and Ailis.

With a grunt Quinn threw the two bodies toward the vessel.

Daniel-Balor and Ailis toppled into the cauldron, the shaft of the spear locking them together.

Bat's fingers continued to move over the strings of the Uaithne, the harp now in control. She couldn't stop the melody. Inside the vessel she could feel it, the seed of godhood fully formed. It called to her, as like could call to like. Idly, Bat wondered if the others could sense what was forming, or if they remained oblivious.

Flash. A form made of starlight and darkness reached out a hand and caressed a sleeping Ailis.

"You idiot!" Scath backhanded the silver-haired man, Quinn. "Only one can go in the cauldron at this point."

Just how much did Scath know of his master's plans? How secret *was* the secret Bat had been keeping?

"Fuck you, bastard. If it was so important, your tight lipped ass should have told us that." Quinn lunged for Mell and the golden spear still impaling his side.

Ari intercepted him, snarling and snapping those needle teeth.

Chaos erupted around Bat once more as everyone was released from the spell of Balor's gaze. A distant part of herself knew this, but she could not see it, could not hear it.

She was completely absorbed in what was happening inside the vessel as she began the last measures of the Final Melody.

Closing her eyes, she detached her mind from her body and opened her senses. She reached for mother sky and father earth and asked for strength. Then slowly, gradually, one note at a time, she altered the melody that her fingers were forced to play.

This was the moment, the one path of opportunity she needed to follow. She did not stop the tune. Instead, she added *herself* into the song. She added her hopes, her fears, her dreams. She added her love for her men and her love for her friends. She added her love for Ailis.

Then she thought one word. *Please.*

What would you have of me child? The vessel's voice was stronger.

I would ask that you place your gift into the woman, and not the man.

There was a pause. *The man contains a spark, still. He has the waters of life running through him. I do not have the power for more than I have already made. I am at my end, child.*

What if I gave you the power?

You do not have enough. A pause. *Unless…*

Please. Oh, how she wished that word was as effective as it was with the fae.

If you gave of yourself.

Bat did not hesitate. *Take what you need.*

I will use a small part. One that you will not have a need of from this day forward.

The vessel reached out and moved through Bat's very soul. It wrapped around a section of her being. *This.*

All right.

The vessel tugged. There was no pain, it was more like... a memory you knew you should know but that would never come again. Or something that was missing but that you would never miss.

Warmth and comfort filled Bat as the vessel withdrew, like a mother stroking their child's head.

This will do.

Then Bat's fingers reached the end of the song, and the vessel shattered.

Chapter Twenty-Six

DUB

*W*hat the fuck just happened?

His head pounded and his eyeballs felt like they were going to explode.

All he could think was how idiotic they'd been to forget just what powers Balor held. Mell and Shar hadn't seen them, but Dub had. Finn had. Con knew, the banshees as well. Finnegan had most definitely experienced them.

Somehow they'd all forgotten.

Dub staggered back a step as control of his body was returned to him. He shook his head to clear his vision and swung his sword blindly.

One minute, maybe two. That was how long it had taken Balor to incapacitate everyone once he emerged from the cauldron. And the bastard had been *playing* with them.

Dub had fought to get to Bat, to Mell, but he'd not had time to break through the line of Fomoiri. He'd spotted Ari by Mell's side just before everything had been frozen in a horrid tableau.

His arm had been poised to strike, but he couldn't move. He couldn't even turn his head. All he could do was listen as Balor backed Bat into a corner, and forced her to play.

But why? Why have her play now? Why did they need the harp? There was more here than merely a return to life. Finn had mentioned the Hunt heading for Tara. If Balor was going to fight that battle, he would need the harp on his side. But that didn't explain why he wanted it played now.

Dub had seen the shadows in his goddesses eyes, had known she was holding back. He should have insisted she tell them what was bothering her.

Because it seemed to be coming back on them now.

A sluagh rushed him and Dub dodged back, putting his strength into increasing his speed. Spinning, he caught the sluagh across the back and wings in a long slice. Then there was another enemy before him, this time a Fomoiri.

"Freide," Dub growled out. He knew this one. He was a lieutenant in the Bull Clan.

"Dub." The man lunged, pushing the younger Fomoiri back.

A melody drifted through the cave, gaining strength with each note played. Bat stood beside the cauldron, her eyes closed, and her fingers flew across the strings. The song didn't touch the fighters.

Scath stood beside her, eyeing her with hungry intent.

That will never happen.

Dub's strength surged and he sent Freide flying into the cave wall, stone exploding behind him. He may not be able to kill without a soul blade, but he could certainly make these people hurt.

Advancing on Scath, he was joined by Cuchi. Finn had moved to the cave mouth where a large Fir Bolg was trying to get in. Shar had taken on the sluagh. The remaining men of ba had teamed up with the pups and attacked the other four of Balor's Fomoiri.

Dub tackled Scath away from Bat, uncaring of Nuada's blade. He needed to get that bastard away from her. They rolled and Scath landed a punch to the side of Dub's head. His shadows reached around the oldest brother's neck and squeezed.

Cuchi tore Dub off and away and engaged the former lieutenant of the Crane Clan. Dub was up in an instant and came at Scath from the other side.

A moment later he was tackled to the ground. Quinn, the silver-haired ass from the Bull Clan, rose over him with a dagger raised to strike. Dub wrapped his free hand around that wrist and squeezed.

Quinn screamed and the dagger dropped.

Just then there was a scream from the cave mouth. Dub sent a crushing punch into Quinn's shoulder. Bone crunched.

When he could turn his attention to the cave mouth, one of the trooping fae was on the ground and Scath was pulling Nuada's blade from his back. Killer leapt and clamped down on Scath's sword arm, dragging the other man to the cave floor.

Cuchi landed a blow to the side of Scath's head and the shadow-Fomoiri staggered, his hold on the sword loosening.

Dub lunged and rolled. He reached for the sword still protruding from his ally's back and wrenched it away from Scath, only to spin back and thrust it through the other immortal's spine.

An image of Bat, her face horrified just as it had been when she found out he'd killed Diarmuid, flashed before him. He growled and twisted the blade of the sword. Even if she detested him for this, he would not regret it. If he needed to he would figure out a way to fix things with her, but he would not allow this monster to remain on the earth. Even if he was locked away in the Tribunal's cells, he would eventually walk free.

Dub would never forget the way Scath had looked at *his* goddess.

A roar sounded from outside and the Fir Bolg was thrown away from the cave entrance by a silver-clawed hand.

Con had arrived.

And the cauldron exploded.

Just as suddenly as it had begun, the fighting ended.

It was the shortest war he'd ever fought, and he still didn't know what to make of it.

Chapter Twenty-Seven

Bastie,
I think I will actually send this note to you.
I need a hug.

- Bat, the goddess who misses you. Really, really misses you

BAT

She sat in the middle of the cave, rocking Ailis in her arms.

It was over. It was over, but it wasn't.

Bat had succeeded, but at what price?

Daniel was gone. The most she'd been able to do after regaining consciousness was to gather the pieces of his soul and send them on.

They had also lost one of the trooping fae—Ogma. One of the Fir Bolg—nearly nine feet tall, a true giant—had escaped the chaos that Con, the banshees, sluagh, and leprechauns were causing and had made its way to the cave. The trooping fae had been assisting Finn in fighting the behemoth, when Scath had run him through from behind with Nuada's blade.

Those were the only fatalities, but not the only damage.

Bat twisted her head to where Mell lay beside her. The Spear of Lugh, Bat had learned, was not soul stealing, but it was fatal for immortals. Ari had managed to hold onto the pieces of Mell's soul until he could be brought to the spring. Finn had added what magic he had by feeding the water to Mell from his hands.

It had worked, to an extent. Like Ailis, Mell was unconscious. Of everyone, the worst injuries were sustained by those in the cave who'd had to endure and face Balor's power. It was a damned good thing there was a magical healing spring within arms reach.

And The Morrigan calls Fate a bitch. Bat snorted. And snorted again. Then laughter spilled from her throat in ragged waves. Balor may have been playing a long game, but Fate's had been longer. Why else set it up so that Balor needed a magical life-giving spring to make his plan work?

The next time Bat saw her, she was going to give the ancient deity a very big hug.

Killer pressed into her side, letting out faint whimpers.

"Oh, baby, I am okay." Bat loosed one hand from Ailis and scratched her pup behind the ears.

"That is good to hear, *a stor.*" Shar entered the cave they'd turned into a makeshift camp and sat down across from her.

"How is it out there?" she asked him.

"Cuchi and Finn finished transporting the last of them."

It had taken hours, but the guards had transported the prisoners one at a time. Apparently both distance and the number of people you were moving at one time affected the transporting spell. You could move one person much farther than a group of people. The captured Fomoiri and sluagh had been taken to the northern guardi headquarters in Armagh, Ulster.

One at a time. *Finn and Cuchi must be exhausted, especially after having to do all that directly after the battle.* "Are they resting?"

Shar nodded. "Back on the boat."

"And Dub?"

"Still down at the bay. One of those ships was Da's. He's searching the wreckage for anything that may be useful."

"To use against your father, or for him?"

Shar just shook his head. "That I do not know."

She let it go. It was not a wound that needed to be healed now. "The harp?" She'd not been able to bear the sight of it after everything. The memory of her fingers moving outside her control haunted her. She'd felt like a puppet.

"With Faolan."

He was a good choice. He'd already kept it safe for her once. "And the weapons?"

"Secure, except for the shard-spear."

Flash. The spear, a gray hand clutching it as blood ran down the shaft. Soft lights played under the skin of that hand. Old Mike wandered the island with that spear until he found a clearing hidden by thorned vines and marsh grass. He buried it there, nodded, and left.

"The shard-spear is not a problem," she reassured him. "The vessel no longer holds power anyway."

It was true. The moment the vessel granted that last act of creation to Ailis, it had used the last of its power, the last of what made it what it was. That was why it had shattered. All the pieces she'd found scattered around the cave had been nothing but pretty stone.

She'd still tucked a piece or two into her pocket. It was pretty. Maybe she'd make Ailis a ring, or a pair of earrings. For when she woke up.

"Does that mean we're ready?" Bat had stayed in the cave with Ailis, Mell, and Killer as everyone else worked. Part of her had felt guilt at leaving it to everyone else to clean up the aftermath, but she couldn't make herself leave Mell or Ailis.

"It does. Saoirse will get us out of here. Then she's going to... 'hunt down Da and make him fix his flimsy-ass security,' I think is how she put it."

That pulled a small smile from the goddess.

Finnegan appeared at the mouth of the cave. He approached her and, without a word, took the five of them back to the boat.

"Here." Shar set a cup of steaming tea into her hands. The

main salon was empty but for the two of them. He sat beside her on the narrow bench seat and she leaned into him.

He'd been the one to stick with her, both after the battle and now that they were on the boat and headed home. She suspected Dub and Finn were keeping their distance to allow the overprotective brother time to assuage his need to see her safe.

"Drink," Shar said.

Bat took a sip, more for his sake than hers. Her mind swirled with too many thoughts—thoughts that only entered her mind now that the fight against Balor was... over. She finally settled on one. "How many do you think were seduced by Balor's whispers? Other than the Wild Hunt and those on the island, I mean."

His arm went around her back and settled on her opposite hip. "I don't know. But, it's not something we need to worry about. That's for the guardi to do." He snorted. "It's *their* job, after all." The faintest hint of contempt snuck into his tone.

"Are you angry?"

"Maybe? More frustrated. I mean, how could The Morrigan or the Tribunal even let this come to pass? Plus, this entire debacle isn't anything I've ever experienced. A war that wasn't a war, battles that lasted no more than minutes. Soldiers that aren't soldiers, enemies working toward the same goals..." His fingers dug into the rounded flesh of her hip. "I think Balor's influence stretched much farther than any of us realize, but I also suspect that most of those he influenced weren't even aware of it. And of those that were aware, not all knew his true intentions."

Bat stiffened. How much had Shar figured out?

They fell into silence. Bat suspected he wanted to ask her what had happened in the end, why Balor's own man ran him through with the spear, why she'd played the Uaithne, why the Egg of Creation had shattered.

After a few minutes, when he continued to hold his silence, she relaxed into him. She didn't know what she would say if he asked, and she didn't like the idea of having to lie to her lover.

"The Fomoiri Clans will clean themselves up. Dub's already called Da to tell him about Scath. And I mean it, leave the rest to the guardi. Finn's been on the line with them almost non-stop. They've already gotten names from the prisoners." He sucked in a deep breath, his muscled chest moving against her side. "Finn didn't tell any of us before, but apparently the Wild Hunt went after a new target when we transported to Londonderry. That's where most of the guardi have been over the last few days."

"Oh."

"Tara. Have you heard of it?"

It sounded familiar, but... She shook her head.

"It's the seat of Power in Ireland. The humans think it's a not-so-impressive tourist sight and something relegated to the history books. It's a hell of a lot more than that. If we had lost against Balor, and he had made it off the island and to Tara, well..."

Bat shuddered. If Balor had gained his true goal, it

would have been so much worse than anything he was imagining.

"Anyway, the Hunt's moved on. They've been spotted in the South, near Cork. Their movements seem to be back to normal. Point is, without Balor to keep them together, his allies will fall apart."

Bat let his words sink in. "So you are saying it is over."

"For us it is. It's time to let the people in charge pull their damn weight. Now, drink your tea."

The boat rocked under them and Bat drank her tea.

Chapter Twenty-Eight

Bastie,

Have you ever forgotten how to laugh?

- Bat

Four weeks later...

BAT

*B*at sat beside Ailis's bed and watched her friend sleep.

Mell had regained consciousness the day after the confrontation with Balor. But Ailis had been asleep now for four weeks. Bat gathered a pale hand in her own darker ones, and squeezed. She hoped for an answering gesture, but it never came.

All they could do now was wait. Bat had discovered a new and deep-seated hatred for waiting. She'd done too much of it in her life, and she'd become used to *doing* things since coming to Ireland. Now she was back to feeling helpless once again.

They'd done everything they could think of. Finn had fed Ailis water from his hands. Oisin had spent days with his head buried in various ancient texts to see if he could find anything that would bring her back. Dub had called upon a couple of Fomoiri healers he was still on good terms with. The pixies had gone on quests for rare herbs rumored to heal even the most grievous wounds.

Even Shar had visited the Rowans—those trees that once guarded the immortals of Ireland, and whose fruit held a kind of healing power. Bat wasn't sure what the visit had entailed—he didn't tell her and she didn't ask—but when he returned he bore a sprig of berries. He'd prepared that sacred fruit and fed it to Ailis one spoonful at a time.

Still she did not wake.

Bat picked up a washcloth and dipped it in the basin of water that sat on the bedside table. After wringing it out, she bathed Ailis's face, pushing back the green hair that was overdue for a touch-up—the blond roots were beginning to show.

"I miss you," she told her friend. "Meera and the other banshees are fun, but they're not you, Ailis." Bat moved the cloth down to Ailis's neck. "They've been practicing their power. Teagan busted three bottles of whiskey, and Meera took out one of the front windows. 'Working on their aim' they said. Dub said they were deliberately terrorizing him and the pub and banned them for a week. They were back in three days."

Bat continued on, filling Ailis in on all the hijinks and mischief their friends were up to. She played with Ailis's hair, and held her hand, not wanting her friend to feel alone. Bat had been reading up on comas, and some people believed that even if the unconscious person couldn't respond, they could still hear and feel you on some level. Bat chose to believe this as well, and she came every day to visit. She would continue to come every day until her friend woke up.

It wasn't the only reason she visited, though.

She also came out of guilt. Mell believed the feeling stemmed from placing her friend in danger. It was only part of it.

No, most of her guilt was for an entirely different reason.

Bat had an idea of what could wake Ailis from her sleep.

She simply couldn't tell anyone.

No one could know what truly happened the day Balor was defeated and the Egg of Creation shattered.

No one could know that Bat had sung the vessel—the cauldron, the Egg—into one last act of creation.

No one could know that Ailis now held a piece of godhood inside of her.

So everyday Bat came to her bedside, and gave her friend small offerings. Tales of the pub, a vase of fresh flowers, a song on her harp, a new blanket, soup she'd made herself.

The others saw it as the care one friend gave to another, and it was.

There was just more to it. *How much power does a god need in order to wake?*

"Oh, Ailis. I miss you," she said again.

A throat cleared behind her. Dub stood in the doorway. "You've been in here long enough," he said.

Bat tilted her head. "How long?"

"Five hours." His voice was even, but there was something under the neutral tone.

Bat's stomach tensed. Dub didn't do neutral. Where were his frowns? "What's wrong?"

He shook his head. "Just come downstairs, please."

Bat nodded. It was about time. She needed to gather more tales to tell Ailis tomorrow.

Wait. He said 'please'?

Dub's brows drew together for a second before his expression cleared. "You miss *her*. We miss *you*."

Her hand crept up and curled around her lapis pendant. "I'm here."

A sigh. "Just come downstairs."

What was going on? What had she missed? What was wrong? They were supposed to all be okay now, their lives were supposed to be back to normal, other than the still sleeping Ailis. The pub was open, the building repairs were complete, the enemy was either being held by the Tribunal or being dealt with by their own clan leaders. The brothers were free of their father and clan—Alatrom had officially let his sons go their own way. There were no gods knocking on the door, no ominous flashes of vision, no ravens cawing for attention.

Dub scowled. "Dammit, woman, just get up and come downstairs."

Woman. That was new. He usually called her *storeen* if he didn't use her name.

Crossing the room, he grabbed her hand and pulled her to her feet. His grip was tight, but not so tight it hurt. Dub dragged her from the room, down the stairs and into the pub. He placed her behind the bar and pointed at the tap. "You're in charge of manning the bar for now." His tone was cold.

Dub left her there and crossed the room. Finn and Meera sat in a shadowed booth and Dub slid in across from them. Neither man looked in her direction.

It was all just different enough to drag her from her constant concern for Ailis. What was going on?

Shar came in from the kitchen, two plates of sandwiches in his hands, and stopped just inside the common room. His gaze was locked on her, his eye wide. A light flush bloomed on his cheeks and he gave her a little smile.

She tried to return it, but her lips lifted a bare centimeter before falling again.

The smile on his face froze and he turned away, taking the food over to a couple of leprechauns in the last booth before returning to the kitchen.

Something *was* wrong. Something was wrong, she knew it, but there were no visions, no flashes to tell her what was coming.

"Goddess, could I get another?" Old Mike raised his pint glass in her direction.

"Of course." Bat grabbed a glass and began building the Guinness. When it was done she moved down the bar to place it before the wisp. "How are you doing?"

"Been better," he said, then downed the last of his first pint. "Got kind of attached to the human, you know? He was all right for being possessed by an evil wanna-be god."

Bat's muscles locked and her lungs froze. "What?"

"Huh?" Old Mike's eyes widened and faint pastels shifted on his cheeks. "Sorry. Didn't mean ta say it aloud. I know I'm not supposed to..." He ducked his head as Bat's eyes grew wider with each word he said.

She opened her mouth but couldn't get a word out.

"The human talked in his sleep," the wisp finally mumbled.

Bat had known that, she just hadn't known exactly what he said. She finally drew in a deep breath. "You can't tell anyone."

"I know." The words were barely there.

"Please," she added.

Mike's head shot up and his grey eyes widened. He nodded.

"Thank you," she added, knowing the two words would convey just how important this was. "Was there anyone else around when he...?"

"No."

She let out a sigh of relief.

Silence fell between them. After a minute or two, Old Mike looked at her again. "Will ya play tonight? It's been a while..."

What did he mean? She played every day...

For Ailis.

Bat hadn't played in the pub since before they set off to stop Balor's schemes.

We miss you. That was what Dub had told her.

Old Mike nodded as if agreeing with her not-man's words. "It's time to come back now, goddess. I know a thing or two about losing your direction—I'm a wisp after all. I hate to admit it, but sometimes it's best to stay on the path."

Bat was stunned. He was right. She'd been... gone. Not physically, but in spirit. She'd been stuck in that room with Ailis for the last four weeks. When was the last time she'd genuinely talked with Dub, or Shar, or even Mell other than the most casual conversation? What about Finn? What she had with the guardi captain was already so fragile...

She'd been caught up in her worries. And they were worries she couldn't tell anyone, not even her not-men. She'd closed herself off, without a word or an explanation...

What had she done? Hadn't she already learned this lesson? How could she be so blind?

She sought out Dub and Finn once more. They stared back at her, expressions blank. Meera cast a frown in her direction, but it didn't hold anger, only understanding. She whispered something to Finn, rose from the booth, and sauntered over to the bar.

"They're not angry, ya know? Well, maybe they are, but they're more worried than anything." The banshee leaned against the bar, her arms folded under her chest.

Bat held her silence, but only because she wasn't sure yet what to say.

"Can I get a pint?"

Bat nodded and started on Meera's drink.

"Ye're going to have ta start talking ta them."

"Did they…" *Did they tell you that? Why talk to the banshee? Why didn't they tell* me *they needed me to talk?*

"No. But I have eyes." Meera's fingers tapped against the bar. "I like ya, Bat. Yer a good one, and I never thought I'd say that about an Egyptian deity. So, I'm going to say a few things, and I hope you listen, because some of us deserve a happy ending." Shadows moved in the banshee's eyes.

Does Meera not expect to be happy? Pressure grew behind Bat's eyes and she blinked.

"Ye're still too used to being on yer own," the banshee continued. "That's fine, centuries of habit can be hard to break. But ye're *not* alone now. Ye've got four men wrapped around yer fingers. Sad thing is they're too used to being alone as well." She scowled. "And *some* of them are too stubborn ta see reason." Her lip lifted in a sneer as she looked over her shoulder in the direction of the booth.

It startled a small laugh from Bat. *Yes, those two are definitely stubborn.*

Meera's brows lifted and her expression softened. "Ya realize that's the first time you've laughed since we got back?"

Was it? Surely… Bat thought back over the last weeks.

It was. Again, she'd just been so caught up in Ailis. Not only in her concern over her state of unconsciousness, but also over her future. What would happen when she woke up?

"Ailis isn't here, so I'm going to be her for a few minutes more and tell it to ya straight. Ye're gonna have ta be the one to fix this. Because those men don't know what's bothering ya, they don't know how ta fix it, and they don't know how ta deal with the frustration of seeing you in pain." Meera grabbed the pint that Bat had only half finished. "Men are idiots. We women are always going to have to take the higher road." She paused. "Unfortunately."

Bat nodded and fell into thought. Meera's words held truth.

How to fix this? She couldn't tell them about the Egg's ability to create gods and goddesses. Yes, it was now destroyed, but that didn't mean someone else wouldn't try to think of another way to rise to godhood if the idea was planted in their minds. There was also the fact that Osiris had truly *died*. Gods did not die, and if the full tale came to be known, someone—whether other deities, humans, or immortals—would try to think of a way to repeat that feat. She'd come to that conclusion back at the cottage, as soon as she'd hung up on Osiris. Her mind hadn't changed.

No, she couldn't tell them the truth, but she could tell them *something*.

She could also... what was that saying she liked? Pull her head out of her ass?

Yes, she could pull her head out of her ass.

And what a weird image that was. Sometimes she wondered who came up with these sayings...

Reaching out, she found Meera's hand with hers. "Thank you, Meera." Bat was handing out "thank you's" very freely today.

The banshee shrugged, but there was a pleased grin on her face.

"Can you watch the bar for a few minutes?"

Meera waved her hand. "Go do what ya gotta do."

Bat curled her lips into a deliberate smile. The feeling was all too foreign. What had she allowed herself to become this last month that a smile felt foreign? She could only be grateful that she now had friends to pull her out of herself when needed.

Leaving the bar, Bat wove through the tables until she reached a small hearth situated at the back of the pub. In front of it, four chairs were set in a semi-circle. Above it was a shallow mantle. And on that mantle was an embroidered leather case.

Bat grabbed her harp and settled into one of the chairs. She paused, thinking of what she wanted to play.

A door slammed closed from somewhere on the second floor. It could only be Mell, her flirtatious, damaged, understanding Mell, with his beautiful laugh and eyes that rarely reflected what he truly felt.

Suddenly, she knew the song to play.

He fingers started slow as she struggled to remember the melody. Gradually, the pub quieted as conversations fell away. Movement in the doorway next to the bar caught her attention and she looked over to see Shar and Mell standing next to each other. Both wore expressions to match Dub and Finn—blank. Mell blinked, and a cutting ribbon of pain and confusion reached her before being cut off.

Oh, Mell. Oh, my laughing not-man. What have I done to you? To all of you, with my selfish worries?

She *had* to fix this.

Bat gave herself a few measures more to gather her

emotions and thoughts, to be sure of the vision she wanted to hold in her mind, then began.

> *Oh, don't you now remember, love*
> *When you gave me your right hand*
> *You vowed if you got married*
> *That I should be the man*

This was the first song she'd heard from Mell. It was the song that had drawn her to him, that had shown her he was so much more than a simple man with a guitar sitting in the back of a pub. This was the song that had charmed her into joining him, that had settled her, that had given her a simple pleasure and delighted her for the first time in centuries.

> *I wish I were a butterfly*
> *I'd fly to my love's nest*
> *I wish I were a linnet*
> *I'd sing my love to rest*

Bat closed her eyes as she conjured up image after image. Her, Finn, Dub, Shar, and Mell in the kitchen, crowded around the central island as they drank tea and she ate her strawberries. She and Finn walking hand in hand down the streets of Sligo, out to explore for a day. Mell and Dub arguing over whose turn it was to take out the trash. Shar working in his garden as she sat beside him and Killer examined the new growth plants. Dub in his forge, a contented look on his face. She, Mell, and Finn playing music together in the pub. The five of them on a blanket spread out on the field under Benbulben as they enjoyed a packed lunch and Killer ran in circles barking at nothing. Dub behind the bar frowning at tourists as Bat tugged on his arm and tried to keep him from kicking anyone out.

I wish I were a nightingale
I'd sing to the morning clear
I'll hold you in my arms, my love
The girl I love so dear

She pulled up more images. Of her bedroom, her snuggled into her men, one after the other. Of kisses and passion. Of them holding her as she finally let out the sorrow and pain she'd held inside for centuries. Of each and every smile she had ever received from them. Of Finn's almost confession of love, and of Dub's assurance that none of them were going anywhere. Of Mell's hugs, and Shar's embraces.

She poured every ounce of the love and longing she felt for them into the song. She wove comfort and home into each note. She bared her hopes and her dreams for them with each word that left her mouth.

The girl I love so dear

As the last note faded, she opened her eyes.

Four sets of eyes locked with hers: two lapis-blue, one deep chocolate, and the last a golden hazel. Four mouths offered her sheepish smiles. Four pairs of arms reached for her in a tangle of limbs.

Then she was being passed man to man as they pressed kisses against her lips.

"Just go!" came a voice from somewhere beyond the wall of broad shoulders that surrounded her.

Dub twisted around, gave Meera a nod, and grabbed Bat's hand. Once more he dragged her along, this time back up the stairs, into his room, and over to his bed. The other three followed close behind.

When the door was closed they stood before her once more. None spoke.

"So, I suppose I should begin?" Bat hadn't intended the questioning tone in her voice.

Shar opened his mouth then closed it. Dub and Finn exchanged a look. It was Mell who finally answered her. "That may be best," he said. "Because none of us know where to start without you talking to us." He sat beside her, his weight causing the mattress to dip and her to tilt toward him. He slipped and arm around her rounded shoulders. "I know you're feeling guilty. I know you're worried. At first I thought it was about Ailis, but now…"

Where to begin? "I am sorry," she finally said.

"Don't want apologies," Dub growled out, frowning down at her.

She smiled back at him. "I just… don't know where to start. There are things I can't tell you." It was the first time she'd outright said it. Back on the boat, Mell and Finn had hinted that they knew she was keeping something from them all. She held up a hand as their faces darkened. "I want to. I trust you. I simply cannot tell you these things." She frowned. "No, that is not quite accurate. I *can* tell you, but I made a decision not to tell

257

you. I made this decision knowing full well that my silence would sit between us in some way. I have also struggled with my decision many times. Despite this, each and every time I examine the facts, I come to the same conclusion—what I know is something I cannot reveal, not to anybody."

They fell into silence. Bat wasn't sure if they were waiting for her to continue, or if they simply had nothing yet to say.

"I did not apologize for not telling you this secret. I will not apologize for it, because it is not something I will change. My apology was for how selfish I have been this last month. You all have needed me, and I have stayed trapped in my worries and secrets." She focused on Finn. "And I know better than that."

Still none of them spoke.

She dropped her gaze and studied the green and blue patterned rug under her feet. "Meera said today was the first time I have laughed since Tir Hudi. I didn't even realize."

Finn sat on her other side. "Can you tell us if this secret has something to do with Ailis?"

Can I? Is that much safe to reveal?

As soon as Ailis woke, it would be evident that *something* in the trooping fae had changed. The green-haired woman would need more than just Bat by her side, helping her adjust. The next few months—maybe years— would be hard on the former fae as she relearned her own existence. She would need people who understood at least that much, and who would be tolerant of any... quirks that manifested themselves.

Bat leaned her head against Finn's shoulder and one of her hands landed on Mell's thigh, giving him a light caress. "It does have something to do with Ailis, though it is not only her." Mell picked up her hand and threaded his fingers through hers. "When she wakes, she will need... additional care. She will need friends around her who will not ask too many questions, and who can watch out for her." Pressure built in Bat's eyes and she blinked, trying to rid the threat of tears. "I don't know what will happen when she wakes. I don't know how she will feel, or what will have changed about her. I don't know... there are no visions." She blinked again. "I feel..."

"Lost," Mell whispered.

Shar knelt in front of her. Bat parted her knees and he scooted forward. He was tall enough that their heads were at the same level. His arms went around her waist, forcing space between her and Finn, and Mell's arm to drop. "Why didn't you simply tell us this instead of drawing away from us? We thought..." He didn't finish, his voice thick.

"We thought you'd decided you'd had enough of Ireland and were going to head home as soon as you knew Ailis was okay." Dub stood over them all, arms now crossed over his chest.

Bat stiffened as her blood surged and her chest tightened. Her eyes narrowed as she glared up at the arrogant not-man. "And what wanker came up with that idiotic idea?"

His gaze flicked down and away as his frown faded and his brows drew up in the middle.

"It was you, huh? And you then went blabbing to your

brothers and Finn instead of coming to me to ask what you wanted to know." Bat pushed at Shar's shoulders, too angry at the moment to enjoy his warmth.

He didn't let her go. "He did come to us. And we didn't... we're not used to this, *a stor*. We didn't know how to..."

She grabbed his braid and pulled his head back, no longer feeling the least bit guilty. "Did you really think I would walk away and leave you all?" Her words were a low growl and power pushed against the four men. "Haven't we talked about this? Haven't I told you how much I love you all? Haven't I bared my soul for your gaze?" She sucked in deep, uneven breaths as she struggled to regain control.

Ah, fuck it.

She freed one of her arms and aimed a punch at Shar's good eye. He let her go and scrambled back. *"Haven't I fucking given you everything I can?"*

"You kept your secrets!"

The accusation came from Dub. His hands dropped to his sides and curled into fists. His eyes were wide and his lips thinned. His chest rose in rapid breaths as though he'd just fought a battle and lost...

"We said no more secrets, *storeen*," he finished as his shoulders slumped.

Her own anger drained away with his. Just how long had this been eating at him?

Bat stood and went to him. She wrapped her arms around his waist and pressed her cheek to his chest. She stayed like that, his heart pounding against her ear, until he finally returned her embrace.

"It is really not something I can share. Please believe that it tears me up to know that I am keeping things from you. Please trust that this is not a decision I came to lightly." Bat pressed herself closer to Dub until every curve conformed to his hard frame. "And please know that it is not because I do not trust *you*. I am simply…" She didn't know how to say it.

"You are simply doing what you know to be the correct thing, even if it is the painful thing," Finn finished for her.

Finn, her guardi who sometimes understood her better than even Mell. She smiled.

But, she still had one bone to pick with Dub. Hardening her expression, she pulled away far enough to look up at him without hurting her neck. "You thought I was going to leave?"

He shrugged and looked away, not wanting to answer.

"Would you have let me?"

Dub's arms tightened around her to the point of near pain. "Are you crazy? You're not going anywhere. I've been busy coming up with schemes to keep you here, or keep Ailis unconscious. I might have started working on a pair of enchanted shackles…"

She buried her head against his chest once more. Only this time she was hiding the grin that spread across her face at his possessive words. "Okay."

He stilled under her. "To the shackles?"

Was that a hopeful note in his voice?

"No." She stroked his back. "Well, maybe. But that's not what I said okay to. I didn't really give my approval of anything. I thought okay could be used as a general acknowledgement of a subject being closed, and didn't have to mean approval?"

"Might want to pick a different word when Dub starts getting possessive and talking about locking you up, *realta*," Mell said. "If you're not careful, he'll take you up on it."

"Oh. Okay." A pause. "Damn, I believe I've gotten into the habit of using this word."

A new hand landed on her back, rubbing over her shoulders. "I think we need new rules," Shar said from behind her.

"Yes, the 'no secrets' rule will need to be amended. What if we promise 'no secrets unless it would mean world destruction and chaos if we reveal them'?"

Silence greeted her proposal.

"Oh, I had not mentioned that part, had I?"

"No-oooooo…" Mell choked out.

"I… could agree to that," Finn said, his tone thoughtful. Bat suspected he had figured things out a while ago.

"I will add an amendment to this new rule," Dub said. "If in the event this secret becomes dangerous to one of us, it will be revealed, *no matter what it is*." He pulled away from her and slid his hands to her upper arms. Meeting her gaze, he gave her a light shake. "I will not have you keeping things from me that may put you in harm's way, understand?"

It was a reasonable expectation. And the only way this secret would become dangerous was if someone else were to discover it, and act upon it. In which case it would no longer be a secret. "Understood." Then she frowned up at him and attempted to poke his chest. He still held her arms, though, and her movement was hampered. "I have another rule to add. No more assuming stupid things." She twisted around to send a mock-glare at the other three men. "For any of us. If one of us is worried, or hurt or upset, or something is bothering us, we have to say something. And if we think any one of us is going though any of those, we must ask. No one may answer with 'okay,' 'fine,' or 'nothing' as an answer unless those are true answers. You may say 'I do not want to talk about it right now.' That is acceptable. However, when the person is ready to talk, they must." She bit into her lower lip. "I think that covers it all? I really do wish Ailis was awake, she would know what else to add to the condition..."

"I feel like we should have written that down, or recorded it or something," Shar said.

"It *was* kind of convoluted," Mell teased.

"I understood it," Finn said, his tone smug.

"Stop being a lickarse, guardi," Dub shot back. The he looked back down at Bat. "I understood it too." He grinned, but there was something malicious about it. "We will also add 'you wouldn't understand' and 'it's not important' to the list of things you can't answer with."

"Great," Mell grumbled.

"Those are two of his favorite phrases when he doesn't want to talk about something," Shar stage whispered to her. "Well, other than just remaining silent. He's really good at remaining silent."

"You'd never know it, though. The sap always has something to say..." That was Finn.

"Will you please stop insulting me, oh dear brothers.

My poor, fragile ego can't handle the abuse." Mell flopped onto his back on the bed. "See, *realta*, I'm expressing. I'm expressing that I have a problem with the way my bothers insult me, especially the eldest." He pouted, but happiness rode out of him in waves. "He's always been a bit of a bully, you know."

Bat laughed, delighted. This, right here, was what she wanted. Them talking together, teasing, getting angry and making up. "I do love you, you know."

Dub crushed her to his chest again and Shar crowded in behind her. Mell jumped form the bed and wrapped his arms around all three of them. After a brief hesitation, Finn joined the group hug, increasing the smother-factor by ten.

They still had not said the words, but Bat didn't worry.

They would.

Because in her heart she knew they already returned her feelings, even her reluctant guardi.

Though there were moments she faltered, she had learned to listen to her heart and to trust in herself.

And to trust in these four men.

Chapter Twenty-Nine

Four months later...

DUB

*P*ink-golden light filtered in through the high windows of the forge. Dub set down a tiny file onto the worktable tucked in one corner of the now clean and well-maintained room, and studied his work.

The file was part of a new set of tools he'd acquired three months before, a little after he, Shar, Mell, and Finn had confronted Bat about her intentions towards them.

Her intentions. He snorted. Sometimes he amused himself, though he would never let his brothers find out the direction his thoughts occasionally strayed into. If they did find out he would never live it down.

They were all such fucking idiots back then. He rolled his eyes at himself. *We're still fucking idiots. Wankers. Whatever.*

Dub admitted it, his thoughts at the time had been out of line. While he knew his feelings for her, and she'd confessed her own, what they all had together was so new —and so unlike any other relationship he'd ever seen—he was thrown into confusion any time he couldn't figure out what she was thinking.

The new rules had probably been of more help to him than any of the other four. They gave him permission to demand she tell him what was on her mind. Over the last four months he'd used that right liberally.

His phone rang. "What?"

"Are you done?" Finn asked.

"What the hell do you think, guardi?"

"I think that if ye're not here in the next thirty minutes the surprise we have prepared will be ruined," was the harsh rejoinder from the man who'd become his greatest rival for Bat's attention.

And also, surprisingly, his greatest confidant. Out of the four men, he and Finn had had the hardest time opening up their defenses to the goddess, even after they'd admitted their feelings.

Well, not to her. Not yet. That's what tonight was about.

"I'll be there in twenty. Everything else ready?"

"What do you think?" Finn slapped his own words back at him.

Dub hung up. No reason to keep talking to the asshole.

Opening a shallow drawer that usually held scraps of the more rare and delicate metals, he studied the five velvet-covered boxes that nestled inside. Pulling out the one that sat at the far end, he placed the last of his creations inside.

They were complete—his offerings to his goddess.

He gathered all the boxes into an embroidered, deep-red velvet bag, rose, and headed home.

MELL

He was sweating. It was ridiculous. He'd played his guitar thousands of times over the centuries. He'd performed more songs than most people knew existed. He'd entranced women and men both with the sounds he could coax from the strings of his favorite instrument.

A pint landed on the bar in front of him with enough force that a line of foam spilled over the side. Mell looked up to meet his youngest brother's eye.

"Drink it. She'll be here soon and you need to relax."

Without a word Mell grabbed up the glass and drained half of the wonderful brown liquid in one go.

"Ye've been working on this for months now, Mell. It'll be great." Shar crossed his arms and frowned. "And even if it isn't, she'll love it."

Mell raised a brow at his brother. That was something he'd expect to come from Dub's mouth, or maybe Finn's. Those two had grown way too close over the last months.

"You could string together nonsense syllables into the most cacophonous melody ever invented and she would love it." Shar paused, a grin growing on his face. "Because it came from you."

That was another change. The largest brother smiled so much these days that most had already forgotten how withdrawn and silent he used to be.

Dub was the grumpy one, Mell was the happy-go-lucky one, and Shar was the silently protective brother who tried to maintain the peace. That was who they were, who they had always thought they'd be...

Until their goddess came and changed them. It wasn't really change, it was more that she...

She allowed them to find new sides to themselves. Sides they had thought were long gone or had never existed at all.

Finn entered the bar from the kitchen hallway and took the stool next to Mell. "Dub's on his way."

This was it. They were really doing this. He'd been *wanting* to tell her for a couple months now, the words fighting to slip out of him, but the time never seemed right. He also didn't want to step on his brothers' toes—and yes, he now thought of Finn as a brother.

"How much more time?" he asked.

"Meera's with her and the pups. She's going to call when they're on their way back."

Mell nodded and took another sip of his pint, his hands trembling lightly.

His lips curled into a rueful smile as he stared at the liquid heaven that was Guinness.

I love you. I love you. I love you. He chanted the words in his head.

The three words he was finally going to say to her tonight.

Who knew three words could turn a man into a quivering mess?

Mell tilted his head back, then looked to Finn and Shar in turn. "Any of you ever told a woman before?"

"Yes," Finn said. "Twice. Once I meant it with all my heart, the other..." He shrugged. "The other was Grainne." The Guardi Captain's words were matter of fact, the past guilt and sorrow that haunted him at the mention of his old fiancée no longer in evidence.

"I have not." Shar frowned. "There were times I wanted to, but something always held me back."

Mell waved his hand, telling Shar to continue.

"I didn't really love them. I cared for them, and I lusted after them, but I can tell now it wasn't love."

"And you're ready now?"

"Yes." Shar's answer was simple, and all the more profound because of that.

"What about you?" Finn asked. "Since we're suddenly in a sharing mood..."

Mell grimaced. "I have. And it was never this hard to say. I've been thinking, maybe that's why I didn't just tell her. I wanted this to be different, because I had said the words when they were untrue. I didn't want..."

"You didn't want them to have no meaning," Finn finished for him.

The three men exchanged a glance of understanding.

SHAR

Shar left Finn and Mell to their conversation. They'd kept the pub closed today in preparation. The plan was to get Bat out for a few hours, then surprise her with their gifts when she returned. After that, he'd think about unlocking the doors and letting the ragtag group of fae that Bat liked to call "family" come in and steal her attention.

He wanted to check his preparations one last time.

Shar examined the offerings laid out on the kitchen island. A bowl of the ripest strawberries. Check. A saucer and cup with a dab of whiskey in the bottom. Check. Tea kettle and tea bag ready and waiting. Check. Fresh bread and butter. Check.

Two potted cornflower plants that he'd been cultivating for the last month and a half.

Check.

He'd chosen these for two reasons. One, he knew she liked the color. Two, she'd mentioned once that she kept a pot of them on her windowsill back in Egypt.

Okay, three reasons.

Finn had said she carried their scent on her.

It was sappy, he knew, but one pot was for her, to keep in her room.

The other was for him. So he could keep a bit of her close to him even on the nights she spent in one of the other men's arms.

His chest tightened a bit at the thought, though it was nowhere near as bad as it used to be. He no longer needed to suppress random urges to beat one of them silly. *It only happened* once, he reminded himself. He'd also stopped contemplating stealing away with her. Well, not as often. No more than once a week.

As time went on, Shar was sure that would lessen to once a month, then maybe once a year. He didn't tell her about these thoughts, nor did he act on them. He'd promised her after all. He would protect his goddess, even if it was from his own urges.

Shar hummed as he fussed with the placement of the dishes on the island before finally putting them back exactly as he'd had them. How much time before she returned?

~

FINN

Finn patted his chest, making sure the envelope was still secure in the inner pocket of his jacket. Stiff paper met his fingers and his lips tipped up at the corners. Mell sent him a knowing smile as he sipped the last of the pint Shar had poured.

The brothers had spent months thinking about and working on their gifts. Their *offerings*, as Bat liked to call them.

Finn hadn't. He'd known since the all too brief encounter in his apartment what he would get her when he was finally ready to return the three words she'd been brave enough to say first.

He'd been ready since the day they returned to the pub from Tir Hudi. Except Bat had been too wrapped up in getting Ailis better. And then Finn had realized he couldn't be the first of the men to say it. The brothers were already holding onto their own control so tightly, Finn didn't think they could take it if he was the first to offer the words to Bat.

Their relationship was a delicate balance that someone needed to maintain. Someone other than Bat, that was.

How did I get in this position? How did I become the damned referee?

Finn drummed his fingers on the bar. Oh, he knew the answer. It was her smile. He'd fucking do anything to see her smile. And when the men all got along, she smiled the widest.

He rested his elbows on the bar and buried his head in his hands. "Fuck my life."

Mell nudged him. "Want a pint?"

"Sure, why not."

Mell rose and slipped behind the bar. Finn didn't move until the glass was set in front of him.

"You know, I think it'll get better," Mell said, as though he was picking up in the middle of a conversation they'd never been having.

"Huh?"

"Us brothers. We'll get better. Shar's already calmer, and Dub's anger surges less every day. You won't have to play referee so much."

Finn raised a brow as he took a sip of his Guinness. "And you?"

Mell bobbed his head and hummed. "Oh, I'm still going to be a pain in the ass for you. But, once I get this—these words—out, I'll try not to be such a pain in the ass."

Finn growled, sounding too much like Dub for his own

comfort. "Are you telling me you've been acting like a brat just because you could?"

Mell's head tilted. "Do you not know me?"

Finn tensed as annoyance gripped him. Then the absurdity of it hit him and he let out a loud laugh. "You are all wankers," he finally said when he caught his breath.

"Well, yes," Mell said simply.

The back door opened then slammed shut.

"Dub's here," Mell said with a wide smile. "Now all we need is our goddess."

~

BAT

Meera had dragged her and the pups out for a long round of window shopping. Not that Bat minded, exactly, but she was worried about her not-men. There was something going on with them.

However, every time she asked them about it, all she got was the same answer: "I do not want to talk about it right now."

It was the agreed upon answer that one of them was to give when something bothered them, but they were not yet ready to share. It had been used once or twice over the last few months, but it had never taken more than a day or two until someone was ready to talk and everything was sorted out.

This had been going on for *six weeks*. And it was all four of them.

Her hand crept up to her necklace as Killer and Mori tugged on the leashes in her other hand. Meera walked beside her, holding Bekka's leash.

Absently, Bat noted the pedestrians moving out of the way of the three half-grown wolfhounds. Killer and his litter mates were well behaved, but they could be intimidating. She sent an apologetic smile to the humans who had to share the pavement with them.

"Are ya still worried?" Meera asked.

Bat shrugged, then nodded. There really wasn't much else to say. She wasn't afraid they would try to leave her, or kick her out. And it wasn't that they didn't want her any longer—*that* was proven night after night.

She and Meera had discussed this until the banshee was ready to either throw Bat into a wall, or bang her own head against one. As wonderful as Meera had been over the last months while they waited for Allis to wake up—and her friend *would* wake up, Bat refused to think otherwise—the banshee's tolerance for what she called "pointless talk" was very low.

"Well, I don't think ya need to be worried for much longer," Meera said now.

Bat's stride hitched. "What do you mean?"

"Oh, nothing."

"You know something."

"Maybe."

"Are you going to tell me?"

"No."

"Bitch." Bat didn't mean it in a derogatory way. She'd overheard a younger girl in one of the shops direct the word at one of her friends who'd been teasing her. It had been said with such frustrated affection that Bat had been charmed. She had yet to come across anything that conveyed that mixture of feelings so perfectly, and decided to adopt it.

Meera laughed, now used to the insult. She knew exactly what Bat meant by it. They'd walked another block, perusing the various items in the shop windows, when Meera spoke again. "Any flashes?"

Bat frowned. "No."

"Not even a tingle?"

"No." And that was another mystery. The level of her power had been steadily increasing as her not-men and the pub's patrons slipped offerings to her one way or another. One of the leprechauns gifted her a belt to match the boots she'd gotten form Dano. The pixies liked to find ways to sneak past the wards and leave flowers on her bedside table. Meera and the other banshees had taken to showing up with random pieces of clothing they claimed she needed to have. Old Mike offered her stories of lost tourists, and Faolan had once put on a shadow play for her. It had been a bit gruesome, but that was only to be expected from a sluagh.

And then there were her nights…

With all of that, her power was higher than it had been in centuries, though it hadn't grown enough to alarm the local deities. The Morrigan occasionally came into the pub to check on just that. But Bat's power *had* grown, which meant she should have been getting the occasional flash of vision even if there were no catastrophic events on the horizon.

"Hmmm… well, ye'll figure it out eventually."

"Yes. I will," Bat replied, nothing but confidence in her tone. Finn had suggested she speak with Oisin, see if he could find anything in the archives about missing or dormant powers. Bat had an appointment to see the sidhe next week.

Her pace picked up. She was eager to get back to the pub and corner her men once more. She may not be able to pry their worries from them until they were ready, but nothing in the rules said she couldn't at least *ask* them if they were ready to share, nor did the rules state anything against *coaxing* them to share…

She *would* get it out of them. After all, what were a few months to an immortal?

They turned right onto O'Connell Street and left the main road behind. It was quieter here, only a few pedestrians making their way along the pavement. Bat stopped before a blue door flanked by large glass windows with scrolling gold script proclaiming the name of the establishment: The Dubros.

The door was locked. She grumbled to herself as Meera laughed and the pups slipped in and around their legs, tangling the leashes into a tricky web.

Bat banged on the door as she shifted her grip on the leashes, trying to untangle them without letting the pups go. They'd been doing this lately when it was time to go back inside. If she dropped the leash ends, they'd be off like a shot, and she'd have to chase them down.

She'd fallen for it *once* and ended up on the other side of the canal, groups of humans laughing at her and the pups' antics. *Never again.*

"*Storeen*, what are ya doing?" Dub scowled down at

her. His expression was reminiscent of her first night here in Ireland, except *this* Dub had laugh crinkles at the corners of his eyes despite the frown.

She was half crouched, one foot held well above the pavement as she worked the leashes from around her ankle. "I cannot let them go, or the pups will run away. I do not want to chase them again."

"And this is how you solve it?"

"What's going on?" Shar appeared over his brother's shoulder. His eye widened at the sight she presented.

"You could help," she grumbled.

Shar shrugged. "When ye're done playing, we have a surprise for ya." Her giant stepped back into the pub, his shoulders shaking.

Killer chose that moment to make his move. He circled behind her and brushed against her thigh, tipping her into Dub. Her face headed straight for his groin and she had a choice—drop the leashes, or find herself in a position she much preferred to save for their bedroom.

It was not an easy decision, but she held onto those leashes for all she was worth.

Dub caught her just before her forehead met a very sensitive part of his anatomy.

Meera sagged against a nearby lamppost, weak with laughter.

Dub picked her up. "Maybe later, *storeen*," he whispered in her ear, his voice husky.

Heat filled her cheeks.

"Mell!" Dub shouted over his shoulder. "Come get the beasts, will ya?"

The middle brother slipped past Dub and gathered the

leashes from her. His face was tight with barely suppressed mirth. He didn't say a word, no doubt afraid he would erupt with laughter if he opened his mouth.

None of them were gaining any points with her today.

"Here," Meera said, tugging Bekka over to the door and handing over the third pup's leash. She gave Bat a mischievous smile then sauntered away, back toward the main road.

When the dogs were out of the way, Dub and Bat stood in the doorway of the pub. She couldn't help but compare this to the first night she'd met them. It had been dark, and she'd been shivering, cold and damp. She'd been armed with nothing more than a printed address and vague visions of rainbows and green fields.

Now, Dub's hands were firmly wrapped around her arms as weak sunlight filtered through low clouds. There was warmth in his lapis-eyes instead of cold suspicion. That night, a fear she didn't even know she possessed had been masked by formalities and defiant curiosity. Now, she'd bared her soul and dreams to the man that stood before her and to three others, and they'd helped her face those fears.

That night, she'd entered an entire world she knew nothing about—a world that held immortals and fae and leprechauns and Fomoiri. Now, that world welcomed her with open arms. She was more comfortable here, in this small pub, than she had ever been back in Egypt. *Ever*.

This was where she belonged. She did not dream of it, or hope for it. She *knew* it.

Dub's eyes darkened as though he could hear her

thoughts, and he tugged her to him. Dipping his head, he caught her lips in a deep kiss.

"Well now," she said when he released her. "What would have happened if you had greeted me like *that* on my first night?"

He just answered her with a heated look and pulled her inside.

There was no one inside except her for not-men. As she looked them over, she wondered—and not for the first time—just how she had gotten so lucky. Mell wore a white button down rolled up at the sleeves. Bat had learned to love the way his muscles and tendons danced on his forearms as he played his guitar. His slightly too long dark hair lay in messy strands around his beautiful face.

He sat at the bar next to Finn. The guardi was her golden man. His red-gold hair was like a beacon to her, asking her to come and run her fingers through it. She loved the contrast he presented to the dark-haired brothers. Everything about his appearance was warm, including the golden-hazel of his eyes.

Everyone knew how much she liked warmth by now.

Finn had become the main partner who… *grounded* her. He was her rock, the one who kept her steady in the chaos the brothers tended to cause in her heart and her mind. Oh, they didn't do it deliberately, it was just who they were. They would never be easy, and she wouldn't have it any other way.

Shar had gone behind the bar, and begun building a pint. He set it on the bar in front of her usual spot.

Sliding into her seat, she picked it up and took a deep sip.

Wonderful. Bat had grown to appreciate a good pint. The Irish truly knew how to make a good beer.

As she drank, Mell stood from his stool and walked back to the hearth where his guitar and her harp rested. Picking up his instrument, he settled into his seat and strummed his fingers over the strings.

Without further prelude or comment, he played.

It wasn't anything she'd heard before. She tilted her head listening. A few of the chords were a little awkward, but overall she liked it. Her foot bobbed in time and she began humming along as the main melody repeated.

Then he began to sing.

And the man
His heart was hollow
For his eyes
Reflected night

Tears pricked her eyes, though she wasn't sure why. Mell didn't put any sorrow into the song, even if the lyrics hinted at it. Absently, she noted that Shar had slipped into the back hallway.

In her arms
He found his solace
This goddess was
His sorrow and delight.

She smiled. Was he singing about her?

The pains

They were left behind
In the end
She held him tight.

Mell's head was bent over the guitar, his attention on his fingering.

In the heart
Of this once hollow man
A goddess
Brought him light

Mell continued to pluck the melody for a few measures more, then his fingers stilled. He bit his lip and peered up at her through the fall of his shaggy brown hair. "Did you like it?" he finally asked.

Something in his voice made her pause. "Did—" she swallowed. "Did you write it?"

He gave her a shallow nod.

A huge grin stretched across her face. She jumped from her seat and rushed to him. Grabbing him around the shoulders, she pulled him into a tight hug. "Was it about me?"

"Yes." His voice was muffled. She'd smashed his face into her chest.

"I love it." She released him. "I love it, and I love you." The words slipped from her so easily now, but she meant them every time.

"I love you too."

Bat froze. *Had he… ?* "Did you… ?"

Mell smiled up at her and grabbed her hand. "I love

you, Bat Sitru, previous goddess of Egypt, now the patron goddess of The Dubros in Sligo Ireland."

Her heart pounded and her head spun. He'd finally given her the words back. She honestly hadn't thought it would affect her this much.

Letting out a delighted laugh, she tackled him again.

A throat cleared behind her. Bat twisted her head around to find Shar, Dub and Finn all lined up behind the bar. A line of dishes sat across the polished wood.

"Come, *a stor*. Eat." Shar pointed to the dishes.

Bat grabbed Mell's hand and dragged him with her.

All her favorites were laid out. Strawberries, fresh bread and butter, and a steaming cup of tea. Beside these was a beautiful potted plant whose flowers matched Shar's eye. "Cornflowers?"

Shar nodded.

"I used to have these back…" She almost said home. "Back in Egypt."

"I know." He paused. "Do you like them?"

"Of course."

Shar stared at her, expectant.

What did he…? It didn't take Bat long to catch on. "I love them, and I love you."

Shar's smile bloomed. "I love you, too."

Bat giggled. Was this what they had been up to? Was this what they had been keeping from her? Maybe she would have to forgive them for tormenting her for weeks.

She looked between Dub and Finn. Who would be next?

Dub frowned at her. "What? Just because these two saps said it, now you expect everyone to?"

She nodded. "Yes. It is only fair, after all." She leaned toward him. "And your frowns don't fool me, Fomoiri."

"Is that so?" He jerked his head at Finn. "You're up, guardi. I'm going last."

Finn sighed but sent Bat a soft smile. Then he pulled an envelope from his jacket and placed it on the bar between the strawberries and the tea. "I did promise you," was all he said.

She opened the envelope and read the contents. It was a reservation for a bed and breakfast in Lislorkin North. Bat raised questioning eyes to Finn.

"We're going to see the Cliffs of Moher."

Bat recalled the painting she'd admired in his apartment. He *had* promised to take her to see them if they survived, hadn't he? "This is perfect." She decided to tease him and held back the words they all seemed to be waiting for today.

He surprised her, though. Finn leaned over the bar until only a few centimeters separated their lips. "I love you," he whispered, then gave her one of the sweetest kisses she'd ever received.

"I love you too," she said as he pulled back.

It was kind of nice to say the words second.

"Lickarse," Dub muttered. He placed a deep-red velvet bag on his side of the bar. Pulling out five jewelry boxes, he lined them up along the edge. He fiddled with them for a few seconds until finally he had them just right.

Dub picked up the one at the end and placed it before her.

"What is this?" Each of her not-men wore serious

expressions and nervousness welled within her once more.

"Open it," was all Dub said.

Her fingers only trembled a little as she pried open the lid on the small box.

Inside nestled a ring. Only... it wasn't a single ring. It was five interlocking bands, all bound together into one ring. Bat picked it up and rolled the bands through her fingers.

"It's a take on the trinity ring. Which has a much older meaning than the one adopted by the Christian faith, actually. It's all about unity, about being stronger together. And I'm not even sure it's originally Irish, the Smith said he picked the idea up from and Russian he met in... well, it's Germany now. Plus..." Dub trailed off as Bat stared at him.

Dub just rambled. Dub never rambles. "Are you all right?"

He nodded, his cheeks burning. Mell's shoulders shook, and Finn coughed.

Bat returned her attention to the gift. "There are five of them. One for each of us?"

Dub nodded, his lips clamped tightly together.

"It's beautiful. Which finger is it supposed to go on?"

Dub reached for her hand. "Let me." He slipped the ring over the third finer on her left hand. His face was flushed so deep a red that Bat really was concerned for him.

"Are you sure you are all right?"

He opened his mouth, no doubt to say "fine," but then closed it. That would violate the rules. "I'm nervous," he ground out.

"Oh." Bat grinned at him. "I love you."

"Love you too." The words came out in a rush of breath and Dub groaned as soon as he said them.

"Is it really that hard?" Bat looked to each of her men.

Finn shrugged, Mell shook his head, Shar nodded, and Dub groaned again.

Then the grumpy not-man picked up the other boxes and shoved one at each man. "Here. Put them on."

"Awe, big brother, I love you." Mell batted his lashes at Dub.

"Shut it." Dub opened his box and slipped his own ring over the same finger he'd placed Bat's ring on.

"Does this mean we are now married?" She asked as soon as each man had put their rings on. "Is that legal? And is there not a ceremony I am entitled to? I have seen the magazines and have watched shows with Meera. There is supposed to be a dress, and a cake, and a man in a dark suit." She nodded her head decisively. "Yes, I am sure of these things." A grin threatened to take over her face as she teased her men, but with effort she maintained a serious expression.

"Uhhh…"

Then Bat laughed and picked up a strawberry. She'd tortured her poor not-men enough for one day. They'd get there. After all, they basically had eternity

Dearest Bastie,
I have decided that even if you never answer me again, I
will continue the messages. You didn't see the other ones I

wrote, because I never sent them. They were more for me to write than for you to see anyway.

I am not sure if you would believe my life here in Ireland even if you saw it with your own eyes. I, who could not keep even one man, now have four. And they are perfect. Well, no they are not. But I would not change them for anything. They make me laugh, and they keep me warm.

I just wanted to thank you, again. If it were not for you I would have never begun this journey.

I hope you are well. I really do.

I will wait for you to write. I know you will, eventually.

Love, Bat

P.s. - Oh! I now have three puppies! Ciara gave me the two left from Fina's previous litter. She said they were causing too much chaos, and that I deserved them. I will be sure to send you pictures.

Epilogue

———

*B*at and Mell sat near the hearth. They had just finished running through one of his new compositions for some of the pub regulars who had stayed late just to listen, when the front door swung open.

Dub scowled at the three figures who stalked into the bar. "We're closed."

"Door wasn't locked." The voice was deep and accented.

Bat, who had been bent over her harp running through some of the trickier fingerings for the new song, froze. She knew that voice, though it had been centuries since she heard it.

Raising her head, she could only stare.

Horus. Horus stood in the middle of her pub, arms folded and chin lifted like he owned the place.

"Where is she?" he asked, his tone filled with all the arrogance she remembered and more.

"Horus." That voice was smooth, throaty, and annoyed.

Bastie was here too?

Bat wanted to jump on her old friend and hug her until she spilled everything about why she had not responded to any of Bat's email notes. But something held her back. Why were they here, now, without a word of warning?

Then she recalled there'd been a buzz in her back pocket at the beginning of the evening, she'd just been too busy to check her phone. Bat pulled it out now and saw she did have one new message, from Bastet.

You have about four hours until the asshole and the whore show up. I'm trying to get in on the meet and greet. Can't tell you much, but they're going to try to persuade you to come back.

Bat's brows rose at the last. They could not be serious. She handed her phone to Mell so he could read the message as well.

He snorted.

At least they were in agreement on that.

She returned her attention to the front of the pub.

"And who is 'she'?" That was Meera. The banshee's eyes flashed, though she kept her anger from her expression, if not her voice.

"That little brat, Bat." And there was the whore.

She is not a whore. Do not fall into using Bastie's language, Bat. And now I am talking to myself. Bat shook her head.

"You'd best be speaking of her with respect." Faolan stood from his usual spot at the bar.

Hathor raised a perfectly groomed brow at the sluagh. "And who are you to tell me how to speak?"

Bat had had enough. She stood, the harp still in her hands. "He is my friend. Why are you here?"

The three gods turned to her. Horus, Hathor, and

Bastet. These three had retained enough followers and believers into the modern age that they had maintained a semblance of power.

They are nowhere near as powerful as The Morrigan, though. It was a striking thought. She was used to thinking of the Egyptian deities as powerhouses.

Hathor pushed the silky fall of her dark hair over her shoulder and spun to face Bat. Her face held the overly sweet expression she wore when she wanted something.

How had Horus ever fallen for this goddess?

Then Horus stepped to Hathor's side, and Bat remembered. They were basically the same. Or at least, now they were. Horus used to have a sweet side... or maybe that sweetness was only reserved for the woman at his side, which was no longer Bat.

She expected the thought to hurt. It... didn't. She felt nothing but general annoyance at their intrusion and a faint wistfulness over shared memories.

I have truly left them behind.

Bat grinned. There was so much relief connected to the realization that she bounced on her toes.

"Hey, you." Bastet took a few steps toward Bat then paused. Her gaze scanned over the gathered fae, lingered on the brothers, then focused on... "Is that the puppy? He's not much of a puppy. Are you sure you know the definition of the word puppy?"

Bat grinned at her friend. She handed the harp to Mell and closed the distance with Bastet before wrapping the goddess in the hug she'd been wanting to give her.

"That the cat?" Dub asked from behind the bar. He

watched the scene unfold with wary eyes and his concerned frown.

"Yes, this is my friend Bastet." She tugged on Bastie's hand and brought her to the bar, ignoring the other two deities in the center of the room. If they would not greet her properly, she would not greet them. "Do you want me to pull you a pint? I am really good at it now."

Bastet nodded and slid onto a seat next to Old Mike.

The cat was unusually subdued.

Bat finished the pint, set it before the other goddess, and waited for her to take a sip.

Bastet's brow rose. "This is good."

Bat nodded. "I know. You should also stay for a song before you need to go. Finn will be here in a little bit, and he was going to bring his fiddle."

"You are truly happy here." Bastet's dark eyes bore into Bat's.

"I am."

Bastet twisted in her seat to stare at Hathor and Horus. The other fae had gone back to their drinks and conversation, ignoring the two deities in their midst.

Those two didn't know it was the usual behavior of the solitary fae and misfits Bat now called her family. She didn't need Mell's powers to see the anger and frustration brewing within them.

"We are not asking her," Bastet told them.

Horus pulled his shoulders back and strode to the bar. "Bat, may I speak to you in private?"

"No." Three voices spoke in unison.

Bat frowned over at Shar, who had just come in from the kitchen, then up at Dub. That was her question to answer, and they had no right to speak over her, even if they were all in agreement.

She turned back to Horus. "Whatever you need to say, you can say it right here." She crossed her arms over her chest and stared levelly at her old lover.

His lips tightened. "This is not something that can be spoken of in such company."

Bat's brows rose. "This is my family, anything you tell me, I will eventually tell them. Besides, I doubt they actually give a shit about anything you have going on."

Horus's eyes widened at her language and Bat laughed. She just couldn't keep it in anymore. The two were so out of their element, though Bastet seemed to fit right in. Bat knew she would.

Hathor glared at her and Horus cleared his throat. "We need the Unifier to return to Egypt. Things have been... unsettled."

"The dead are restless. More and more souls are not making it to their judgment," Bastet said with a sigh.

"And why do ya think tha' has anything ta do wi' th' goddess here?" Old Mike drawled out his question in the thickest accent bat had ever heard from him.

She had to stifle another laugh. She did love her family.

The H's—*yes, that is what I will call them*—brows drew together in confusion as Bastet grinned at the older fae. "Because the trouble started when she left," the cat said simply.

Old Mike nodded. "I could see tha'. It would mess things up quite a bother if she left *here*."

The wisp's message was quite clear, and rumbles of agreement built throughout the common room.

"What do you need, exactly?" Shar asked.

Horus finally said the only thing that could soften Bat at this point. "We need her help. I know we have treated her unfairly, but—"

"She's not the one you need." The soft voice cut through the room.

A slim figure stood in the doorway to the kitchen hall, one shoulder propped against the jamb. Her green hair had long since grown out and now a good six inches of blond showed at the roots. Her legs trembled and her face was pale and thin, but she stood on her own power.

"Ailis!" Bat shoved Dub and then Shar out of the way and nearly tackled her friend. "You are awake! Oh thank the stars." Bat pushed away, keeping her hands on the fae's—no, the *goddess's*—shoulders. "Do you know?" she whispered, the words barely audible even to her own ears.

Ailis nodded. "We'll talk later. For now..." Her gaze drifted to the Egyptian deities in the pub. "I think I got ye'r visions, Bat. I woke up and pictures flashed in front of me, so fast I couldn't really understand them. Then I saw myself standing with the three of them in some kind of temple..."

Bat laid her forehead against Ailis's. She'd suspected something like that when the visions remained gone even after eight months. She'd also noticed her ability to distinguish and delve into souls was... diminished. It was not gone, but reading even one soul took thrice the effort it used to, even when she held plenty of power. "You are sure?" Bat asked her friend.

"I'm sure." Ailis's voice held not one quiver of doubt.

"Well, then, I have someone I'd like you to meet." Bat wrapped her arm around Ailis and led her through the now silent fae and toward the seat next to Bastet. "I've always thought you two would get along." Bat turned to the H's. "You two should sit as well. I do not think this will be a short night."

"Don't care as long as they know ye're not going anywhere," Dub said with a shrug.

Shar nodded. Mell laughed and wrapped and arm around her shoulder. "Yup. Ye're never getting away now, *realta*." He pressed a kiss to her cheek.

The H's slid into a booth near the back of the room, expressions of wary disgust on their faces as they eyed the dark wood of the benches.

Just then Finn walked in the front room. He froze as his head came up and he drew in a deep breath. "Well shit on a stick," he muttered.

Bat tapped her lip. "I think this situation calls for tea."

And thus begins Ailis's journey...

A NOTE FROM THE AUTHOR

I am going to preface this with: Please do not read unless you want to see this author spilling her guts and getting a little emotional about this last book for Bat and her not-men...

I realized something while writing this last book. I've never told you what the guys' endearments mean! So, here goes: Dub calls her *storeen*, which loosely translates to "little treasure". Mell calls her *realta*, which means "my star." Raise your hand if you have read my Blue books... (I swear I didn't do that on purpose, I only realized I did it after the fact. Originally I meant it to refer to the silver sparks that appeared in her eyes when she used her power, and the fact that Bat is considered a sky goddess, and the personification of the Milky Way in some references.) Shar calls her *a stor*, which is "my dear." Not particularly fancy, but neither is he... Finn began to call her *acushla* when he didn't call her simply goddess. This is an endearment that came from a phrase meaning "vein of my heart."

How did you all like my take on Tir Hudi, the mythical island? While I did find a few references to it as an actual island, most of them only noted that it was enchanted in some way that made it findable only under certain circumstances. So, I added my own spin to it, of course. (wink, wink)

Yes, this is the last book for Bat and her guys. The next adventure will belong to Ailis as she figures out how to be a goddess instead of a fae of Ireland, and as she navigates Egyptian pantheon politics and potential new relationships. Oh, and not to mention figuring out just what is going on with those restless souls...

Some of you may have noticed a few... unresolved bits of plot line, or hints at greater opponents or evils that could come. I did that very deliberately. (And if you didn't notice, just disregard this whole paragraph and pretend I didn't draw your attention to them.) I did it for a few reasons: 1) Maybe I'll get the urge to play around with a few more world ending evils in future books in this world, even if Bat is not a main player. 2) Even if a person or goddess has gotten themselves in a good place, if you look around this world there is always something that could be better or that should be fought against. In Bat's case, these are evils that are either contained, or asleep. 3) Like anyone, Bat and her guys are still working on things. Their emotional wounds are not going to magically disappear (though I could probably make that artificially happen with an enchantment or two... hmmmm...). They've gotten themselves into a pretty good place in their relationship, but that doesn't necessarily fix everything they've experienced throughout their lives. They'll keep helping each other to grow and heal and let go of the past. The important thing is that they now have each other, and they *know* it. 4) The last reason is that I simply couldn't make myself wrap everything up. I needed to leave myself little avenues to revisit these characters...

Why is it so hard to say goodbye?

I hope you guys have grown to love this world as much

as I have. And I hope you stick with me through Ailis's journey and beyond. At this point, I don't think hers will be the last tale I need to tell for these characters that I have grown way too attached to...

About the Author

Cecilia Randell was born in Austin, Texas and grew up in a home with her very own Cheerful Bulldozer. After some brief adventures in various places such as California and Florida, she returned to her hometown and took up a career in drafting.

A lifetime lover of words and stories, the transition to writing was two-fold: a comment from a relative and a short line from another author, saying to write what you want to read.

And thus the new adventure was born.

Now she can be found most days curled up in a comfy chair and creating new tales to share with others.